PEOPLE OF THE VALLEY

BOOKS BY FRANK WATERS

Midas of the Rockies (1937)
People of the Valley (1941)
The Man Who Killed the Deer (1942)
The Colorado (1946)
The Yogi of Cockroach Court (1947, 1972)
Masked Gods: Navaho and Pueblo Ceremonialism (1950)
The Earp Brothers of Tombstone (1960)
Book of the Hopi (1963)
Leon Gaspard (1964)
The Woman at Otowi Crossing (1966)
Pumpkin Seed Point (1969)
Pike's Peak (1971)
To Possess the Land (1973)
Mexico Mystique: The Coming Sixth World of
    Consciousness (1975)
Mountain Dialogues (1981)
Flight from Fiesta (1987)

ALSO AVAILABLE

Frank Waters: A Retrospective Anthology, ed. Charles L.
    Adams (1985)
A Sunrise Brighter Still: The Visionary Novels of Frank
    Waters, by Alexander Blackburn (1991)

PEOPLE OF THE VALLEY

FRANK WATERS

SWALLOW PRESS

Athens

03 02 01 00 99 98   10 9 8 7

Swallow Press / Ohio University Press Books are
printed on acid-free paper ∞

Library of Congress Cataloging-in-Publication Data

Waters, Frank.   1902–
  People of the Valley.

I. Title.
ISBN 0-8040-0243-6 (pbk.)
PS3545.A82P4   1984   813'.52   78-137435

Cover photograph of Frank Waters by Cynthia Farah

Cover design by Chiquita Babb

To the people of the beautiful blue valley, and to those who have loved it: *Gente muy remota, muy cerrada— amigos bien recordados, muy cariñosos.*

1

To three races and four generations, through all its many names, it has been known simply as the beautiful blue valley. It is not as beautiful as it is blue. Nor always blue. Yet the tone persists when the vegas turn sere and tawny under drought, and the pine slopes white with frost. And seen from above the haze of Indian summer and the winter mists, from the top of the nine thousand foot pass, the valley appears always what it is—a crescent lake of blue draining the shadows of the steep-walled cañons which hem it on all sides.

It drains more than shadows and the shadows of the men with a wild remoteness in their eyes. A thunder cloud snags on the western cliffs of the Sangre de Cristo, and from the converging box cañons of Luna and Lujan the water foams down along the ridge rock of Los Alamitos. The trout stream at Guadalupita swells from a rain in the north, and rises higher at Turquillo from the drainage of La Cañada de Carro. Melting snows rush down the glacial bed of Rio de la Casa, swamping the beaver dams. To the east and south the Coyote and Cebollita overflow the pastures, the fields and valleys of the Big Onion and the Little.

And the tiny river no longer meanders, poco a poco
through the beautiful blue valley. It rips through the willow
uproots cottonwoods, tears out old acequias so patientl
banked by hand. The chalk cliffs crumble; the rutty road
dissolve into rivers of slimy glue; corn milpas look like
muddy rice fields. Dead chickens are cast up on the beache
of flooded corrals. A drowned calf, neck broken, hangs over
patch of fence. Adobes wash out too, crumbling back int
the earth from which they rose and will stubbornly rise again

Each swollen tributary, in turn, marks the seasons, alter
the landscape if only by a foot, and brings crops and peopl
God's blessing or the devil's own.

But sometimes a cloudburst up one of the cañons mark
the year as one of many to be remembered. The decades ar
labeled by such washouts. And the people divide their live
by what has happened once.

Twenty or thirty years it has made. Quien sabe? It was the
flood. A cloudburst. It broke on the ridge and poured dow
both cañons at once. Two. Not one. Two, Señores. Madre d
Dios! The water! How it came! Here to my very feet it rose
Verdad! From El Alto de Talco to El Alto de los Herreras
from Cañoncito to La Cueva, the valley was one lake. Th
floor of the church was wet when we heard mass. Santísima
That's how it was.

So now they are building a dam.

Who?

They. El Estado. The Governor. The políticos for whom
we made crosses on our votes, as instructed. Perhaps the
Presidente himself. . . . Who knows these things exactly whe
he is busy in the fields?

What dam?

Burro! Fool! The dam so that we won't have any more
floods. Across the valley, at the mouth of the cañon.

But I don't see any dam. What kind of a dam is it that a
man cannot see? Forgive me, friend, but I am of the people; I
do not understand. But I don't see any dam. No, certainly, I
can see nothing there but that fence which Fulgencio Garcia
Valdes should have fixed when I told him about his two
cows in my oats. And that old mare, too, the one with the
evil eye. . . .

Sacred Heart of Jesus! There is no dam! But they are
building it just the same. On paper first, as is the way
nowadays. A big dam. A dirt dam. A check dam.

Oh sí! Sí. Sí, Señor. A dam de checks! Of course. Of
course. There must be many checks—to pay us for hay for
their horses, for adobes, for work perhaps. I have seen in the
store such checks. Little pieces of paper good for money. We
shall all be rich. . . . But still, amigo, why do they build this
dam? There has never been one before; it is not the custom.
The floods come, like sunshine and the drought. They are all
God's will. Else why should there be floods? No doubt it is
wrong to stop them. No; I do not see why there should be a
dam. Why should there be a dam, Señor?

It is explained to everyone, there in the sloping campo
where even the pines march down to listen, soughing among
themselves like the echoed whisper of the multitude.

The wary, flint-eyed men who have ridden out of the dark
mountain fastness of Las Colonias and El Quemado still sit
their restless mounts, swaying like reeds in the breeze.
Families and neighbors who have bumped since sunrise over
the rocky roads from Vallecito and Lucero squat patiently in
the crowded box wagons. Barefoot women and ragged men
who have plodded down the trails from west, north, east and
south; from El Alto with brown faces tinged red from Indian
Picuris; villagers, shopkeepers, strangers—all, mouths agape,
huddle under sun and dust and flies.

Of course it is a fiesta. Only a fiesta could bring them
together. Since yesterday afternoon the long barbecue trench

has been fed till it is two feet deep with glowing coals. Fou
steers, two sheep and three pigs have been basted with a mes
of brown sugar, vinegar, black and cayenne pepper, tomat
paste, salt and chile; have been cut into chunks, and wolfe
down with bread and one hundred and fifty pounds o
potato and onion salad. Now, with something solid in th
belly to counteract the unusual stimulus of mind and spirit
they stare fixedly at the platform in front—the back of
truck covered with planks and hung with an American flag

There are many speeches and many speakers. Flower
speeches from local políticos for whom the little crud
crosses were marked on the votes, and demanded. Lon
speeches from city Anglos properly sweating in white collar
and buttoned coats. Speeches crisp and awesome with fact
and figures from visiting ingenieros who are building the dan
on paper, first.

Such a big dam to be built on paper! Where does it al
come from, this paper?

A thunderbolt sentence, a flowery phrase. An outflun
arm, a pause. The speaker spits out dust, runs a forefinge
under his limp collar. The interpreter beside him duly
translates.

So it goes on all afternoon.

The dam looms up, bigger, clearer. Here, in this valley
There, at the mouth of the cañon. So long, so wide, so high
And there will be a lake behind. Imagine, a lake! Strange
There has never been a lake here before. It is not the custom
And a new road, a slick shiny road. Many automobiles wil
come whizzing by where one chugged, bogged down and wa
dragged out by teams before.

Progress is coming to the beautiful blue valley. It sound
muy importante. The people are properly impressed.

El Estado, the Governor, the políticos for whom the
made the tiny crosses as instructed, the Presidente himself—
how is it that all these should be so good, so generous, so
truly thoughtful of the people of the lonely valley so long

orgotten in the mountains? Pues, the dam! they are going to
uild a dam. Like the one on paper.

But what is this? A rippling tenseness draws the crowd
ogether. The dam must have many varas of land. The lake
must have land. Also there must be room for the road to run
through the fields. Whose land? Our land. Don Teodosio's
and, Maria del Valle's land, and the land of Refugio Montes
nd of Gertrudes Paiz . . . everybody's land perhaps. That,
ompadres, is a horse of a different color! We have never sold
our land. It is not the custom. The land is our mother. It had
uckled our fathers, our father's fathers. What would we do
without land? Even with a dam?

Up on the platform somebody slyly kicks the speaker on
he heel. "Sssht! Easy on that now. It isn't time." He stops
with a flowery phrase.

The last speaker rises unsteadily. He is a little drunk. His
traw hat sits on half his head. His bow tie jerks up and down
over his Adam's apple. He brushes the interpreter aside with
ordly grace.

"Caballos and Caballoses!" he shouts. "Yo pienso que
i . . . que es pretty good por la public waino for maka this
dam aqui!" He totters, regains his legs and flings out his arms.
"Caballos and Caballoses! Muchas gracias!"

They catch him, behind by the coattails, and slide a chair
under him just in time. He sits there, eyes glazed with
ncomprehension, before the shouting throng.

It is the best speech of the day. The inarticulate good will
of drunkenness is something understood by all. But ground
has been broken for the dam.

It is the crepusculo vespertino. The green of oats and
wheat and corn, of pine and spruce and piñon, has lost its
yellow component, but still retains its blue. The indigo
shadows are not yet black. It is the blue hour between yellow
sunset and black night. The bell of the village church strikes
t with a faint silvery chime.

On top of a ridge above the valley a box wagon halts in th
rutted road. It is loaded with people returning from th
fiesta. On the plank seat rattles a little bag of bones. The ba
is a pair of stained trousers with the fly unbuttoned, a rust
coat and a little black hat. Out of it protrudes two splintere
bones gloved in dry yellow skin and holding the limp rein
Beside it, stiffly upright in imperious silence, sits a woma
older still. The rest of the crowd squat patiently on the floo
behind: thin, barefooted women huddled in black cotto
rebozos, men rolling cigarettes in paper less brown than thei
stubby fingers, and children sleepily nodding at a dog, tongu
out, which has been plodding behind.

They cross themselves, hearing the church bell, and loo
back down into the valley. The barbecue pit is still faintl
smoking, adding blue to blue. The village lamps are comin
on. In front of La Cantina Palomita is a dark crowd drinking
smoking, spitting into the street, and discussing the day'
speeches.

"Of course," observes a man in the wagon. "Before th
baile tonight there will be much talk. It is necessary. Perhap
we should have stayed."

But his wife sees him wet his lips. "For what?" she ask
"To get drunk and have your throat cut for nothing?"

"It is a great thing, perhaps, this dam," ventures anothe
"But who knows what to think? Who shall tell us?"

They look up, warily expectant, at the old woman i
front. Her stiff straight back does not unbend. She maintain
her imperious silence. Suddenly out of her dusty rebozo
sharp elbow strikes the bag of bones beside her.

The little black hat rears up. The skeleton hands slap th
gaunt carcasses with the limp reins. It shouts. "Andale! Fo
the love of God! Have you no breath? We shall be late wit
the milking."

The scrawny team plods forward. The mongrel, behind
opens his mouth and starts a long pink pendulum t
swinging, like a clock jolted to sudden life. Then he trots t

is post under the rear axle. And the wagon load of people lips down the rocky road into the shadows of the pines.

The silence is thick and heavy, a little triste and holding the wild remoteness of the dark, narrow cañon. It is a flood which washes up to and around the plodding horses, the panting dog and creaking wagon. The upright old woman holds it at bay with a greater silence.

Three little wooden crosses beside the road are passed. An adobe. The pale yellow lamp in the window stares after the wagon. A dog barks and is choked by the silence. Then looms a scatter of six or seven steep-roofed adobes, aspen corrals and anthill ovens—a village, as villages are in these remote cañons.

Past it the road turns right, curves upward again. A trail leads tangent through a steep corn milpa amongst the forest. The wagon stops.

The clothed skeleton on the front seat rattles with a threat of clambering down. "I shall go with you to your house, Madre," it squeaks politely. "I will see that everything is all right before I return."

The upright old woman has already got down, a little stiffly, and jangling the singletree. She wraps her rebozo about her shoulders. "Fool! Since when has Maria del Valle required the help of a man she has suckled like the sick pig of a litter?"

The skeleton sinks back with a sigh of relief into the same comfortable heap. "It is as you say, Madre."

A match flaring up in the wagon box lights the old woman's dark, wrinkled face. Its powerful and primitive features, timeless with sorrow and fecundity, are savage and enduring as if cut out of rock: a rock beaten, smashed and worn by waves but still jutting the promontory beak of nose, high cheekbones and solid jaw into the surge of life. The eyes are small and black and bright, the eyes of a hawk. Only the dark, red-brown flesh of her seamed and sagging cheeks appears touched and worn by time—but still timeless and

enduring as the red-brown earth forever furrowed by th
plow. She has one tooth. It is clamped down on the stub of
cigarette protruding stiffly from her loose, parted lips.

She suddenly, imperiously, reaches forth and grabs th
match to light her own stub.

"A thousand pardons, Señora! I did not see. . . . Go wit
God, Señora."

"Yes, Yes. Adiós! Adiós, Doña Maria!"

"Muchísimas gracias! It has been a great fiesta. Buena
noches, Madre."

Abruptly, before she throws away the match, a man lean
out of the wagon and asks quietly, very politely, "The dam
Doña Maria. It is too great a problem for my simple soul. Th
many speeches confuse me. It is good, this dam, Señora
I. . ."

The old woman lifts the match, peers forward. A lo
rumble from deep in her throat rises to meet a thin water
hiss in her powerful, jutting nose. Her loose wrinkled lip
draw back. She spits vindictively upon the ground a vigorou
expuition of great contempt. Then suddenly the match i
out, the corn is rustling, and the old woman is stalkin
sturdily upright through the darkness.

"Ándale! For the love of God! Have you no strength? W
are late with the milking."

The wagon crawls on, squeaking.

Soon in the darkness a voice speaks softly. "The Señora
doesn't think well of the dam, perhaps."

"Pues. Doña Maria perhaps does not like the dam."

"Don Teodosio! Hey there, amigo! Is it possible, perhaps,
that the Madre doesn't like the dam? What do you say,
compadre?"

The bag of bones straightens up a bit on the seat. "I have a
cigarette rolled these many minutes. But no match. Who has
a match? I want to light my cigarette. But I have no match.
Not in this pocket, nor in this . . . ."

Hurriedly, respectfully, a commotion produces a match.

Don Teodosio lights his cigarette. The little flame lights up half his thin, wrinkled face with its expression of cunning indolence. The other half, doubtless, is no better. He puffs a time or two. Now, a little self-conscious with authority, he says, "No. Of course. It is possible that Doña Maria does not like the dam. Who knows? But I think it is possible the Señora doesn't like the dam."

The wagon creaks on. The people nod to themselves in darkness.

It is possible that Doña Maria really doesn't like the dam.

Mid-November it is, and the Saint's Day of the village. The late morning stillness of the deserted fields is broken by a faint wailing chant. A thousand crows, polished like ebony, flap up cawing from the tawny stubble. A lone mallard shoots like an arrow from the marsh. A shaggy stallion wheels from his mares, flings up his head and stares over the fence.

The chanting wails louder. It comes from twenty men in a column of twos crossing the fields from El Alto de los Herreras. Their boots are muddy, their denim trousers ragged, but they wear neckties and wrinkled Sunday coats. All are bareheaded. Their eyes are raised to a banner of red silk lettered with faded gold. It flaps between two poles which the men in front are carrying.

As the column crosses the creek by the old mill and enters the village, the wail rises higher and falls lower. A red rooster flees squawking. A wagon draws aside to let the men pass. Clutching their rebozos to be sure their heads are covered, a few hurrying women fall in behind the column.

All cross the little plaza behind the general store. Beyond the rows of empty wagons and tethered horses the bell of the church is ringing. The tall poles dip, and the red banner slides through the adobe arch of the courtyard wall. The chanting ceases. The bell stops ringing. And in silence, down the dark nave between the cottonwoods, the people pass into the church.

Soon they come out again. The whole church empties. First the two fat, lace-robed priests. Then four men carrying on a litter Santa Gertrudes. She is almost life size, and stands swaying on a pillar in her white and dark blue robe, and wearing a manta of yellow. Her right hand carries a Bible. In her left she holds a long staff. Up it crawl two of the five mice that were carved upon it long ago when her paint was fresh and her dark cheeks not yet cracked and weathered. Behind her, head down, troop the people: humble women wrapped in their black rebozos, squat muscular men carrying their battered Stetsons, and children squeaking in new shoes. And in the rear, carrying their faded red banner, the twenty chanting men from El Alto.

The procession straggles up the one dusty road of the village, crosses the creek and winds back to the church through the scatter of log corrals and squalid adobes.

Santa Gertrudes, whose gentleness befriends even the timid mice, has blessed village and people again, and sanctified another year.

Now the people in knotted strings line the church wall, the sides of store and cantina, the courtyard and the plaza. They gossip, gesticulate, roll cigarettes. But warily, a little furtively, they watch an old woman sitting imperiously upright on the seat of a rattletrap buggy in the middle of the plaza.

Santa Gertrudes comes out once each year into her name-village with her gentle cracked smile, her mice and mercy. Already she is being stuffed away, forgotten, in her gloomy niche.

But Doña Maria has appeared for the second time with her vindictive lips drawn tight, squeezing as usual the life out of her cigarette stub. Her dark cheeks are weathered too, but not cracked. They are hard as two seasoned piñon knots. And her small bright eyes stare coldly, contemptuously, over the crowd. Perhaps, like all dictators, she knows her people better than Santa Gertrudes their transient regard for gentleness and mercy, and their enduring respect for tyranny. So she sits, straight as a pine, and as if oblivious of their sly attention. A tattered queen in a topless chariot whose old leather is as hard as its brittle hickory.

"Buenas días, Señora!"

"Cómo está, Doña Maria?"

"A very fine procession. Verdad!"

To their polite greetings, their fustian phrases—to themselves cringing past her, the old woman pays scant heed. Her acknowledgment to their obeisance is a shrug of her shoulders, a curt nod.

One of the priests comes out. He has doffed his lace and locked the church. As he waddles across the plaza the people rake off hats to hold against their breasts, bend their knees, shove children forward for his greetings. He comes abreast of the rattletrap buggy, pauses.

"Ah! Doña Maria! A splendid mass this morning! You did not come? But God still waits for you. It is never too late, Señora. Even after forty years."

Doña Maria shrugs wearily without bothering to turn around, as if more bored at his pleas than at his former maledictions. But when he has passed on, his plump face red as an apple above his stiff collar, she stares triumphantly at the crowd. Her reward is their embarrassment.

They nod slyly, poke each other in the ribs, gaze away and whisper, "You saw? She is not afraid of the Father. Of God or the devil either! What do you say now?"

They move about now in the morning sunshine, greeting friends, gossiping, begging tobacco, offering a swig of cheap whisky or a taste of stale beer—satellites swarming around a common sun, but at a respectful distance lest they be scorched.

Along the courtyard wall lounges a group of men. Another rides up, dismounts and flings the reins over his horse's head. Greetings from one cañon to many others. Talk of weather, crops, people. And finally the subject common to all.

"No doubt you have heard more of this dam, compadres? Myself, I have just this day left my work for Santa

Gertrudes."

"They are building it, primo. No doubt."

"But my wife has heard that Doña Maria del Valle doesn't think much of the dam."

"Verdad!" exclaims another, looking up from his paper of punche tobacco. "It is what we have heard at Sisneros. From my primo who came to look at my new calf, from Carmen. And his wife had it from her sister at La Jara."

"The devil take these women! They sit at their pots seeing no one all day long, and yet news comes up the cañons to them on the wind . . . Jesú Cristo! Who knows what she thinks and why?"

"It is she who sits there in Don Teodosio's old buggy," says one quietly. Then slyly he adds, "Why don't you ask her, compadre?"

All smile. It is as if each has been asked to light a keg of dynamite while the others watch from safety.

The one scowls—he in homemade leather chaps who has ridden down into the valley for the first time since summer. "A witch of an old woman! Shall my life, my new cow, be cursed for my pains? Sorda hija de tal!"

"Hush! For the love of God! She has ears for the wind, Señor." Self-consciously and apprehensively, he peeks around at the old woman still waiting alone in the buggy.

Defensively now, another adds in haste, "Still, she is a wise and powerful woman. There is none who has such power with herbs. It has made years since my Pablito had the poison from yedra. She came to us quickly, being near. No medicine. Nothing she did but spit. And the boy also she made spit, spit vigorously and copiously. Mother of God, how they spit! And the poison went. 'Remember,' she said, 'when one touches a harmful weed, when one comes in contact with the evil thing, one must spit out the evil.' "

"Cristo Rey! Listen! Is it not as you have said? It came, I have heard, from old Don Teodosio himself: when the Señora was asked about the dam. True, she did not answer. But she spit. She spit as you say. Does that not make the dam evil?"

"Look! Don Teodosio! We shall call him. . . . Hola! Hey there, amigo! We are saving you a drink—a little drink, the last in our bottle."

Don Teodosio's bones rattle in their stained trousers and rusty coat; his fly is still unbuttoned. He stops in front of the group, takes off his little black hat and brushes back his thin white hair before replacing it.

"Sit down. Among friends. In the sunshine. Ah! And here is the bottle!"

Don Teodosio watches a broad brown hand wrap around the bottleneck, as if around a rooster's throat, and yank up. He takes the opened bottle, squints at it toward the sun, then drains it at a gulp. "Hah! Fine weather, amigos! Pues!" He sinks down in a heap, props up his legs, and holds himself together with both arms.

Greetings, talk of weather, crops, people, and then. . . .

"Don Teodosio. This dam. It is too big a problem for our simple minds. We wish counsel of someone wise and learned to tell us what to think. . . . You perhaps, who have seventy years of which no more than thirty show . . . or even your esteemed mother, Doña Maria. Now if the Señora would let us know—out of her wisdom—we. . . . "

Don Teodosio has never been known to have an opinion of his own; he is liked by everyone. But his flinty brown face assumes the gravity of a priest in charge of an oracle.

"The Señora has not yet spoken. No doubt when she has consulted this year's herbs still drying . . . but already there are signs. Sí. Signs I have seen already. . . . But as I have said, there are signs. . . . "

He is arrested during his fumbling for a match by the sudden stare of Doña Maria who has just turned around in her buggy. He rises to his feet, not forgetting the proffered match, and makes off without another word.

"By all the devils of Hell!" shouts the wrinkled oracle. "Where have you been? It makes an hour I have been kept here waiting. Did I not feel my left nostril twitch? For what! To see you loafing in the sun with a bunch of lazy pigs! Get in here—old fool, sick pig of a litter. Burro!"

"Pues. Madre mia. Of course," Don Toedosio answers affably, taking up his reins. "The people are but inquiring your opinion of the dam."

"The dam. Mother of God!" The old woman leans over the side and spits, then throws back her head. And as the buggy rattles past the group of men sitting against the wall, Don Teodosio lifts his whip to them like a finger raised in admonition.

"You saw!" exclaims one, gazing after the buggy. "You saw her spit as she is said to spit each time the dam is mentioned? It is the sign."

"Sí. She is a powerful woman and wise. The time will come when she will open her heart about the dam and tell us what to think. Till then I will remember the sign equally with the talk of the políticos. 'A little shadow is worth more than a long length of sunshine.' Eh, amigos?"

The wheat has been cut, the oats, the barley. Corn has been gathered for chicos, roasted in outdoor ovens, then dried and shelled. Some has been soaked with lime to remove the husks, dried for posole or ground for nixtamal. And now the brittle stalks rustle in the wind. Rueditas, the "little wheels" of small squash have been sliced and dried. Big pumpkins have been cut round into "tasajos"—long thin strips wound up like rope and stored away. And now the withered vines glisten in moonlight with silver rime. Green chile has been roasted and peeled. Popote and popotito have been stored, and peaches, and all the herbs: cota for rheumatism, yerba del manzo for stomach pains, oshá for colds, and yerba buena to warm the insides of pregnant brides.

Time and weather have changed. Summer has gone, and all the usual crops are in. But other seeds keep growing despite the ground frosts and the snow caps eating down the mountain slopes: the seed of Doña Maria's sowing; the seeds of doubt.

She is a wise and powerful woman, and she doesn't like the dam.

2

The age of the beautiful blue valley and of Doña Maria is not, strictly speaking, a hundred years. Each is older, each echoing as they do one timeless and changeless pulse. But for a century they have been known by man—the valley ten years longer, Maria ten years less.

At the beginning of that short span six Hudson Bay trappers came warily down over the snowy pass hunting for beaver. On the banks of the frozen stream they found first three human skeletons left by Comanches, and so named the long blue crescent the valley of "L'Eau du Mort"—the Waters of the Dead.

All were Frenchmen. Roubidoux was one, and Ceran St. Vrain whose own skeleton lies yet beside the meandering stream, in the little Campo Santo rising out of the flat and covered by scrub oak. Their tongue still persists in the names of the little cañon settlements of Gascon and Ledoux, just over the hill; and it sounds at times in the general store of gruff, wooden-legged Pierre Fortier. In the church, behind, were French priests. The old linden in its courtyard, too, was a seedling brought by Father Guerin from France—one of the two which have rooted in these high western hills.

But it was up the Chihuahua Trail from Mexico, up the Rio Grande and over the Pecos, that the settlers came. Their soft fluent Spanish slurred the valley's name to "Lo de Mor," changed phonetically to "Lo de Mora," and finally shortened to "Demora." It was a place of berries, too, according to their translation: wild raspberries and strawberries thick along the streams and carpeting the clearings between thickets of chokecherry, gooseberry and wild plum. The steep, narrow cañon of Rio de la Caza, the place of the hunt, softened musically to Rio la Casa—and the beaver houses attested its change of name long after deer, wild turkey and bear grew scarce.

There were seventy-six settlers when they petitioned in the name of the Mexican nation for a land grant. Not only the long deep crescent was granted, but all the tributary cañons, the mountain uplands and the grassy plains below. And the beautiful blue valley to the north and to the south of the jutting cliffs which marked the handle of its curving bow, took two more names. The Valle de San Antonio above, and the Valle de Santa Gertrudes below.

The two villages were lifted slowly, a handful at a time, from the rich red-brown earth, roofed with vigas hand-hewn from the pines and interlaced with slim aspens. The adobes clustered thickly together for protection and according to the superior decree: "two hundred and fifty varas from East to West, leaving thirty varas outside for drippage and a common road and the meadow for the benefit of all, with its entrances and exits free."

But as the beautiful blue valley it persisted through its second name and tongue: more beautiful, more blue, as the thickets gave way to meadows of grass and the lower pine slopes to milpas of corn.

Yet little by little a third tongue, name and race crawled in. They came not over the pass from the north and west as had the first, nor up the Chihuahua Trail from the south as had the second. They came from the strange, unknown and barbaric east, over the vast buffalo plains. In great lumbering wains they came, with wheels high as a man and which left their traces forever imbedded in the soft limestone, with sheets drawn tight over the curving wagons bows—ships riding the pelagic plain. Men with eyes colder and bluer than the valley, in buckskin and with long emphatic rifles to punctuate their taciturnity. But where the wagons stopped to rest before the last climb, a fort grew up. Great walls it had, barracks and stables and courtyards where soldiers laughed, cursed, threw dice and shuffled cards. But they needed corn and wheat and oats, both men and horses—and the men wanted women and excitement.

So the beautiful blue valley over the hills prospered. For gold the village supplied liquor, gambling, horse races and cock fights. The people supplied the corn, wheat and oats for silver, and sometimes the women for a quicker exchange of lead and flashing steel. And duly, apathetically, they petitioned the new Jéfe, the Señor Presidente of the gringos, to confirm their title to their land. Again it was granted "with the stipulation that the United States herein expressly reserves to itself the buildings and improvements situated on the Fort Union Military and Timber Reservation, together with the possession and use of the same. . . . "

Save this, all the tributary cañons, the mountain uplands and the grassy plains below—a wilderness empire, remained theirs. But only the valley mattered.

New teams, new masters for the plow, but the land remains. The land that is mother to us all. An enduring truth that only her sons can know.

For the French disappeared with the beaver, leaving only their names and Pierre Fortier cursing and stamping his wooden leg. And soon the last of the gringo wagons passed over the trail, leaving the fort to crumble on the hillside and the colonel's grand piano to leer with a mouth of missing keys through the dusky parlor of the old inn.

Only the people remained rooted to their soil in a valley muy retirado, muy cerrado, that grew more isolated, more closed, within its mountain walls.

Through three tongues, three races and many names, then, the beautiful blue valley persisted; and yet it was but twenty years old when Doña Maria came. Old enough, but not too ripe, to be her mother.

Dawn-dusk drew the charcoal outline of a hut on the mountainside. Then the dirty gray light of day, like a soiled brush, thrust through the pines and smeared it with drabness. Its walls, waist-high, were heaped up stones chinked with adobe as were the gaping logs laid on top. The roof sagged with dirt and sprouted a growth of wild timothy.

A pig might have waddled out, but it was a woman who emerged into the clearing. She brought life and color into the drab monotone. About her bulging body she held a faded, striped, burnt-orange blanket. On her bare feet she wore sparse-beaded moccasins. Her long blue-black hair hung down around a smooth brown face slightly tinged red. The face was young but its pleasant immobility was marred by a strained expression of pain and anxiety. It was the look of a woman near childbirth, who watches for a man she knows will not return.

Without pausing she waddled across the flat stones in the stream and struggled up the trail. It rose through the gelid darkness of the pines into the pallid gray of scrub oak. Head down and breast heaving her protruding belly stretching the blanket in wrinkles across her broad hips, she climbed blindly, as if she had known it an incalculable number of ascents. Abruptly, across a face of frost-shattered granite, the path ended.

Below her the valley was rising out of a mist. She was standing on the tall weathered cliffs that jut out to separate the upper and lower halves of the one long valley so beautiful and blue. It curved like an Indian bow to left and right, as though the woman flexed it with her longing.

She looked toward the first mud clumps of Santa Gertrudes and San Antonio. Jets of pale smoke rose, adding blue to blue, but never the dust of a horse's hoofs from the plains below. Then the arrow of her gaze flew west to the wall of mountains.

She was Indian, Picuris, and the pueblo lay hidden behind the pass. Like her, others would be drawn out of its decaying squalorous, mud-black walls to the tiny new settlements in the valley below. They would drift together to live about the hot springs, and be forgotten with the Mexican men who drew them hence. Only the faint red flush showing through the dark cheeks of their sons and grandsons would mark El Alto as different from the others—the rising end of the scale as Picuris lowered in oblivion.

But now, alone, she stood between them. It was day, and the rising sun marked her time on its dial.

She slumped down on her broad haunches, clasping her quivering belly, her face grown oily with sweat. Then with a last look over the precipice, she rose and stumbled weakly back down the trail.

The inside of the hut was growing gray with light. Its small room was windowless and without furniture save a deal table lashed together with rawhide, and a leather trunk. Patches of the dirt floor were hard and smooth and black with the goats' blood mixed in the adobe. In one corner was a small fireplace. Before it lay a straw mat and another blanket.

The woman pawed back the ashes, and blew the coals awake. In a nest of sticks she set a copper kettle, dropping fresh yerba buena into the water. From an earthen pot she drew out the last handful of parched corn and chewed a few kernels slowly. When the water boiled she drank the tea to ease the increasing pains of her pregnancy.

They kept mounting, bubbling up within her and sinking down, a geyser of cramps. She lay writhing on the sleeping mat, then rousing against the wall to wipe the sweat from her face.

A shaft of sunlight fell in the doorway and slowly revolved about the room. A blue jay screamed from a pine outside. Two magpies quarreled on the roof, dislodging a thin trickle of dirt between the smoke-stained vigas.

Shortly after noon the woman awoke from a sleep that was not a sleep. A deer was standing in the clearing outside of the door. The great petals of its ears were thrust forward, the sunlight glistened on its porous, rubber-black nose. Weakly the woman gathered up from the blanket a few dropped kernels of corn to toss outside. With the gesture the deer, stiff-legged, rose into the air and vanished with a twitch of its white tailpiece.

The woman's big body was now a volcano trying to erupt. Spasms of pain rolled her from side to side. From knots of cramps her arms and legs unraveled, twitching. Her face was no longer dark rose-brown. It was muddy orange. She chewed, as if starving, a corner of her blanket.

The tea was cold. It could not quench the fire within her. She rolled on her back and lay snorting through her wide nostrils.

After the next spasm she got up. The beaded moccasins she took off and laid away carefully in the old leather trunk. The blanket around her she removed, folded, and placed out of reach. Now barefooted, her wheat-sack body covered only by a loose, black cotton shift, she stood before the fireplace.

In the niche in the wall stood a small dusty Cristo carved out of cottonwood. It had been lacquered with the gelatinous glue of cow's horns and gypsum, painted with egg yolk and ochre, and rubbed with mutton tallow. All this had soaked into the wood leaving a dark, muddy Rembrandt-brown figure with a long sharp nose, a bitter mouth and one broken leg. It was her man's Santo. The woman propped it up and lit a candle before it. She stared at it wonderingly in the vain attempt to discern power in such an inimical form.

Then she brought out a small buckskin sack, touching with it her nose and mouth, her breasts and belly, the secret parts of her body, after which she hung it back around her throat

Another recurrent convulsion doubled her like a felled tree. She straightened slowly, her moon face glistening with sweat, and laboriously looped over a rafter a long horsehair rope which dangled to the center of the floor.

Now began her labor.

Hands above her sagging head, she hung and pulled on the rope. What she needed and wanted were the strong hands of her man or of midwives around her waist: dragging their weight on her bulging body, slipping down from breasts to broad hips, squeezing, compressing, forcing out the new little life clamoring within her for outlet.

Instead, she hung there alone, doggedly straining in the dusky hut before the guttering candle. With one hand she prodded and pressed her belly and groin. Every few minutes fresh labor pains gripped her. Then she hung on with both hands. Her knees and feet twitched. Her hands slipped down the rope. Head down and moaning, her bare feet dragging in the dirt, she revolved more slowly, came to rest.

Little by little she hitched herself up, panting, waiting for the next spasm. The Cristo with his long sharp nose and bitter mouth looked on as if ironically amused—an amusement that yet seemed to have in it the compassion derived form severer suffering.

By midafternoon the floor beneath the woman was dark puddle of sweat. She could no longer hold herself up. She slipped down to her knees, legs outspread, and ripped off her soppy shift. Her long blue-black hair stuck to her broad back like a shadow.

Suddenly she rolled sideways upon the heap of blankets, howling. Her eyes filmed over. Her hands fought the air, fell and sought in the blankets something that was neither there or anywhere.

Time now had meaning. It hammered out its truth as if on

ι great drum. The pulse beats throbbed through her and
through the earth below, they shook the mountains and the
evening star in its socket above. It was her time and another's
too, and all to which they were bound in unbroken sequence
by the one pulsing beat which echoes dreamily and power-
fully through the earth of the flesh and the flesh of the earth
alike.

And so it passed. . . .

They found her that evening—Two goatherds passing the
hut, who heard the child's cries.

"Mother of God! It is she. The India. The woman of that
stranger who ran away again to join the great wagons of the
gringos. She has been here all this time . . . Cristo Rey! What
a mess, this of woman bearing children . . . Señora!"

This man's name, where had he come from, would he
return . . . what does one do now with such a tiny babe . . .
would the Señora like some tea, a scrap of fat meat and a
cold tortilla? Señora! Señora India!

To all their questions, pleas and exhortations the woman
made no answer. They got out of her a wild and frightened
look, a last choking gasp and one intelligible "Maria."

It was the only name she spoke, and so it became the
child's. Red and tiny, it lay on the edge of the stained
blanket. One minature hand was closed upon a bit of dirt. It
was her birthright. Doña Maria never let it go.

Maria grew up with her goats. She was as scrawny and
stringy-legged as they from scrambling up the rocky hillsides.
Her hair too was long, coarse and tangled with burs and pine
needles. Like theirs, her large, dark eyes could, in an instant,
become wild and wary as though a pebble had been dropped
into their placid depths. They were her only companions by
day, her bedfellows at night. She drank their milk, ate their
cheese and sometimes chewed a piece of their flesh. Their
odor clung to her as if it were her own. Her life was like
theirs save in one respect: she did not eat grass. At ten she

was a little she-goat.

Their goatherds were two old philosophers. They kept back the mounting tide of life with a rampart of stones heaped across the narrow throat of a cañon. Behind it was an aspen fence and a roof of branches. To most of the valley below it looked like a corral. The inclosure did keep coyotes and an occasional bear from the flock at night; and interlaced with spruce branches in winter it kept out some snow and wind. But across the top of the high stone barricade gleamed a row of pale goat and sheep skulls. They were symbols of a school of thought, and its two exponents stared down between them into the valley with all the irreproachable dignity of their calling.

The older one sprouted on his long dark face a few gray chin whiskers like a he-goat's. Around his shoulders he wore a dirty sheepskin. He carried a staff and wielded it when pressed as Jove a thunderbolt. The other, scarcely over sixty, still betrayed a lingering worldliness by wearing a battered sombrero with its last tiny bell still dangling from its rim, brass earrings and leather leggings. It was obvious that he was conscious of his weakness. He kept wrinkling his seamed and weathered face as if he knew that the veneration accorded age and wisdom in men depended on thier outward mien.

These two viejos lived in a small hut in back of the corral. Maria ate with them. On stormy nights she also slept with them on the floor. It was a privilege granted her with new-born kids, an ailing ewe or a goat maimed by wild beasts. During blizzards the whole flock was let in.

The kids whimpered, the ewes blatted. When warm grease was smeared on a lacerated leg a new voice added to the bedlam and muted the shrieking winds. Maria did the smearing. She sat on the goat's head and kept ducking back from its threshing legs.

The two old men squatted in front of the fire, watching. Generously they offered tidbits of advice from their feast of wisdom. They minded neither the stench, the noise nor the gusts of smoke that filled the hut. They were immersed in life yet never wetted; salved too, as it were, by the protective goose grease of their inherent aloofness.

Both had come up from the desert wastes of Chihuahua. The lush grass and innumerable streams of the beautiful blue valley they could never quite believe permanent. Twenty times a day, at every stream and rivulet they crossed, the older would stop and drink his fill.

"You will kill yourself with drinking, compadre," said the other, observing his companion's gasping red face and drum-tight belly.

"My son," replied he, "it is not thirst I indulge but safety. Fate has led us here, and without doubt it shall lead us back again into a desert wilderness where streams and water holes are a day apart. If here I grow lax and fail to drink my fill at every stream. thinking the next near by, I will surely perish there."

Thus they maintained caution.

Parsimony they practiced also, and tyranny over Maria. As the little herd under her care increased, her daily rations of tortillas and cheese decreased in wise proportion of her safety. A glutted child, they said, makes a careless climber.

This caution, parsimony and tyranny they regarded as custom, simplicity and benevolence, and so justified philosophy which is ever blind to the crass and superficial aspect of things seen by lesser men.

To prove it, Maria flourished. She often went out into the hills without food, and never asked for another covering when her old sheepskin wore through. The two viejos admitted satisfaction. "We are doing well by the child. She grows hardy as a weed."

Maria did not tell them that she sucked udders of milk from her herd, or that before entering the hut she hid the faded, burnt-orange blanket stolen from them. What they liked about her best was her silence.

This was the form of their lives. Its substance was

impregnated by their peculiar philosophy whose symbol
gleamed palely along the top of the high stone rampart, wer
stacked around the outside of the hut, and held their rap
gaze inside.

The men, by night, were always squatting down before th
fire with a skull between their legs. With little twigs the
measured the span between its eye sockets, from gapin
mouth to top of head. These lineal measurements the
recorded on the dirt floor. Little triangles and squares the
drew in the flickering light, and these they compared with
the seasonal patterns of moon and stars on the skull of th
heaven above.

Often they rose and brought out from the corner a bundl
of bound twigs. Each was marked by a knife cut, a strip o
peeled bark or a broken branch. These too were laid ou
carefully on the floor to compare with a skull.

"Yes. The wild plum branch marked with the cut of a new
moon. It is the one that shows where the water rose highes
in the little stream to the west."

"Pues, brother. I remember this skull well. A lively young
ram—he who climbed highest always. To the gray cliffs with
moss so thick in the cracks. Observe these wrinkles, com
padre. What a head!"

With such remarks they punctuated hours of silent study
Maria lay on the floor, belly down, watching their intent an
timeless faces. Their sharp, shrewd eyes bored through th
skulls at their feet. The vast skull of the heavens they probed
and added to the zodiacal signs read in the brittle bone. Ever
the earth they seemed to strip of its flesh to sound the depth
of springs, of winter snows and underground streams.

To them, it was all one pattern endlessly repeated in
magnitude and miniature. By goat skulls they read the record
of floods and droughts, foretold heavy snows and drying
springs, measured the movement of stars—and little by little
as men ventured up from the valley, they began to prophesy
love and illfortune, wealth and sickness, danger, drying wells

nd to supply remedies for heavy hearts.

To the villagers below they were charlatans and greedy hieves, or men wise and learned in the ancient learning of he hills, depending upon the opinion of those badly cheated n trade, who slyly suspected where their missing goats had one, or happened to seduce their chiquitas soon after urchasing a love charm. To all the beautiful blue valley they vere at least markedly eccentric.

But to Maria they always remained philosophers.

She was a wild and wary little goat. She saw through their charlatanry and maintained silence. Their tyranny she endured for the spot of benevolence it contained. With simple, unsuspected guile she combated their parsimony, and was not above trading a kid to a passing stranger while excusing its oss by referring to a marauding bear.

Of it all nothing endured but the intent of their teachings. The great dome of the midnight skies, and the dome of the arth rounding from horizon to horizon: both forever epeated with the triangles and squares of stars, and with the vrinkled watermarks of freshets and spring thaws, upon the esser, miniature skulls of beast and man. This was the lesson f her childhood. She never suspected it was philosophy. She nly thought that she was learning about goats.

The two viejos, then, were wise men. In their wisdom they choked out life with a high stone wall across the throat of the añon. It had one little gate. Out of it went Maria each day vith her scrawny goats, and into it was permitted to pass an occasional visitor from the valley. Inside, the two old philosophers prophesied water and weather, attended personlly to their precious sheep, and confounded all men with heir alarming eccentricity.

They made only one mistake—one miscalculation of water nd weather. It was as though the life they shut out in front crawled around and struck them from the unsuspected rear.

It came in the form of a flood down the steep-walled,

cañon. The thunderclouds broke against the face of the clif
were transformed into great glacial boulders as round an
gray and smooth as enormous skulls. They snapped pine
tore out dirt and brush, and swept down in a raging torren
that scarce thirty minutes before had been a twinkling litt
trout stream.

The high stone wall, shutting out the flow of life in fron
had created something of a vacuum in the pocket in back
Now the flow from behind rushed in to fill it. It was a grea
lesson, this trite truth that nature abhors a vacuum, but th
two philosophers had no time to learn it. In a twinkling the
were immersed in a torrent six feet deep. The protectiv
goose grease of their inherent aloofness was battered b
rolling stones and twisting logs. Soon their heads were too.

The little hut unfolded like a flower, the aspen fenc
collapsed like straw. Men, sheep and a few goats, pitiousl
bleating and shrieking were dashed against the stone wal
For a minute it held. Then with a crash it collapsed, and th
flood swept down into the valley to leave an apron of debri
a few bloated carcasses for the buzzards, and the bodies c
the two viejos whose fate had perverted their philosophy b
neither drawing them back into a desert wilderness no
developing their thirst in proportion to the water the
received.

Maria, up in the hills with her goats, stumbled upon
half-collapsed hut in which they took up new quarters. I
stood in a little clearing just below the tall weathered cliff
that jutted out to separate the upper and lower halves of th
one long valley. Often she climbed the overgrown and almos
imperceptible trail to the edge of the precipice. Here
immobile as one of her goats, her long hair blowing in th
wind, she stood staring fixedly down into the beautiful blu
valley.

Below, the great white-cloud wagons kept passing, the for

ew up. It was all very strange. But she was a stranger. Most
ople turn from the thing called life to the thing called
ilosophy. But Maria from philosophy was confronted by
e.

3

At fifteen she was considered a little fey even by the mos
superstitious. This opinion was tempered by a grudgin
admiration for her goats. She and the flock were know
throughout the valley, from mountain to plain. By day th
vecinos might catch a glimpse of brown and gray tricklin
like water between the pines. At night they could sometime
hear in the darkness a strange voice answering the tinkle of
bell.

"It is that queer Maria with her goats" they would say
"We shall buy cheese again tomorrow. But watch sharply
She cheated us last time. Watch but say nothing. Remembe
it is said she has an evil eye."

Mostly she stayed in the clearings near her little mountair
side hut. But sometimes, penning her goats, she came dow
alone into the village. She moved as a young pine migh
move, neither proudly nor humbly, but self-reliant. Sh
walked in the middle of the road as mountain folk walk i
town, needing some assurance of space. And all that she saw
she devoured with the hunger of the solitary—the hunger tha

et can be appeased so quickly and for so long.

Her eyes were quick and bright as a bird's. Her tongue was
harp for she used it not often enough to dull its edge. She
ore a tattered dress of course, dull trade stuff. Under it her
reasts hung like August plums—small and firm, not green
or yet wholly ripe. Her arms and legs were brown and bare.
1 the sunlight her long black hair rippled with the same
ueer aliveness that permeated her whole body. She was not
eautiful, but she had the beauty of the wild.

Before her, fresh-plastered, new-adobe Santa Gertrudes
himmered in the hot afternoon. The walls of Bishop Lamy's
ew church rose clean ash-gray with adobe brought from
iuadalupita. Behind it, chattering like a flock of blackbirds,
he Sisters of Loretto watched their convent school being
iven its first coat of yellow tierra amarilla. In the row of
tores, trading posts and cantinas, Maria recognized the
elumbroso from the red clay banks around Turquillo. And
orth and south, the scattered adobes reflected white and
lay-blue from Cañoncito and Chacón.

It was a single village street sprawled along the winding,
utted road between the pine hills and the cottonwoods
ning the river. But with its colors the girl saw in it all the
lay banks and the cañons, the hills and chalk cliffs of the
ne long valley she wandered from end to end.

Over all hung a haze of dust. It never settled. Great wains
oaded with hay and grain for the new fort stirred it
ontinually as they rumbled through town. Horsemen clat-
ering in and pulling up their mounts on their hind legs in
ront of St. Vrain's store or old Fortier's, sprayed the
oungers with powder. The twinkling centipede feet of a
•urro train loaded with firewood, even the plodding bare feet
•ehind, kicked up little gritty geysers.

Men filled the long portales which jutted margins of shade
nto this river of dust. A few tobacco-spitting trappers in
•uckskin who lingered yet in the twilight of their time, a row
•f squatting Indians hunting lice—all hugging in their silence

the silence of the hills. Wagon-masters and mule-skinners too
bragging on their exaggerated eight miles a day across th
Jornada; a gambler with polished boots and the shirt studs o
Sutter's gold; a sharp-nosed Armijo who ever deigned in hi
haughtiness to see the gringos at its end. Paisanos and gent
de razón, strangers and homefolk, they spit and swore
laughed, drank, gambled and swapped knives, talked o
discoursed in pregnant silence, and were jostled by the strean
of villagers plodding past. A lady between high French heel
and a Spanish comb stepped daintily over a pile of manure i
the street. Father Abel lifted his hat in passing and garbled
Spanish phrase. There was a sudden roar and clatter; th
whole street hushed. It was old Fortier, the trader, stampin
his feet and howling in French—he had run out of suga
again. The street resumed its talk.

It was the beautiful blue valley's three races fusing in thei
short and transient hour. Their color and life, their custom
and tongues, the strange and the familiar, the goat girl saw a
she passed slowly down the street. But it was the gray, gritt
dust that bit into her senses. The vast cloud that covered an
muted everything, the dust to which all would finally return

It was, in a way, the philosophy through which Mari
always stared as if through a curtain.

But even it seemed to lift and dissipate when lights leap
out to sting the hide of approaching darkness. There wer
campfires beside the wagons and along the stream, ocot
torches stuck in wall crevices of the little mud huts. Candle
guttered on crowded bars and inside the church. In the store
brass lamps lit up shelves, boxes, bales. . . . Thus successivel
they lighted Maria's way back up the road.

She had done her little trading: goat cheese and two pelt
for a bit of salt, a piece of cloth and four iron nails. Alon
she had eaten beside her own fire at the edge of town. An
now refreshed by food, by light and smell, she was arreste
by a strange and wonderful sound.

Ójala! What a beautiful, wondrous sound! It was at onc

ppling over rocks, a child's laugh, the tinkle of frosty stars. t was the blood of springtime beating an arpeggio at temples nd fingertips.

But it seemed to come from the corner parlor of the huge, prawling inn fronting the plaza. A crowd of loiterers on the ortal was staring through the cracked shutters of the front vindows. Maria crept round the corner, along the dark road oward the river.

The garden gate was open. Inside she could glimpse the mall placita, and beyond, the enclosed garden. A light athed the flagstones with milk, and shimmered like moon-ght through the branches of a great locust. Around the tree vere tethered some horses. By the saddles she knew they elonged to soldiers from the fortaleza.

Between them she crept closer to the window. A hand on heir flanks, a muzzle fondled, a whisper in their ears—they vere still.

Maria crept closer against the adobe wall. By standing on er toes she could see the light. It hung from the ceiling by hree golden chains, a great glowing drop of goat's milk ainted with red flowers. But it revealed nothing of the vonderful sound, the tinkle of the unseen frosty stars. Maria aid down her bundle, crossed hands over her breast. The moke rising from the porcelain lamp was the incense of her ribute.

When the unseen music ended, Maria opened her eyes.

Underneath the lamp a table stood in the middle of the oom. On it lay a big conch shell and a brass bound Bible. Around the walls hung a few tin daguerrotypes. Under them, n stiff red plush chairs, sat the gringo soldiers more stiffly pright in their uniforms. All faced, in the far corner, a large ox of shiny redwood. Out of it protruded a brass crank.

This polished box was muy importante. Maria had seen it he day it came—from across the plains, and even across the ea, the men said. It was raining, and the wagon had bogged lown in mud. Four mules couldn't drag it out. The gringo

colonel had sloshed around cursing, his men had thrown ov
the box their own coats, and stood there heaving li
whipped dogs.

So Maria waited outside, her curiosity fixed on the bo:
her longing on the wonderful sound now stilled.

Beside the box sat the gringo colonel's lady. Her dre,
foamed out from her narrow waist like a waterfall, but h
face was carved from a cold white icicle. She had a narro
cruel mouth and shallow eyes which froze when she spoke t
those of the soldiers without much braid on their uniform
She sat with her gloved hands in her lap. The soldiers sat wit
hands in laps.

They were gente de razón, and so they talked as people c
reason always talk. The movement of their lips was ceasele:
as running water, and the murmur of their strange hard voic
aroused in the girl a subdued apprehension. Talk withou
gesture, without smiles, frowns or animation—the gringo ta
which holds all and gives nothing.

So held by a mystery greater than silence itself, Mari
stood peering into the room as into a lake in moonlight.

Then into the passionless stability of the parlor strode th
step of life. It bore a tall, square-shouldered cavalryman. H
blue eyes smiled, his curving silent mouth spoke louder tha
their greetings. He was a Samson whose tawny strengt
flowed from him in long waves that hung to his collar.

He was young but a man. The soldados, even they wit
beards and much gold braid, answered his manhood wit
quick bows. But it was the woman who answered his youth
The icicle of her face flushed, she rose and gave him her tw
gloved hands.

Maria saw behind the colonel's bearded smile, and smile
to herself in the darkness. "There will be a fight," sh
thought. "Perhaps with knives. Or maybe with the shor
guns. It is good!" And her strength flowed forth to that o
the young man, he like a lion with the tawny mane.

But instead, a Mexican criada shuffled into the room o

are feet carrying glasses and a bottle. They drank cautiously
s men afraid of their wine, and from glasses no bigger than a
oat's teats.

Suddenly the young soldado jumped up, laughed and went
) the big polished box. He twirled round the brass handle,
pened the lid and put in his hand.

With the first sound from the music box, Maria shrank
gainst the wall. Una caja de música! she thought ecstatically.
Iagic box!

It spoke. It sang! With the voice of rippling water and of
vind, it sang, with a child's laugh and the tinkle of frosty
tars. And all these voices were one voice, and it was the
oung soldado, its master.

He stood there, one hand on the box, staring directly into
er eyes with cloudy eyes and a quiet smile. Maria shook in
ne darkness. Her blood became water, wine, fire; her
noughts nebulous as clouds drifting across the face of a
noon. She shrank back into the darkness, but not away. Her
ace grew hot. She held her breasts as if they were the warm,
truggling body of a new-born kid in her arms.

Then suddenly the music stopped; he turned around,
nughing, to his companions.

Maria ducked, grabbed up her bundle and fled. She had
ot yet learned that there are things one cannot escape.

For two months Maria kept out of Santa Gertrudes. She
id her little trading in San Antonio, and led her goats into
ne northern cañons. The short grass of an August drought
vas the excuse that brought her back across La Cañada and
ne Coyote.

She sat on the slopes overlooking the beautiful blue valley
ow sere and brown in summer sunshine. Her goats scram-
led at will up the rocky hillside, straying through scrub oak
nd dribbling between the metallic, dusty pines above.
Always the faint tinkle of a bell marked their casual
vhereabouts. Maria seldom turned around.

What held her gaze was the continual stream of dust that rolled, wave after wave, up the cañon to the fort sixteen kilómetros away. In these waves, as they passed below, she detected loaded wagons or burro trains, valley horsemen, or occasionally the uniform of a galloping soldier. Maria shrugged. These gringo soldados! In hats they all looked alike.

Late in the afternoon she rose and led her goats down to water. The little stream crawled half-alive through thickets of chokecherry and wild plum. Here she splashed in a tiny pool and rubbed her body with grass. Slowly she pulled on her single coarse dress and stretched out like a lizard in the sun to dry her hair.

That afternoon Maria was asleep when one of the waves of dust, like a worn out ripple, subsided in the road a half mile away. Out of it a lone horseman turned off into the brush. His polished boots were covered with dust, his tunic unbuttoned, his face red and sweaty. At the glade he dismounted, throwing the reins over the head of his horse which stood unmoving while he walked down to the water.

He was master of the song which had caught up with Maria, but mastered for a moment by silence. A big bluebottle fly buzzed among the plums. A single pine murmured in the breeze. Far off came the faint tinkle of a bell, and nearby the patter of another goat. Maria still slept.

Before her the gringo soldier lay at the edge of the stream as some men lay at the edge of a precipice: belly down, arms outstretched, head cautiously forward. Drinking his fill, he raised up to a squat and splashed his arms and face.

"Major! Here boy!"

As the horse trotted obediently forward to take his turn, Maria roused. She awoke instantly alive and with the intense awareness of an animal—head up, a hand on the huaraches under her head, one bare brown leg outstretched for instant flight.

What she saw before her was a wet tangle of tawny hair,

taring blue eyes, a familiar red face and the uniform of a
ringo soldado. He too was caught in a posture of surprise, in
he act of wiping off his mouth with the back of his hand as
\c turned around. It was as if he had stifled a song on his
ips—this tawny-haired master of the singing box whose heart
\ad once spoken to her in the darkness.

"Cómo le va! Cómo . . . . "

His Spanish was terrible, his breath faintly warmed with
he smell of the drink which had flushed his face. But in his
:yes was mirrored something of her long, bare brown legs,
he dark fell of her freshly washed hair, and the quick, dark
ook in her own eyes—the unsung song which answered his
)wn.

Major stopped, his black velvet ears flung forward: it was
)itched too high for even them. He tramped heavily down to
he stream. Drinking, he raised his head and regarded the two
)n the bank. Then, as if seeing no more than he heard, he
urned his back and began to munch grass.

His master had taken off his tunic to sit on. "No habla
nglés?" he stuttered. "Caliente, eh? . . . Jesus, it's hot! I've
3ot a long ride back."

"Sí" A flat, uncommunicative sí. The goat girl's tattered
dress was still up around her bare smooth thighs, but she had
brushed her tangle of hair. She wiggled her toes, and chewed
\ blade of grass. Her casual manner marked an inward
trepidation. She felt a weakness and a strength stealing upon
her, both at once and the same, a strange thing.

"Fumar . . . cigarro?" the man mumbled, sitting up to
fumble through his pockets.

Without waiting, Maria reached behind for her bundle, and
took out a little sack of punche and a roll of corn husks. She
rolled herself a cigarette and smoked. Now, propped up on
one elbow, she could see him more closely: the fine gold
hairs on the backs of his hands; the straight line dividing his
sunburned face from his white chest—like a cut throat; and
the dancing stars in his eyes.

"Me . . . yo montar a caballo. . . . To the fort. Over there.
He pointed over the hills. "Soldier, sabe? I go pretty quick.

But he didn't. He only rubbed his brass buttons, dusted o
his boots, whistled a bar of "Yankee Doodle," grinned.

Maria's face remained calm, inscrutable, almost somber
the look of a child which is interested in everything, knowin
nothing, and hence incapable of surprise. It is the same loo
of old women of the world who have seen through it an
expect nothing. But the smile had quickened her blood to th
beat of a song that seemed oddly old and familiar though sh
could not remember its tune. And he kept smiling—close
now.

He suddenly pinched her bare toes. Maria yanked up he
legs, broke out into a giggle. To recover from this astoundin
relapse into the unfamiliar world of childhood, she raised u
and whistled shrilly through her teeth. Far off in the brus
answered the tinkle of a bell. Reassured, like a general, of th
legion at her command, she was again calm and enigmati
But the young adjutant had not released her toes. His han
slid casually up to her knee and settled there lightly as a bir
on a branch. This time Maria did not giggle, nor did sh
whistle to her goats.

"I got to get back. To the fort. Over there, sobre la
montañas," he said after a time in an empty voice, as if t
himself.

"Cómo no?"

Why not, indeed? For it was a strange thing that as thi
weakness grew upon her, so did the strength it held.

So through the afternoon neither moved. The goats stirre
like phantoms through the brush. Major crunched grass witl
the bit still between his teeth. A magpie chattered in th
pine, a hawk hung suspended overhead. The stream ripple
noisily in the silence. It was all one song, a song heard b
none but sung by all. And in the yellowing sunlight the wil
August plums hung darker, softer—green no longer, but ye
not wholly ripe.

Man and woman sprawled closer together now in a sleep
hat was not a sleep nor yet wakefulness. It was the still
rance of August and twilight, between day and night, when
ll things have grown and wait in tranquillity for harvest and
ulfillment.

They sat up suddenly, as if conscious of the shouts of mule
kinners passing on the road as they had all afternoon.

"I ought to be goin' back to the fort," the soldier said,
taring at a tuft of dust shot through by the fire of the setting
un. But instead he tethered Major our of sight in the brush.
Maria called softly to her goats, as if merely to hear their
crackling in the thicket.

The shadow of the pine grew longer, blacker. A breeze was
coming up. And yet neither man nor woman spoke.

When the sun went down they moved back into the wild
plum thicket. Here it was warmer, darker, and there was
nothing to be seen or heard, not even the faint ecstatic
trembling of the plums overhead. . . .

The moon was lifting when they came out. The cliffs were
gray and ghostly across the stream. In the open glade the
ewes stirred uneasily, full of milk. Major whinnied. It was a
strange place. It had changed tone. The man and the woman
looked around them as if they had emerged to unfamiliar
surroundings.

The soldier came back to reality quicker. "Dammit to
hell!" he growled, loosening his horse. "The colonel ordered
me back at dark!"

Maria understood his tone but not the words. She stood
caressing his hat, and did not answer. He grabbed it from her,
slapped it on his head. Now he swiftly buttoned up his tunic.
What a strange man, once his tawny hair was hid. In hats and
brass buttons all gringo soldados looked alike.

He was on his horse now, and Maria, barefooted, was
standing quietly, arms down at her sides.

"Here!" He suddenly leaned down and thrust some
trinkets into her hand. "Adiós, muchacha! Don't let the goats

run off with you!"

Maria watched Major lope across the moonlit glade, h
great strides springy as a cat's on the grassy turf. And far u
the road, in darkness, she could hear his receding gallop.

When he was gone, she examined the thin little gold piec
in her hand. On one side was engraven a star and through
tiny hole ran a piece of blue ribbon. This was very nice. An
he had left her also one of his brass buttons.

She tucked them away in her bundle, and then went out t
count her goats.

At the foot of the pine Maria buried her brass button an
the gold piece with its blue ribbon. It was a shallow little hol
between two roots, and covered with a flat rock—very easil
dug out every week or two when she returned with her goats

On one of her visits something strange happened. The thi
gold piece broke open in her hands. In one inside half was
little picture. It was the face of a gringo lady. Maria gave
little scream of delight. "Bonita! Qué bonita!" She looke
closer, and then murmured awesomely, "Verdad, verdad!
Without doubt it was the face of the colonel's lady. This wa
a wonderful thing, and Maria was more pleased than ever.

She stayed there all day, the brass button in her lap an
the gold piece hung round her throat on its ribbon so that sh
could look at it from time to time. Lackadaisically sh
watched the road, but was never disappointed when thei
giver did not return. Like all gringo soldados, he was a littl
unreal, evanescent as his song. The trinkets he had lef
became themselves unreal, and had no value in nor connec
tion with her daily life. As fetishes they were simply symbol
of an August eve, and so she left them each time in the onl
spot where they had validity.

The twilights came quicker, they faded from gold to brass
took on the greenish hue of leaf mold with the first frost
The picture streaked and faded, the blue ribbon rotted, th
brass tarnished, the gold became encrusted with loam. Wit

he passing of summer they too lost their power. Maria left
hem buried there, and no longer returned. By winter she had
lmost forgotten them.

One day in early April, Maria came down from her hut
nto San Antonio. As she left the trading post, an old woman
obbled out into the muddy road after her. She was lean and
vrinkled, with one sharp eye, and for fingers the prehensile
alons of a hawk—the village midwife. The eye played over
Iaria's broadened hips, the two wild plums of her breasts
10w full and ripe, her cold pinched face. One long curved
alon prodded the girl in the side. Then she thumped Maria's
elly.

"You—daughter of many goats—things are going well?"

"Cómo no, Madre?" Maria answered easily.

"You are plumper than a full moon. You are shorter
vinded than a blown cow. Mark my words, you will not
limb after your goats long."

"Verdad, Madre. But the trail down was steep and the
lrifts deep. I shall work off my weakness with spring; have I
10t always followed my goats?"

"Pues!" snorted the old woman. "You are with child. It
vill be but another moon."

Maria lifted her foot out of one puddle into another, and
wung her gaze along the snowy ridgetop. "Sí. It is what I
1ave often thought, of late, that I shall have a child. Pues!
Iave I not seen my ewes bear each spring?"

"Mother of God! Are you girl or goat?" For a moment she
egarded the girl with the shrewd appraisal of her one eye. "It
vas a soldier then? Another gringo soldado from the
ortaleza? Todos Santos! He knows already, doubtless. Or
hall I be the one to tell him, who have caught so many
others loose-tongued over their bottles?"

To this prodding Maria gave a puzzled frown. "A soldier?
Oh yes. Doubtless, Madre. But how should he know, and
vhy? I have never seen him since."

"Ah, a soldier then! As I knew." The old partera threw

back her dirty rebozo and rubbed her hands together. "Now
tell me. Did he have many brass buttons or few? Was he one
who spoke or one who listened to a master? Was he of those
who are black, or one of the six with flaming hair? He
whispered his name in your ear, perchance? You know the
sound of his horse's feet in the dark? Speak quickly!"

"Mi Madre," answered Maria quietly, "you talk only in
words. In hats and brass buttons all soldiers look alike."

The old woman vainly braced herself against this assault of
ignorance or loyalty. In either case she saw her expectations
of bribery and a fat fee dissipate like smoke.

"Fool! Fool! Burro! Fool! It is what one can expect from
a girl in the hills, wilder than her goats—and one who is
blinded by the song of a crow! But stay, child, listen!" She
caught Maria by the shoulder. Her cracked, greedy voice
lowered to a confidential whine. "It is the way of the world,
of women and soldiers. You have known another? We shall
tell him, eh? Trust it to me, niña! There are men in this world
who are fathers but for my words. Who knows the difference
save God, the priest, and a few chosen few?"

"I do not understand," said Maria. "It is cold. My bundle
is heavy, my legs tired already. I go. Adiós, Madre."

"Go? When then shall we talk business? Come, niña. We
shall agree on the price. You neither know the soldier or
another who would do as well. You are entirely without man.
You are poor. Your time comes quickly. Shall we say a goat?
Perhaps that old ewe I have seen straggling behind?"

"Por Dios! For what? That you should have my best
ewe?"

"Santa Maria! Are you a goat to crawl in a thicket when
your time comes? Who shall watch the phases of your moon,
petition the saints, gather herbs, make tea, measure your
belly, count the heartbeats of him inside? Who shall alleviate
your pain with wisdom, stroke your forehead, mark the cross
on your breasts and seize upon the instant as a swooping hawk
to pluck forth the first fruit of your womb with untellable

:ase? Who but I, who follows men's passions and women's railties from mountain to plain, who has delivered nigh half he souls of this valley to the sun of day—the best partera from Las Colonias to the Cebollita. And the cheapest, niña! Come! Shall we say a fat ewe? With perhaps a bit of cheese each week until the happy throes of pain clutch at your belly, and you cry wildly for these practiced old hands, this stout heart and all the knowledge of the new ways?"

"I had not thought it so important—this simple thing of having a child," murmured Maria vaguely. "But perhaps, as you say, a bit of advice . . . a simpática. . . ."

"Bueno! A ewe then! And the cheese? A bit now on this cold winter day?"

"Pues, but Madre. A child—truly that is something. I have never had a child before. But a goat. Yes. A goat is something else. They are my friends, my compadres, my children too. And the cheese. Mother!" she said resolutely, "we shall say perhaps a goat. But certainly not my best ewe, who lags behind because her bag is heavy. But a goat. Yes, perhaps a goat."

So a month and a shaving later, Maria parted with one of her herd. It seemed a needless extravagance, and never again did she succumb to the luxury of a partera. What she really bought was a vast knowledge of midwifery, and the sound of another human voice and the touch of a hand in the loneliness of her little mountainside hut.

The child, she reflected, would have come anyway. It was a boy. The old woman called it Teodosio—her favorite name. So did Maria later.

His coming made little difference in her life. He simply added to the weight of the bundle she carried about, leading her goats. In truth, Teodosio was never much. He was rachitic and sickly, and his apathy grew into the incurable disease of laziness. Maria always called him the runt of a litter. Her phrase contained the germ of endearment. It did not come until she really began to notice him. He had black hair, dark eyes and iodine-colored skin. This lent her some satisfaction, for by then there was throughtout the valley a scatter of queer-looking children, dark skinned youngsters with red hair, and some with thick lips, wide fleshy nostrils and negroid cheeks.

It was not Teodosio then, but the first ripe August after his coming that reminded Maria of the gringo soldado and the trinkets buried at the foot of the pine. She carried the boy there. Squirrels or water had scooped out her hiding place between the roots. Without its fetishes, the place had lost its validity. It seemed just one glade of many.

Maria settled down, her back to the road, and suckled the child on her lap. There had been rain in the mountains, the stream ran full and noisily. In the glade the grass was high. The thickets were heavy with plums. In the hot stillness of the afternoon her goats wandered sleepily after the tinkle of a bell. Maria was well content.

4

Maria at eighteen had given up rambling the cañons with her goats. She had moved down from her mountainside hut to live with a young muleteer at the bottom of the cliffs. They had a new girl child whose smiling aliveness balanced Teodosio's sullen laziness. In front of their squat, two-room adobe, their few varas of land sloped down into the valley. Behind was a rocky corral to hold the last of Maria's goats, a pig, four mules and a great wagon.

The piece of hillside with its adobe lent them stability, the mules and wagon a meager living, and the children sanctified their love.

A little of the wildness went out of Maria's eyes. Her body, grown heavier, no longer moved with the alert stealthiness of an animal. Her voice lost its faintly hollow sound as her ears grew accustomed to hearing it answered by something besides an echo. She did not become soft. She was up an hour before dawn to beat Onesimo's tortillas thin, and her furious calp-clap-clap resounded again at dark like an assault against time and loneliness.

Onesimo was a man of twenty-two. His long thin body
covered with hand-dressed leather looked like a monk's in
brown sackcloth. He had a lean ascetic face sallow in tone. It
sloped backward from a weak chin jutting a few uncut hairs
to a narrow smooth forehead, and the slant was continued by
his straight black hair combed back over his small round
head. He thus appeared to be continually gazing upward—like
a martyr tied to a cross and searching the heavens for an echo
of his faith. He was a simple, credulous fellow, he had long
and kind though calloused hands, and was an excellent mule
skinner.

Onesimo hauled grain, hay and wood to the fort, leaving
Maria with her girl child, her work and goats. Often he took
Teodosio.

"Who knows?" Maria would say. "Perhaps there will come
the day when you recognize his father, he with tawny hair.
You have asked among the others, Onesimo? Qué lástima!
No doubt he grieves, believing his loins dry and seedless."

"I ask, but am answered with laughter. It is as if God
permits his ignorance. . . . But still, as I have said, there was
talk among the soldiers of him whom the colonel sent
angrily away because of this lady. But I shall ask." And
Onesimo mildly drove away with Teodosio beside him.

Maria shrugged and went out to the wood pile with her
axe. It was difficult to remind herself from time to time of
the almost forgotten gringo soldado. In her happiness she
somehow felt that she had done him ill. But at the fort
soldiers came and soldiers went. And soon no more new
soldiers came, and troop by troop all the old ones left—even
the red-faced colonel. Onesimo told her that the fortaleza
was empty as a last year's magpie nest. Only the dust
marched down the parade ground, the wind and the rain ate
at the walls. She herself felt Santa Gertrudes go dead and
barren. And in the great inn the French music box with its
quadrilles, polkas and valses alone remained to gather
cobwebs in the unused parlor.

Onesimo lost his big wagon and three of his mules. With the fourth he plowed his bit of rocky ground. Maria followed behind. With a sharp stick she poked holes in the earth, and dropped into each a kernel of corn. All over the valley people were doing the same. The gold and silver, the laughter and riot, the soldiers and all the gringos had gone. But the land remained, and the people dug in to sink their roots.

Maria and Onesimo were still ambitious. They wanted to get married and have the children baptized, all at once—perhaps on Christmas. This, thought Onesimo, would be very nice.

"On the very nacimiento of Nuestro Señor," he would say at night. "On the day that the Christ child lay in the little barn with the cows and horses and chickens and pigs about him. Humble like ourselves, Maria." And he would reach down his long, kind and calloused hand to a goat or a pig huddling up to him for warmth. "He, Our Lord, will bless our love. We shall be man and wife on paper like any gente de razón, and be much respected. And the children. Ójala! The holy water will dedicate them to God. Niña, what shall we name the niña, the first of my seed? It must be just so. Inocencia? Is not her smile chaste? Quiteria? Purísima Conception?—though to be sure it was but the desire for your ripe breasts and eager body that drove me up the cliffs those many nights before you came to me here. Serafin? Ah, but wait till you see the angels painted in the church, like God's doves, with silver wings. Macedonia? Fidencia Eutima? Pues—it will come, the proper name for our niña. The priest will reveal God's will."

Maria had little to say. She had never been to church. But from Onesimo she was learning much of God, of Jesú Cristo and all the Saints. She could not be fanatically devout as Onesimo who wore a cross under his shirt, carved another for the house, spoke of the Saints more familiarly than of his friends, and to whom the Passion was the greatest thing he could conceive. Maria lacked the imagination which makes saints of fools, martyrs of fanatics, and lends grace and strength to the most humble of men.

In all the stories she saw only the human frailty and the human triumph of their holy participants. Joseph in the pit Peter at his nets; Daniel walking unarmed among lions— "Verdad? And no staff, not even a knife? Santísima! I cannot imagine such mountain lions!" Judas she forgave. "For why did not El Señor give him the thirteen pieces of gold first? He who could make a thousand fishes from one surely would not begrudge a poor man a few pesos for his tortillas. Could He not take care of Himself as well?" But Jesús she liked. She imagined him riding down the dusty valley road astraddle a burro, "the short and simple animal of the poor." A long lean man, with narrow kind hands and thin ascetic face, His long legs dangling to the ground. He reminded her of Onesimo. And when He found He had no power really, and the soldados drove great iron nails through His narrow kind hands and limp dusty feet, and He leaned His head back upon the cross to stare upward into the heavens for an echo of His faith—ah, then Maria's heart cried out with comprehension. "Pobrecito! Pobrecito Jesús! And no doubt the crows and buzzards swooped down to eat out His eyes. How much better had this poor Jesús gone into the hills with some goats, had He trusted to the earth and not the heavens!"

They were great men, these Saints, the Father's Son and His Holy Twelve. But deep in her heart their religion seemed less than that of those two old philosophers who had taught her that even the skulls of goats reflect the pattern of the stars and the power of the earth below. So secretly she climbed the cliffs to the little hut wherein she had lived alone, there to consult signs of the future.

They told no more than Onesimo's little wooden box with its diminishing silver pesos which he had been saving for the ceremony. "There are but half enough," he would say. "No longer they grow, but dwindle. Yet the priests are kind. They will take the money and a promise to God for the rest. Have no fear."

On Christmas Eve they set out for midnight mass. Maria on the mule, wrapped in rebozo and blanket, and carrying the niña. Teodosio behind on the rump. And Onesimo walking ahead to lead the beast. Like Joseph, thought Maria, leading another Mary to another village on a cold December night. And she watched his tall lean figure plodding in front, head up as if he were guided by a bright, mounting star, his left hand stuck inside his leather coat to feel the little buckskin sack of pesos against his breast.

The night was clear and cold, the valley a long crescent lake of blue between the steep black hills. There were patches of snow on the lower pine slopes. The peaks cut sharp and white into the sky. But because the roads were hard and dry, the valley was alive with travelers. They were coming down the cañons from Chacón and Guadalupita, up from La Cueva, across the campo from Los Altos and over the hills from Ledoux. Lone horsemen. Groups of six or seven on patient, pattering burros. Families en todo huddled between straw and blankets in creaking wagons.

"Adiós!" they called in passing, their muffled voices rising into the dark, cold stillness.

"Adiós!" answered Onesimo in his low proud voice.

Adiós! Adiós! The synonymous word of greeting and farewell of a people who know their transiency upon the wide and bitter earth.

It was nearly midnight when they plodded into Santa Gertrudes. Two bonfires lit up the crowded plaza; on top the walls luminarias were burning, little rows of flickering flames. It all had a queer, still aliveness, a vatic hush. Even the chiming of the frosty bells. So that the people walked quickly, stealthily and without greeting from their tethered mounts and wagons.

The posadas were over. But in Pierre Fortier's window, lit by two candles, gleamed the manger of Bethlehem. The box was filled with straw. In it lay the Holy Family, tiny wooden figures, and horses, cows, goats, a rooster of red cedar. Overhead hung a tin star.

"Bonita! Qué bonita!" Maria clapped her numb hands. But Onesimo knelt stiffly in the road and raked off his hat in silence.

Now, swung with the stream, they stepped humbly into the church. Maria gasped. With her first look, religion took on for her the awesome splendor of gold and gilt and brass, of silk and lace, of shinning light. She forgot the long lean man with a thin gentle face, the humble Jesus riding down the dusty road on a burro. She forgot how His narrow kind hands and limp dusty feet had been peirced with great iron nails, the meekness and humbleness of His teachings. She forgot, as all men since have forgotten, the creed of the spirit. And she saw only what all men see—the ornate, splendid and confusing temple of its impressive and meaningless outward form.

Maria was not aware that in one instant something within her had refuted forever Onesimo's faith. She was too dumbfounded at that cavernous temple of unbelievable splendor with its huge carven vigas, each in its time a lofty pine and now bedecked again with fresh branches, with its hundred santos and tapestries, its thousand candles gleaming everywhere, its altar magnificent beyond her imagination. Madre! Was it possible? Here? In Santa Gertrudes?

Onesimo was abashed too, and Maria could not understand his hesitation. Was he not devout, no stranger to this church of God? They were still standing just inside the doors. Onesimo, hat off and carrying Teodosio, and Maria with her rebozo covering both the niña and her own face so that only her eyes peeked out.

The church was packed; a few rows of benches in front, then more villagers sitting stolidly on chairs they had carried from home, and in back and down the aisles more and more people crowding in to kneel on the hard, uneven planks.

Pushed from behind, Maria started forward. But Onesimo

gently plucked her shawl, and humbly led her to the cold back corner. "We shall kneel here with the poor and the sinful," he whispered. "I have not paid for these many months. Besides, it is only the gente de razón who have seats in front."

Above them a candle in an iron socket dripped tallow down the wall. By its guttering light Maria could see Onesimo's face. It held a strange soft look of adoration and abnegation. He head was tilted backward, so that his long uncut hair hung down on his greasy leather coat. His eyes were closed. He was mumbling inaudibly through trembling lips.

So in cold and candlelight, in wonder and adoration, they knelt praying God to forgive them their ununderstood sins and the weak flesh that cramped and cringed from the hard, cold floor. A column of children filed past carrying pine branches and candles. An unseen chorus wailed "Ave Maria." A priest paraded, head down and swinging a little pot that perfumed the air. And all this sound and smell and movement beat vainly, like waves, against the jutting altar.

An incomprehensible ritual held them at bay. Candles were lit and snuffed, books opened and snapped shut, altar cloths laid and folded up. Two priests controlled the magic. A young slim one who had paraded with the fragrant pot, and an old fat one. When they knelt, stiffly as if in a great hurry, Maria could see the young one's close-cropped bullet head. When they turned around she watched the old one's white fat hands fluttering at his chest like birds, also in a hurry. They rang little bells, lifted crosses and forever kept up a low mumble in a strange tongue. This impressed Maria. She knew it was the language of God which only they could understand.

But now the old fat one spoke the Spanish, and then the gringo. His Spanish was queerly slurred. He spoke it as one of the arrogant viejos contemptuously referred to by the people of the valley as "Don Thinco Thentavos de Athucar." But

Maria listened patiently. He was talking of José y Maria, the gentle Jesús and how all men should be simpático, simple and poor.

The mass ended. People pushed forward for a sip of Christ's blood and a taste of the bread which was His flesh. Many, like Onesimo, crawled all the way down front on their knees. Maria waited in the corner. She suckled the niña again, then roused Teodosio from the sheepskin on the floor.

The doors were opened. Christmas Day stood on the threshold, cloaked in darkness and bitter cold. The people with eyes still lit by wonder trudged out to their horses and wagons. Only Onesimo and Maria remained, each with a child in his arms.

"Come, Maria," he said smiling gently. "It is the moment. The Christ is born. We shall be united in His name."

They walked slowly down the empty church, and halted at the railing before the altar. The young slim priest was hurriedly snuffing candles. He had taken off his robe, undone his collar.

Onesimo laid down Teodosio, still sleepily whining, and threw over the boy his sheepskin. "Padre, mi padre!" he called softly. "Un momentito, one word in the name of God." Hat in hand he walked toward the priest in the flickering candlelight. Maria waited patiently in the gelid gloom. The silence was sepulchral. It was broken by Onesimo's low impassioned voice and the sharp queries of the priest.

"Sí, Padre, sí, sí! We would wait no longer. Our bodies have been joined by the the fire of passion. Let now our union be tempered with the Holy Water and the cooling faith of Him born this night. Mira! Our niña waits for a name."

"But now? Near dawn? What is this? Does not the good padre give days for marrying and send word from village to village? My eyes see yet another child. He is well grown. You and this woman have waited long. How now would you hurry? The mass has tired the padre. I myself am sleepy.

Come again, my son."

"But I have money. Look. In this little bag."

The priest hefted the buckskin bag in his hand. "There is very little, more will be needed," he answered reluctantly. "But I shall call the padre. Padre! Blessed Father!"

From a room behind the altar the old, fat padre came out. His eyes were small and cunning, his jaw resolute, his hands fat and white. Maria, from the darkness, saw that he had laid away the grace of God with his robe. He scratched himself like a man.

Onesimo did not see the scratching. He had knelt at the padre's feet for a blessing. The fat white hands were over his head, but they were counting the pesos poured from the little buckskin bag.

"It is a strange request," the young priest was saying. "There is the matter of writing the papers, for one thing. There is tomorrow and the day after, there are the regular days for marrying. Perhaps the Lord will not permit His gracious servant to be so unduly tired at such a time of night. All this have I pointed out. Yet there is this to be said, God always welcomes new lambs into the fold. See, there are two. Look also, the man is humble but devout, though stubborn. And he has brought money. Did you count it, Padre? Pues! You have promised the rest soon, my son?"

"Sí, seguro! Certainly, mis padres. To God I promised the rest. Are we not humble but honest?" Onesimo stood up then with a face illumined by anticipation.

The padre scowled. He had pocketed the pesos: they would, no doubt, stop his scratching. As he carelessly handed back to Onesimo the limp buckskin bag, his fat white hand lifted. He grasped Onesimo's long lean face by the chin and turned it into the full glare of a candle.

"God permits my memory to fail, but my eyes never. I have seen you before." His small eyes glittered coldly. "Yes, I saw you often. Then suddenly you came no more."

Onesimo's face, released, dropped into the shadow. His

long thin body went boneless. "I had no money," he said tonelessly. "When the gringo soldados left the fortaleza I had no work. Three mouths there were to feed. But God I did not forget. Padre, I remembered! I am here now." His voice strengthened. Maria saw him raise his face.

But in the padre's she saw a sullen anger. It flamed up in his eyes, his voice.

"Do you lie? Here before God?" he thundered. "Confess where you have been, and others! That certain group of men who think to take the worship of God into their own hands. Los Hermanos they call themselves. Brothers of Sangre de Cristo. Brothers! Brothers of iniquity! Brothers of sin and evil practices! Have I not denounced such practices, according to the blessed instructions of the Archbishop Salpointe from God?" His voice beat at Onesimo, at the young priest, at Maria waiting in the darkness. "That is where you have been, evil man, Brother of Evil! On your knees, sinner! Confess that from such cursed practices you have crept into this Holy House!"

But strangely, it seemed to Maria, Onesimo did not fall to his knees. Boneless and contrite, yet curiously resolute, his long thin body stood before the priest.

"Pecado, pecado," he said in a hushed, low voice. "I have sinned, but my sins will be forgiven for I have remembered God. And so I have come with my woman to be united in His name."

The padre's fat white face had gone red. The little blue veins stuck out. He shook his fist at the high honey-colored vigas. "You do not confess! You do not name your evil Brothers! Mother of God! But I shall learn. Dios tarda pero no olvida. Yes! God delays but does not forget. In His name these cursed Brothers, these evil flagellants will be excluded from the Church. Hah!" He seized Onesimo by his leather coat, stood peering into the lean ascetic face. "And then what? They will be excommunicated!"

Maria heard the young priest gasp beside him. But from

Onesimo she heard nothing. Only his face seemed to have grown more sallow as he stared upward over the padre's head.

The priest misjudged his silence. "It is a warning to you who would escape God's eyes and come here for His blessing. And now," he added curtly, "go and reflect upon your sin. Until you return to confess there will be no talk of marrying. And see that you tell others—that I, their good father, have the eyes of Heaven."

And so in cold and darkness they plodded home under the frosty stars. Maria on the mule, wrapped in rebozo and blanket, and carrying the niña still nameless. Teodosio on the rump. And Onesimo's tall lean body plodding in front, head up as if he were guided by a fading star, his left hand tuck inside his leather coat to feel the empty buckskin bag against his breast.

Maria was a little confused.

"I do not think we shall be married," she said when the plodding mule stopped before their hut.

Onesimo gently lifted down Teodosio, then took the niña in his arms. "No, I do not think we shall be married," he assented in his low proud voice.

Maria sighed without understanding or regret. The pallid wintry dawn was seeping over the valley walls. The earth, timeless and immense, had not changed. It was all as before.

In spring too the valley is beautiful and blue, but the beauty is muted and the blue diminished by the intense white light of the steadily rising sun. The mountain walls shrink back. The valley lifts. It is only one ampitheater of many in a vast continental plateau. And so it reflects the mystic strangeness and inimical austerity of the greater whole.

Occasional clouds of apricot, peach and wild plum blossom soften the harshness in the river bottoms below. They repeat the variolitic white splotches of snow and ice and sleet in the cañons above. Both are ephemeral white shadows on the face of the dark enduring earth. Its features are the red sandstone cliffs, the sandy hillocks of yucca, the bare red-brown earth and the chocolate mud banks along the lower river. Its expression is fixed and inimical, and the same look of strained attention and repellent remoteness is seen in the faces of the people. It is as if the brilliant blinding light reveals their common soul.

Maria could see it in Onesimo's vacuous, bloodshot eyes as she saw it at twilight when the Sangre de Cristo took on the color of their name. Thus she first understood the Brothers of Light, the Brothers of the Blood of Christ, divining dimly the ununderstood truth that faiths like everything else spring from and are distorted by their earth.

Onesimo was still kind and humble, simpático always. He never referred to his disappointing visit to the priest, to their conversation, nor did he ever return to church. Yet little by little he changed. He neglected his rockly fields to wander up the cañons. When he returned at night he would sit brooding in the corner. His eyes became vibrating pools of light. His tall lean body grew leaner, his long ascetic face thinner. Suddenly he lay with her no more, and slept beside Teodosio on a sheepskin.

This religion business! Maria fought faith with faith. She clapped out his tortillas ever thinner, hoed the weeds, held her tongue, and was more than mindful of Teodosio and Niña.

"You are a good and a discreet woman," said Onesimo gently. "But there are things women do not understand."

Gradually she learned a bit here and there from other women working in the fields. They too were not slept with, held their tongues and maintained caution lest the padre at church learn too much. Their men too were Hermanos— Panocha Eaters as they were known in the idioma, for now they ate little more than the gluey brown pudding made from wheat sprouted, dried and then ground into flour.

At nights, for she could be trusted, a neighboring Hermano came to visit Onesimo. He too was a simple, poor paisano and

ad the Light in his eyes. In the dark he would knock softly
t the hut, and Onesimo would open the door.

"Who gives light to this house?"

"Jesus."

"Who fills it with joy?"

"Mary."

"Who preserves it with faith?"

"Joseph."

Thus they talked: catechism and answer. Then the visitor
entered. He bought an old paper book of faded writing. Its
leaves were tattered as if a goat had fed upon the edges. It
was a book of hymns; and because Onesimo could not read,
he rezador was teaching him the chants. The two men sat in
he corner huddled over a candle. Verse after verse the words
went on:

> *In these arms outstretched*
> *Here is the Divine Light!*
> *In His brotherhood we take*
> *Our Father Jesus . . . .*

> *De la tierra fui formado,*
> *La tierra me a de comer;*
> *La tierra me a sustantado,*
> *Y al fin yo tierra ha de ser.*

On Ash Wednesday, Onesimo climbed the hills for a piece
of flint which he chipped and sharpened. That evening as he
left the house he asked solemnly, "You will have a bit of
Romero Weed boiled for me when I return?"

Maria nodded silently and watched his tall lean figure,
head upraised, striding swiftly across the campo. It was dusk.
The blue mountain peaks were topped with snow. Up the
cañon, on a bleak water-gashed hilltop, stood a squat
windowless adobe. Before it rose a cross. It was tall and lean.
It looked like a man with arms outstretched. Quickly, before

dark, she went out for a bit of the weed.

It was boiled when Onesimo returned. Hearing his stumbl Maria lighted the candle. His face was more sallow, his ey brighter. He lay down on the sheepskin, lifted his blood shirt. There were three gashes down, and three gashes acro his back.

"What is this?" she asked quietly.

"It is the thing of obligation," he answered softly.

So in silence she washed him with tea of the weed.

The Lenten penance had begun. For weeks it continued Onesimo stumbled home with three lashes from a yucca whi on each side of his spine.

"What now is this, Onesimo?"

"For the love of God, the Three Meditations of the Passio of Our Lord." He would say no more.

Thus successively he stumbled home with the Five Wound of Christ, and the Seven Last Words, and lay uncomplainin while she washed him with the rosemary.

But one night they brought him home on a burro. Tw stern-faced, sad-eyed men held up his long, wilting body They stretched him on the floor. His back was raw, th wounds of the lashes tangled like goat hairs. This, for the lov of God, was the Forty Days in the Wilderness.

"I fainted. I could stand but few. My sinful flesh wa weak," moaned Onesimo with shame.

"But his will be the glory," said one of the men, and the stood with unfathomable respect and pity in their dark, sa eyes.

Maria did not speak. Neither did she weep. But her hear bled like his back. And as before, she bathed his wounds wit rosemary. What is the strange love of a woman to the strange lover of a God? What is the meek rich ripeness of the earth t the brilliant blinding light? So in her misery she doubted th enduring even while she endured.

When a stranger happened to inquire why Onesimo was i bed that next day, she replied casually, "Why, Señor, tha ranky old mule kicked him in the leg. He will soon be up, nd with a club in his hand." But she did not invite him in.

At the beginning of Holy Week the two priests from the hurch rode up the valley. They went from hut to hut, from anchito to ranchito. By the time they arrived at Maria's their cowls were black. But they affected a pleasant greeting, sked for water.

"Ah, you have not come to be married! You wish to live in vil yet, perhaps?"

"No, Señor Padre."

"Good! We will talk to your man about it. We will talk bout the services to be held soon, on Holy Thursday, on ;ood Friday, on Sunday when the Christ rose again. You are oming no doubt?"

"Oh doubtless, Señor Padre."

"But where is your man?"

"Oh, he has gone up into the mountains for wood."

"But we see much wood behind the house."

"One always cuts wood."

The fat padre bit his lip. "I see no man in the fields. I see nly women. Are they all cutting wood?"

"Oh doubtless, Señor Padre." And Maria watched them ide away, scowling.

Onesimo was gone all week. He was up at the morada, on he water-gashed hilltop up the cañon. She took her turn vith other women carrying up bowls of panocha, sometimes . bowl of sopa. The walls of the morada were four feet thick, t had no windows and its one door was closed. She could ıear chanting or praying inside. So she set her bowl outside ınd trudged back down the trail.

On Wednesday a light snow fell. Late afternoon the sun :ame out. The sky was gray, the earth was gray and bitter as alt. The morada on the hilltop squatted before the dark ›ines. Its cross spread its lean arms against the sky. From it at wilight Maria watched a line of men emerge and file up the :añon. She could hear, faintly, the thin piping of a flute and

the low soughing of a chant. Several of the tiny figures we
bent under crosses they were carrying. The rest swung the
arms over one shoulder and then the other. She knew the
were swinging braided yucca whips, beating their backs.

On Holy Thursday she saw them again from the door o
her hut, her heart bleeding like Onesimo's back. "Pobrecit
Pobrecito." And she gathered still more rosemary against h
return.

On Good Friday she awakened early, and with a prem
nition of evil. She bundled Niña on her back, and yank
Teodosio up the arroyo behind the house. They climbe
higher—to the tall jutting cliffs above her old deserte
mountainside hut. Across the valley she could see the squ;
morada. The brilliant blinding light beat down upon th
snowy hilltop. The faded white cross gleamed nakedly again
the pines. The earth was still, and the stillness was oppressi
with the sin of man.

Again the procession came out of the morada, climbir
into the dark cañon—the Procession de Sangre. Maria cou
hear no chanting alabados, could see no carried crosses. Just
long file of tiny men naked to the waist and steadily floggir
themselves in silence. An hour later they came back and shr
themselves up in the morada.

Far down the crescent valley, in Santa Gertrudes churc
bells began to ring. The roads filled with people dressed up i
Sunday clothes for the padre's mass. Maria looked up at th
sun. It was high noon. It was the time when the Three Hour
Services began, commemorating Christ's agony and death o
the Holy Cross.

A flock of black shadows raced south over the snow
fields without cawing. A buzzard hung overhead. Mar
shuddered. The silence thickened. Through it she fled swiftl
back down the rocky trail, and shut herself up in the hr
with the children.

Onesimo's faith gripped her by the throat. She lay dow
on her bed, and put her hands over her eyes to shut out th

d marks on Onesimo's back of the Three Meditations of the
ssion of Our Lord, the Five Wounds of Christ, the Seven
st Words, and the Forty Days in the Wilderness.

"Madre de Dios!" she whimpered. "What now?"

She tried to sleep.

The room seemed bare, dark and silent. It was neither. A
rrow slit high up under the eaves let in a bit of strong,
hite, north light upon the white-washed back wall. Candle-
ht illumined the altar in front—a plank table covered by a
rty white cloth on which was sewn a row of huge black
osses. On it, besides the dripping candles, stood several
ooden Santos: a large sad Cristo in lace petticoats; a smaller
ae naked and bloody with clotted red paint, and hanging to
cross; figures of the Virgin, of San Juan Bautista and San
sé. Before them lay an earthen bowl of flowers, a Bible and
old copybook of hymns, both opened. On the hard dirt
or knelt some twenty-five men. Their hierophantic bodies
d low voices, the garish altar and weeping candles did not
l the room's sepulchral emptiness. They were part of it.

After a time the praying ceased. The phalanx of kneeling
en became a wedge driven between death and silence, and
e and light. Tears ran down their strong simple faces. Their
own bare backs were dark with clotted blood. Anguish dug
eir mudshoed feet deeper into the dirt floor.

The life and light came from a calm-faced, broad-
ouldered man in the candlelight who began to read out of a
ok on the altar. He was the Hermano Mayor reciting the
st of the Passion.

The death and silence was embodied in a man who knelt at
e back of the room under the slit of white north light. His
ng thin body was naked except for a loin cloth. His arms
ing limply at his sides. His lean ascetic face was tilted
ward and sloped back from a weak chin to a narrow
rehead. Neither his lips nor eyes moved. He simply stared,
th a hypnotic look of gentle adoration and somber

fatalism, at a figure on the right wall.

It hung by a cord around the throat, and with the terrib
broken limpness of a body dashed down on rocks from
great height. It was dressed in rusty black cloth and sma
child's shoes. From its pale white head drooping forward
gawked huge, round, black eyesockets. In its limp, skeleton
hands dangled a bow and arrow. It was a figure of Death.

The recitation ended. With a clear, sound voice th
resolute, broad-shouldered man prayed God to forgive th
sins of all the men in this world. The kneeling phalanx rose
sobbing. One of the men took the large sad Cristo in his arm
another picked up the open copy-book from the altar.

The almost-naked, lean ascetic still knelt in the back of th
room as if in a trance. A compañero touched him gently o
the arm.

"Brother. The time has come."

The tall, lean man rose and smiled. He followed the other
outside.

Below the water-gashed hilltop lay the long, crescer
valley. The late afternoon sun, like candlelight, gave it life
The snow had melted. The new plowed fields smelt rich an
pregnant. The stream gushed noisily down the rocks.

But the wall of mountains above the morada was slate blu
under leaden clouds. It shut off the sun from arroyo an
piñon slope. A cold white light filtered through the pine
upon patches of snow. The cañon was a dark mouth tha
swallowed a narrow trail. It held death and silence.

To it the men turned after locking the door of the morada
They formed a long procession which crawled up the narrow
rocky trail into the cañon. The broad-shouldered ma
carrying the Cristo. The reader carrying the opened copy
book, and leading the hymn. The lean ascetic staggerin
under a heavy cross. And the rest, following behind, chantin
and flogging themselves with whips.

Their deep male voices rose and fell in a monotonou
miserere. So did the yucca whips—over one shoulder and the

e other. Soon the sharp slap of the cactus on their backs
came a soggy thud.

They kept climbing steadily but slowly. The lean ascetic
ith his cross retarded their progress. The leg of the huge,
nd-hewn timber dragged on the ground. One arm stuck up
rtically into the sky. The man's thin body bent under its
eight. His sallow face flushed with exertion. Sweat ran
wn his gaunt cheeks.

He fell often: sliding in the mud at the bottom of the
royo, stumbling over rocks as the trail rose upward, and
pping in the soft snow above. Face down he plunged, arms
tspread, the heavy timber on top of him. For a moment he
y quietly, his breath whistling through the thin lips fixed in
eir unalterable smile.

His companions waited patiently, drawing their soggy
cca lashes through calloused hands. When the cross bearer
d struggled erect they moved on, chanting. The snow banks
ead grew deeper, whiter. Behind, on each side, they were
ecked with spots of red.

The trail led up into a small clearing behind the ridge of
e cañon. Around it stood great serried pines and spruces. In
was a deep round hole. Here the line of men became a
rcle.

One of them stepped forward a pace with the sad-eyed
risto in his arms. Another got down and dug out some fallen
ods from the hole. Two others laid the huge cross on the
ound, and bound the bearer upon it. Carefully now, and
ntly, they lifted the butt of the cross into the hole,
amped it solid and stepped back.

Over the ridge and down the cañon, spring had come to
e valley with light and life. But here it was yet unresur-
cted winter. The pale white effulgence, without source,
ade a well of light in the dark forest. The bitter, pungent
nell of leaf mold and soggy brown pine needles exuded
eath and decay. The great trees wept. Yellow tears hung on
eir bearded faces. The whole earth gave itself to the stark

parable of the Crucifixion.

The man on the cross did not stir or whimper. His wris and ankles were bound to the timbers with horsehair ropes. dirty, white cloth band passing around his waist helped hold him upright. Above it the ribs stuck out from his lon thin body. His lean, ascetic face was tilted backward again the beam. It still maintained a fixed and gentle smile. H dark eyes sought the heavens for an echo of his faith.

He was no longer a man. He was a great, obdurate fact— fact timeless as the earth itself which ever dies to b resurrected again, the only enduring truth.

The outer circle of pines soughed faintly. The inner circ of men breathed hoarsely. And still he hung there, tossed u by the mute and unresistant earth, a hostage to the cruel an bitter skies.

But his long lean body had sagged. Little slivers of ski curled over the chafing horsehair ropes. His bony knees stuc out. After a time his head straightened. He was starin directly into the face of the Cristo held up to him.

There was something wrong about this face. It was a littl too Spanish-Moorish with its sparse black beard carefull combed; and its sad eyes contained a bit too muc resignation. This Cristo did not know that death of the eart which is a bitter thing and not accepted lightly. Nor did h know the terrible birth pangs of spring, that eternal resu rection which is a struggle worse than death.

But the man on the cross knew, being part of that earth s cruel and unresistant, so gentle and yet so enduring. And s his smile seemed slightly ironic and he closed his eyes as the heavens were pitilessly empty of the faith he had sough

Suddenly his head drooped forward. His body slumpec yanking at his fetters.

The circle around him broke. Men leapt to dig out an lower the cross, to untie him. The thing was over. They wer no longer estatic Brothers. They were men with sore an bloody backs, half-starved from fasting on panocha. The

egan to talk, to shiver in the cold, to wind up their soggy
ucca whips. Somber reasonableness came back into their
red, wild eyes.

A few drops of blood still splashed the sky above the pine
ps, then night erased them with a gray hand. The men were
athered about the unconscious lean one untied from his
ross and recumbent upon the ground. Lackadaisically they
hafed his wrists and legs, waiting for him to come to. Now a
ellow came up from the stream with water. He splashed it on
he unconscious man's face, his wrists and belly.

Suddenly he stooped down. He stared at the ascetic, sallow
ace on which was engraven the gentle, bitter smile. He felt
he thin wrists and let them drop stiffly back. And now,
uickly, he bent an ear to the lean still torso.

"Mother of God!" he cried, jumping to his feet. "His eyes,
is wrists, his heart—He. . . ."

The men surged forward.

"It cannot be! He is but young and frail. He is over weak
om fasting. He lost too much blood for long. He spent his
trength too freely. His faith has been too devout. . . ."

"Jesú Cristo! . . . God will not permit it! He has not
ermitted such a thing to happen for these many years!"

And still that great, obdurate fact lay there before them.
ts lean nakedness was colder, whiter than snow in the
hadow of the pines. Its deathly silence was more tumultuous
han the thunderous mountain shapes. It was an immovable
act greater than their faith. In the chill darkness its wet loin
loth had already begun to stick to the damp ground.

The earth, of which he was a symbol, was already eager to
ake him back.

It was dark when Maria was awakened by a pounding on
he door.

She sat up and stared, stupid with sleep, around the room.
he knocking had stopped, but an echo still beat in her mind.
t seemed an echo of something greater: of the hour after the

Christ had died upon His cross, when the heavens darkene
the earth gaped and the graves burst open.

Teodosio had fallen asleep on the floor, but Niña w
pulling at her breasts and howling with hunger. It was th
that finally aroused her.

She got up, lit candle and fire, laid out three bowls
warmed goat's milk.

Her mind had cleared now, but she still felt uneasy abo
Onesimo. Pues! He had always come back. He would tonigh
Pobrecito, pobrecito. She set to boil a huge kettle
rosemary. Then she opened the door to stare out across th
fields toward the morada on the water-gashed hilltop.

On the doorstep lay an empty pair of shoes. She closed th
door and carried them into the candlelight. The shoes we
old and shapeless, caked with mud and spotted with drie
blood. They were Onesimo's.

The sudden meaning of their appalling emptiness stabbe
her like a knife. It carved out her heart and bowels and min
She stood more empty than the shoes, one hand clawing
her face, holding her breast, then pressing against her bel

Teodosio and Niña were gulping goat's milk from wood
spoons. Maria bent down to her own bowl, and lifted out
hair from the milk with her forefinger. Suddenly sh
straightened. With a fearful howl she flung open the door ar
rushed out into the night.

5

ues, there is this about all martyrs: the people they would
ave saved turn upon them and their memories alike, and the
uses they die for grow cold and are forgotten. By their
oble deaths they prove nothing but the supremacy of life
ith all its foibles. Even this Señor Jesús, the Cristo, and
nesimo who had died as He.

And Maria, lashing out against her anguish, banged His
tle cottonwood image over the fireplace, and cracked the
into in two. She knew now exactly what Onesimo's death
as worth to the people of the valley. At first the neighbors
ad given her commiseration, respect and help. Then slowly
ese changed to commination, fear and avoidance.

She heard talk.

"He was too young. . . . He was too weak. . . . His faith
as not whole."

"What business had he to die? It is not the custom.
antísima! Now there is the devil to pay. All because of him.
e foolishly let himself die, and so we must bear the anger of
ie priest and the curse of the church."

So, alone, Maria bent under the burden of their conden nation, the hunger of her fatherless children, and th niggardliness of her rocky field. And between the people an the church drooped somber storm clouds of mistrust and fe; and hate. It was not only Onesimo's death and th unsanctified Brothers of the Light, but everything that w; wrong.

The people no longer lifted their hats to the padre ridin through the fields; the padre no longer rode forth to mee sullen faces and silent lips. The masses were ill-attended an heavy with threat. The archbishop had come and ordered th padre to excommunicate all flagellants from the church. Bu who were these Penitent Brothers? No neighbor took off h; shirt in front of another at the stream's edge lest his scars b seen. Few went to church, they did not get married, they di not take their children to be baptized. The priest thundere against the people, and the people muttered against th priest. And over all, house and field and valley, droope lower the stifling storm clouds of mistrust and fear an hate. . . .

Maria did not know why she went to church that day. Sh did not know why her neighbors went, nor did they. Bu there was something in the air—something light and fleetin that flew from ear to ear; something heavy and stifling tha compressed people out of the cañons, and drew them to th church.

Inside, all was as she had seen it before; the honey-colore vigas gleaming in candlelight, the Santos and gilded crosse the magnificent altar. She listened to the songs, smelled th fragrant little pot paraded around the room, watched th incomprehensible ritual of the mass.

But it was not as Maria had felt it before. For now, witl bitterness in her own heart, she felt the distrust and fear an hate that oozed out from the hearts around her. It cam through their taut heavy bodies as through fissures in th earth. It tinctured the air like the cloying odor of perspi

tion, like fumes of poison. They crowded about her, these
undreds of villagers and valley folk, with faces fixed and
meless as weathered rock, with faces dark and hard as hers.
hey waited.

Through candlelight and silence, the old fat padre came
nd stood before them. No sound greeted him. Not an eyelid
uttered before him. Yet before their stifling negation the
riest went through his ritual. His stiff blue lips mumbled.
lis trembling white hands crossed and recrossed. He slumped
o his knees and rose unsteadily. And now he was standing
efore them, and holding a little glass of Christ's blood.

"Padre! Oh my padre! Stop!" A woman's shriek rent the
ilence with frightened wings. It soared up to the timbered
eiling and raced frantically around the walls. "Stop! For the
ove of God! The sacramental wine. It is poisoned!"

The room erupted. It moaned, groaned, hissed, shouted,
hook. It wept. The priest lifted his hand, and the volcano of
oise and movement ceased.

Now he held up the little glass. It did not tremble, nor the
and which held it. His legs were no longer weak. Firmness
moothed out his white face. Strength parted his blue lips in
gentle smile.

Maria, watching him, felt the bitterness gush from her
eart. Hot drops of anguish rolled down and cooled her
heeks. He was no longer the hated padre. He was something
nore. It came out of his voice.

"My children, my children whom I love," he said clearly,
trongly, kindly. "The wine is poisoned, that I know. Yet it is
vine of man poisoned by the hand of man, and so I know it
ot. For it has been blessed, and so it is no longer wine. It is
he blood of the Christ which will redeem us. Shall we refute
ur faith in a moment of weakness? No, my children. This is
ny cup. In the name of the Christ who redeemed us with His
lood, I cannot refuse it."

Wonderful words he spoke, smiling his sweet kind smile.
le implored their forgiveness, forgave them their sins and the

cup in his hand, entrusted them to the hands of God, the
His children and his. So he prayed, standing there strong
his faith, kind and gentle.

And at its end, very simply, he drained the cup
poisoned wine. . . .

The padre's death lifted the storm clouds of mistrust an
fear and hate from the land, and the bitterness and angui
from Maria's heart. She patched together the Santo she ha
broken, covered him with fresh yeso, and stuck him up in h
old niche. But only as something Onesimo had treasure
greatly.

Strange the faiths of men! Onesimo and the padr
enemies, had both died in His name, and their deaths ha
proved nothing but the strength of their own faiths. And no
together in the same earth they lay silent: the padre in th
Campo Santo, and Onesimo up the cañon above th
water-gashed hillside.

> De la tierra fui formado,
> La tierra me a de comer;
> La tierra me a sustantado,
> Y al fin yo tierra ha de ser.

Long after the memory of Onesimo began at last to fad
she remembered this one of the many alabados he ha
learned. And to the earth, the living earth which alone wou
endure, Maria turned again.

She sold Onesimo's last mule and the pig, traded off th
few sound sticks of furniture. She lugged rocks from th
field, pulled up weeds, carried water by the bucket to th
scrawny corn rows. Quelites, the wild greens, she fed h
children, with milk and cheese from her goats. Fro
dawn-dusk to dark she worked, and it was not enough.

The little crop withered without water, then a late ra
washed the stunted stalks down the rocky hillside. The hou

vas stripped of everything but a few pots, a heap of blankets,
nd two straw mats. Teodosio and the Niña's bellies were
mpty, like the house, and so was Maria's heart. By winter
he emptiness began to show in her eyes. They were the
nouths of two black caves that no one entered, an appalling
acuousness that wind nor rain nor snow ever filled.

Sometimes in the wintry twilight the villagers saw her
oming across the fields. She stood at the door, unbending
rom the storm. One numb brown hand threw back the black
hawl from her face. The other offered a cake of cheese for
rade. And when she left with a bit of corn, they watched her
top furtively at the corral to gather up a handful of straw.

"It is that strange Maria," they would say. "The one with
he evil eye. That woman and her goats! She would steal
nything."

At dusk she reached home. Inside her rebozo she carried
n armful of straw for her goats which she let into the
kitchen. She raked up the fire on the hearth, stirred some
orn meal into hot milk. Fed, the children fell asleep. Maria
huddled before the fire, staring at her drowsy goats. Their
vrinkled horns and skulls contained the only ineradicable
ecord of this day's storm, this day's despair and victory—the
nfinitesimal mark of time, and the almost imperceptible
warping of eternity. Their shagging pink-lit faces showed
nothing of the change. They were the faces of philosophers.
Maria understood them. She had accomplished the day. It
was a victory. She slept without turning over, without a
dream.

Winter passed, and spring and summer. Through them she
fought her way from tortilla to tortilla, from meal to meal.
She combated time with time's only weapon—the thrusting
moment. Slowly she won her way through the years.

She did not try to plant and harvest the rocky hillside. She
made the valley pay. At harvest she followed the falling
crops. Where the wheat grew thickest, the oats tallest, where
the corn drooped heaviest—there trudged Maria with Teodosio.

"Señor. Por favor. For the love of God, Señor. You will l
me glean behind you? I have your permission, no?"

"Of course, poor woman! Would Fulgencio Garcia
Valdes have it said of him that he denied to the poor th
gleaning of his fields? There along the acequia in the mu
There close to the chokecherry thicket where it is difficult t
swing a blade. A fine stand it is! Almost a row!"

So by day Maria rivaled the crows, and by night sh
rivaled the stray stock loosed in the fields according t
custom. Her reward was blanketfuls of grain hid in th
thickets and brought home at night. Her own feet, Niña's an
Teodosio's and those of her goats threshed it on the ba
floor. She separated it carefully: the small wrinkled grair
and the nubbins to be eaten, the fine full grains and fa
kernels to be packed and hidden, never touched by hunge

In early spring she made the rounds.

"Señor, you are breaking this new field. It has never bee
broken before. It is a good field. It needs fine seed. The bes
That I have. A little but the best. You would like to look a
it, verdad? But a moment it takes to look."

"Ah, compadre! What talk I hear you make in the tienda
That you are short of seed when the earth cries for renewa
That you would buy seed brought across the mountains b
strangers. Verguenza! Is that the custom nowadays? Is it tha
the good earth no longer cries for its own seed, that a mothe
would no longer suckle her own? Compadre. You remembe
last year's wheat? The great yellow grains, how firm the
were, how they gleamed in the sun, the weight of them i
your hand! Five measures of them I have saved for you. Wha
do you say to that, compadre?"

But not a fanega would she sell, not a handful. Tw
measures in the fall for one in spring. That was her price
Two measures of the best. She would pick them out hersel

Maria was wise and shrewd. From the cliffs of Lo
Alamitos to the flatlands below La Cueva, from valley wall t
valley wall, she doled out her seed. Not to men living to

ose together, nor much to each.

She was also niggardly. For as the grain bags heaped she
id them beneath straw, secreted them in the loft, and
onccaled even in her goat's hut. She became known not for
much, but for a bag or two that was always available. Of the
est. She had a power, this stange Maria, even with seeds.

The Niña grew, and was a great help. Teodosio grew, but
as never much. Maria bought a buggy and a pair of
way-backed skeletons covered with leather to draw it. In this
ie made him drive her all about the valley to deliver and
ollect her grain. She went north into the mountains where
ie snowy peaks rose out of pines, westward up the steep
añons where summer lingers but a month, south to the dry
lains, and east. She began, twice a year, to cross the pass to
ie little settlements beyond the valley's rim.

The beautiful blue valley grew and prospered. So did
Iaria. But it was she who became known. Maria from the
alley. Maria del Valle. She became the valley. In her buggy
he brought its sunstruck wheat, its ripe oats, the sturdy
orn, its wrinkled peas and round barley, and the look of the
ich ripe earth that bore them. In her eyes she brought its
epellent remoteness.

Back to it from across the wall of mountains, from the
iver bottoms beyond, she brought great necklaces of scarlet
hile that turned blood red and brittle hanging from her
afters. She brought tomatoes, the little sweet peaches,
pricots, and melons, the low-country fruit and vegetables.
And all these, in season, for a shrewd profit. Herbs she did
ot forget, both those that grew in the valley and those that
rew without. In cans and boxes and bottles, tacked on the
valls, hanging from the rafters and drying in the loft, was
oleo for colic, oshá and yerba de manzo and topalquin to
reak a fever, cota for rheumatism, ruda for paralysis,
anaigre for soft gums, yerba buena for pregnant brides and
equisquite for gas in the belly.

She knew the secret uses of weeds and kept them handy:

tumbleweed, horse weed, milkweed, frog weed, waco and
wild marjoram. Brown grass she dried and bound, popote fo
brooms and popotito for brushes. The long dry stems o
sunflowers she kept for lighting cigarettes from the fire.

Natural colors for spun wool she knew how to obtain, and
how to make native dyes. Chamiso for yellow and the lichens
for light orange; peach leaves and cedar bark for green; oak
bark for wine; walnut hulls for brown; chokecherry roots and
berries for purple; urine with cedar twigs for Indian red.

Foods she knew how to dry and preserve in the old way
the way of the poor who know neither sugar nor salt, the
way of the hungry who watch each apple fall, chicos, posole
nixtamal, panocha; ribs dried in the sun, jerked beef, dried
corn and squash and apples, green chile roasted, peeled and
hung up to dry, quelites dried and stored in sacks to cook
with meat or gravy.

All these foods and seeds, herbs and weeds that filled the
house, and were hidden carefully, Maria herself used
sparingly. Never meat when a taste in gravy would do as well
never an apple without a spot. Time and hunger she knew she
could never vanquish. She was content to hold them at bay.

Yet it was not alone these things she sold and traded. It
was the advice, instruction and power that went with them.
For she never abandoned her goats and the wisdom derived
from reading their skulls. An old he-goat she sold. Another
died. Their skulls came back to sit with others upon her
rafters. They were pages of a book she bound together year
by year. They were a chronological record of the span of life
that flowed past her. And sometimes she caught glimpses of
its course ahead.

So slowly money began to come in. No one knew where it
went. Teodosio was lazy and ragged, Niña industrious and
ragged. Maria went around in her worn, rusty rebozo, and
shoeless half the year. The occasional peso squeezed out of
her for staples—for salt and thread and lime—seemed wrung
from her very flesh. She was almost self-reliant, and she

eemed quite content.

Like buffalo, the black-humped clouds stampeded over the ramparts of the valley. The thunder of their hoofs shook the sky-plain. From their locking horns leapt zigzags of fire.

Suddenly rain fell. Great warm drops hissed on the dry, dusty earth. Then slanting silver threads unraveled abruptly the whole texture of the shower. Within two hours the storm was spent.

A rainbow brilliantly colored as a Chihuahua serape hung over the shoulder of the sky. Pines and piñons glistened with water. The sharp smell of sage cut with a whetted edge. The black plowed fields began to steam. The whole earth seemed quickened, in heat, and straining at invisible bonds.

Maria with arms crossed stood at her window. She was holding her full and strangely aching breasts. Maturity had filled the hollows of her face. The sun, coming out again, enlivened the dull red underneath her brown cheeks. Her black eyes were no longer dead and empty; they were alive and restless. Her firm body had reached the softness of a ripe peach that waits to be plucked, to rot with decay or wither.

The devil take it! She whirled around and put on her shoes. She grabbed down her rebozo and hurried out of the house. Three o'clock in the afternoon. Quitting her work, her house, and going to town for no reason whatever. Mother of God! What gets into a woman?

What comes over the whole earth at times like this? Maria stopped and plunged her hands into the black steaming loam, crumpled the wet clods under her nose. In the pasture beyond, a roan stallion raced blindly and alone, tearing up the turf. The crows applauded insanely.

At the edge of town Maria stopped in the road. A bedraggled gray hen squawked past her and cowered against the fence. After her flapped a rusty rooster. He flew at her, screaming, drove her out of the weeds with beak and spurs. Before she could break away, he leapt upon her.

Maria stood watching. The gray hen squatted in a puddle without struggling, her wings half outspread, her head bent meekly forward. On her, his talons dug in her wet feathers, titillated the rusty rooster with his powerful, rocking tread. In a moment he stepped off daintily, shaking his feathers. He glared around haughtily, but with the fierceness gone out of him, and stalked away.

The little gray hen remained the victor. She chuckled over his betrayal, smoothing her ruffled wings and lifting her langorous yellow claws, one at a time, to shake free of mud. She looked smug and self-sufficient, as if the road had encircled the world to meet in her plump, bedraggled ball of feathers.

Maria went hot with anger. She stooped and threw handfuls of mud at the hen who only walked away disdainfully. "Cochina! Pig! Sorda hija de tal!" The hen threw a look and a cackle back over her shoulder, and ducked through the hedge. Maria, still steaming, walked angrily into town.

At Pierre Fortier's she banged back the door and stalked inside. Pierre left the men grouped at the stove and clumped to her on his wooden leg. "Ah, it is Maria! Whom I have not seen for these many weeks. You are well? And the children? And doubtless needing new supplies. . . .What a shower! I feel spring in my bones. It makes me hungry for life and meat. Fresh meat. Look! Behind, there in the corral, they are butchering. I have bought two steers. Look. A bit of fresh meat to take home for a change. Fresh beef from the mountaintop pastures. Maria. . . ."

Maria spit on the floor. "Beef! Santísima! You are talking to a poor old woman? An old woman who praises God when she can season the pot with a piece of goat flesh? Pagh! You and your talk!" She glared at the men crowding the stove. "Well, come and talk here at your desk, over your papers, about how much I owe you. Why you have cheated me, on paper, thinking my memory weak. Talk! Sí! It will take much talk."

It was as good as anything to vent the nervous excitement that had filled her veins—this long harangue over salt, sugar, thread, lime. Pierre, with spectacles on, sat his stool quarreling. Maria squinted at the fly-specked paper as if she could read. Neither was angry, neither misjudged the accuracy and shrewdness of the other.

At the end Pierre Fortier slapped his leg. "What a magnificent memory! The like I have never seen!"

"So that is what I owe?" mumbled Maria. "Well, it is good for both of us to know that when I have the money I shall pay. Certainly. But not now. Does silver grow on trees?"

Pierre reached behind him and took down a red cotton kerchief—the most faded and fly-specked of the dozen that hung on a rope. This he flung around Maria's neck and knotted. "A present. For my best customer. This most beautiful of all my fine scarfs. Madre! It makes you look like a girl! What beautiful red cheeks!"

Maria stamped her foot. "Fool! You think to shame me before all these men?" But she stole a look into a mirror, and swiftly reckoned the amount he would somewhere squeeze into her bill.

"Now. That fresh beef," Pierre reminded. "You will walk by the corral? You will see the fresh, firm red meat? Then you will return tomorrow for the piece I shall save?"

"I shall walk by," promised Maria at the door. "But no more. Am I a wealthy woman that I can eat beef like the rich and yet keep my friend waiting for his money?"

Pierre sighed. "It shall go on the paper. Do I not know my people?"

It was as he had said; in the corral just off the plaza the men had waited to slaughter until the shower was over. Maria leaned over the fence.

Two steers had already been killed. Dripping blood, they were hung up to be skinned. Two others waited their turn in a small corner enclosure. Their hoarse, frantic bellowing, the stark fear in their eyes, roused no pity in Maria.

The puddles in the corral seemed to reflect the sun lowering on the Sangre de Cristo. The mud itself was red and slimy. It seemed to give off a heat that crawled under her clothes. It smelled. The smell was aphrodisiacal. Maria's black eyes glittered. She loosed the red kerchief about her throat and panted quick pale breaths into the cold afternoon. Crowding close against the fence, she kept rubbing her breasts back and forth over the top aspen rail.

Two men had come out of the log enclosure. One was a bearded old man in a leather coat who carried an axe. The other was a tall lean man naked to the waist, and carrying a long knife. His strong smooth back revealed long ropey muscles writhing under the skin. Maria sucked in her breath and shuddered as the hard tips of her breasts drew back over the rough bark. Then she pressed forward again upon the fence, the pink end of her tongue showing between her lips.

The bearded old man threw open the gate, stepped back and lifted his axe. As the frightened steer came out plunging, he swung once, twice. The blunt end of the axe thudded on the steer's forehead. He dropped to his knees.

Before he could roll over, the tall lean man stepped forward and drove up from his thigh the naked blade. He gave it a twist. From the steer's throat gushed a warm flow. It covered his knife, hand and wrist as he stepped back.

"Santána! What a steer!" he laughed, turning aorund and shaking his arm. "As full of juice as a ripe peach!"

Through a film of dizziness Maria could see the cold pink peaks, the corral filling with blood and its hot sweetish smell. She could see the man's chest now, hairless and sharply outlined as if carved out of wood, his flat muscular belly, the strong sharp lines of his jaw and cheekbones. He was laughing. His teeth gleamed white, like a wolf's.

Then, just as he turned around, he saw her. His look was dark and quick, sharp as a knife. It cut through the film over her eyes which dropped away like a curtain. It twisted; she opened to receive it, and something deep inside her gushed forth to meet his knifelike gaze.

A moment did it. Maria straightened, adjusted her new red kerchief, and moved a few paces along the fence. The man had stopped laughing. He was tense, impatient.

"Carajo!" he called to his companion as the steer was dragged away. "Why do you wait? The sun sinks. Let us have the other." But he kept glancing obliquely at Maria sauntering along the fence.

The last steer plunged out to meet axe and knife, to roll over sideways in blood and mud. The man stepped aside, drawing the blade between his bloody fingers. Maria had reached the end of the corral fence, and was walking demurely into the road.

"There!" he called loudly. "It is the last. I have bargained for no more. There is just time to return to the mountains before dark." He walked to a hollowed log trough and began to wash.

"But compadre," complained his bearded companion, "how is it you do not wait? A good drink to finish a nasty job. Has it not always been so?"

"Carajo!" sputtered the answer through cold rain water. "Am I a butcher, a meat carver, a shopkeeper? From the hills I delivered my beef. I killed them as was agreed. I go. Adiós. Adiós, compadre." He threw on shirt and jacket, saddled and rode out of the corral.

Maria was not a kilómetro up the road when he drew rein beside her.

"Cómo está, Señora?" he spoke in a voice soft as the dusk.

"Bien. Y usted?" she answered quietly.

But again the sharp dark look passed between them.

They walked along without speaking. Maria trudging along the side of the road, and the man jogging slowly beside her on his horse. He had put on his hat, and rode head down. His boot and trouser leg were stained with blood. The horse smelled it, threw up his head and twisted from side to side.

The leather squeaked. The bit jangled faintly.

When the tall cliffs jutted out, Maria turned aside without speaking. The man followed her up the lane on his mount. They stopped before the house.

"It is where I live," Maria said simply.

"You are the woman with the strange power," he answered in a deep, quiet voice. "Perhaps to this one you will bring luck?" And he stared down quietly from his saddle.

"Quien sabe?" she smiled. "Come."

He dismounted and followed her into the long back room. The dusk was thicker inside the hut. He could hardly see the rows of pale skulls, but the smell of drying herbs wrapped around him. He rolled a cigarette with fingers that trembled a little in the light of the narrow window. Then he sat down before her on a stack of sheepskins.

His breath was coming quicker now. His shirt front was open at the collar, and at each breath his smooth powerful chest swelled toward her.

Maria reached out and took his hands. She turned them palm up, squinting at the few lines etched into the firm calloused flesh. Their heads lowered, almost touched. Their breaths made one heat. Now Maria laid his hands in her lap. Her finger tips began to trace the lines up his corded wrist. From the touch little zigzags of fire leapt up his arms. Others leapt up her legs as he rubbed the backs of his hands over her knees. The room was darkening as with a storm. Its clouds flushed the cheeks of their bent heads. Abruptly he grabbed her by the wrists.

Maria stiffened, raised her head. From outside came the sound of wagon wheels and voices. The man drew back, wary, remote. Maria rose. She laid her hand on his warm throat, pulled his ear, then stalked to the door. Teodosio with Niña had just driven up in the buggy.

Shrieked Maria, "Sick pig of a litter! And you, lazy one! Can you not see there is one here to consult me? Are you blind to his horse tied there, that you would interrupt? Go!

Stay as you have stayed away all this day. Go to the tienda and there obtain the bit of fresh meat Pierre is saving me. Ungrateful children! Shameless ones! Go!"

When the wagon turned down the lane into the dark, Maria closed and latched the kitchen door. Then she walked swiftly into the long back room, taking off her new red kerchief.

Thus it was. A quick look from a man's eyes, the chance touch of a hand in the plaza, a meeting in the dark. They came unbidden, unlooked for, but with the imperative gestures of destiny to punctuate the monotone of Maria's life.

Later, heavy with child, she saw the man riding by into his cañon without stopping. She met another in town with his wife, and only nodded casually.

"What! Another child? And who this time can be the father?" she overheard, and Teodosio's answer, "Pues. Am I a son who is his mother's master? How is it that I should know these things—who is driven to work from dawn till dusk? It has happened before. What man can say it will not happen again?"

It mattered little. Maria accepted her nameless children as she had accepted the quick look of their fathers, the touch of a hand, the meeting in the dark, the beginning and end of the one enduring mystery.

They grew. Maria grew. They valley grew. It was all one rhythm, but with changing tempos like the seasons.

The French had disappeared, the fort had crumbled; the trappers and traders, the white-topped wagons came no more. The land was no longer Mexico but Nuevo Mexico. It was a Territorio of the east and not of the south. Now this was a strange thing, gringo land but no gringos. How was this, that the beautiful blue valley high in its sierras should remain untouched, unchanged by change? Because, Señores, the Jéfe, the gringo Presidente, loved his people here and wished them to retain their land.

They all filed down the trails to stare wonderingly at the anunciados, at their great gold seals, and to hear the news that the "Said claim known as the Demora Grant" had been "recommended for confirmation by the United States Surveyor General."

Bravo! Bravo, Señor Presidente! The land will be ours, as it has always been. But whose?

Well, it is like this, compadres. The beautiful blue valley will be divided under the eyes of the Presidente among those seventy-six who came first to break its soil. But some have died. Some have sons. It is true that these sons have sons. So the land must be subdivided among all in the eyes of the Presidente: to each his share, with a little piece of paper from the Presidente, that hereafter there will be no quarrels.

And so the people stand in a long line before a man at a big table covered with papers. He is a gringo with light hair. He is one of the intelligent, wearing spectacles and holding a pen. Under a flag he sits. He is, in fact, not a man. He is authority. He is the right hand of the long arm of the Señor Presidente. Beside him stands an interpreter.

The people present their claims. The right hand of the long arm of the Señor Presidente writes swiftly.

We have lived on our land, we have loved it, we have worked it, Señor. Myself, my father, my father's father. Now I have this paper which says so and more—that it shall be my son's and his son's. It is very well. Gracias, Señor. And to the Señor Presidente, my devout respects.

The interpreter duly translates. The man bows, steps back humbly, hat in hand. Next!

But there are difficulties, there are squabbles.

You see, Señor, this land is very old. It is not measured in acres. It is not parceled in squares of meadow, of grazing land, of mountain slope. For then it would be unfair. It runs in the old way, in strips, "from the river to the mountain top" or "from mountain top to mountain top" across the valley. In this way, each man has a bit of meadow to plow for corn, a bit of pasture for his cows, a bit of forest for wood. The vara is the measure, Señor.

The Devil!

The vara, Señor, is thirty-three inches.

The Devil, I say! What is this, a strip three varas wide? Are they crazy, to work land scarce nine feet wide?

It is this way, Señor. A man takes an equal share with his neighbor when the land is new and plentiful. But should he hold it when he cannot work it? The land must be worked, Señor.

Or again. A man has six sons. He dies. To each he leaves a strip, perhaps twelve varas, perhaps less. From mountain top to mountain top. So that each shall have a bit of meadow, of grazing land, of forest for wood and vigas and fences. Is it not reasonable, Señor?

So it goes on for hours, for days. And each man goes out with his piece of paper. And the ownership of the valley is slowly confirmed, officially, as the Señor Presidente wishes.

Now comes a woman, shoeless, in a rusty black rebozo. With her stands a listless, loose mouthed man with his fly unbuttoned, a ragged haired girl and three small children. She is greedy for land, for papers to the tall cliffs jutting out into the valley's throat, for the forest slopes above and the vegas below. But certainly she has a right. She is one of the first settlers in the valley, her man was son of another. She has lived on the land, no one has denied her claim, it is the will of God. . . .

Come, come. Let's get at the root of this. Methodically.

"The Devil! Doesn't she have a name? Ask her what her husband's name was," the man at the desk demands of the interpreter.

"Maria of the valley. Thus only she is known."

"Maria del Valle! Why didn't you say so!"

Well, yes. But no. This woman had no husband; she has never been legally married.

"It is often the custom," advises the interpreter. "Marriage

by God and not by church. There are no illegitimate children
they are 'natural' children."

So! And Teodosio, this long lazy one with his fly
unbuttoned, and Niña here with straggling hair go down on
paper for the strip of land which is the share of one Onesimo
their father.

But what about another strip, the share of Maria and these
other three children?

The Devil! All these children and no fathers at all! All
right, all right. Not that it matters, a few minors' names
scribbled on a paper. "But what do you call them? This
one?" He jerks a thumb at the next oldest boy.

Maria recollects. His father came from San Antonio in the
upper end of the valley. "His name, Señor, is Antonio."

"Antonio what?"

Well, thinks Maria, he watches the cow in the pasture.
"Antonia de la Vega."

And this girl whose father lives in Santa Gertrudes. Will she
not be able to help with the crops, such a quick hand?

"Gertrudes Paiz."

Ah. But this little barefoot chamaco, wild as a deer. Maria
smiles. That was passion! The hot leaping blood, the quick
moment under the willows, and then receding hoof beats of a
horse bearing his rider to refuge in the mountains.

"His name, Señores, shall be Refugio Montes."

Thus it was, "In witness whereof, I, Ulysses S. Grant,
President of the United States of America, have caused these
titles to be made patent, and the seal of the General Land
Office to be hereunto affixed."

And Maria stalked out with her papers. She had her strip
of land from the tall weathered cliffs, across the valley to the
pine hills. And her children, priest or no, had proper names,
on paper. Bonita! Qué bonita! Such pretty names. Yet who

hall know their fathers—as if it mattered?

Maria sighed satisfaction. It was a good day's work. That ight she allowed herself a cup of chocolate, and permitted Refugio Montes del Valle to lick out the mug.

6

Maria at fifty was short and shapeless, her skin dark, dry and
wrinkled. She was like the talus slope behind her house, the
decomposed granite eroded from the cliffs, integrated by
weather and weight, and now congealing into stone again.
She looked juiceless, settled—and at any moment was likely
to come roaring down with invective into the valley. To
vecinos and townspeople she was a power and an enigma, to
her children a despot. All called her Doña Maria.

To escape her tyranny, Refugio Montes took to his heels
into the mountains. Maria sighed, erected a little wooden
cross to his name in the Campo Santo, and appropriated the
land due him at age. Antonio de la Vega she allowed to marry
and build a hut in the pasture; as tribute he took care of her
cows and goats, and his wife supplied her with cheese. The
Niña had borne somebody's child. Little Gertrudes Paiz
helped nurse it to free Niña for work in the fields, and Maria
bossed both. These three women and Teodosio comprised the
happy family that crowded Maria's small adobe.

"And now! Mother of God! You would bring yet another

o spit upon the hearth!" she attacked him vigorously.

"Cómo no? Marriage is a man's fate. I have escaped it long nough."

There was in Teodosio's voice the smug assurance of a veakling who at last has found someone weaker than he. Maria looked over with amazement his long skeleton covered by a spotted suit with the fly open, his sallow, saturnine face. Her small black pig-eyes snapped.

"A man's fate! Carajo! You sick pig of a litter, who thinks himself a man. You who do nothing but drive half asleep rom road to road. Who will drive me now when you have a vife cackling at your heels? Pig! Lazy one! Listen! Tomorow you will begin a new house. There in the orchard, there along the stream. Then we will see about this marriage."

Teodosio sighed and rolled a cigarette.

Maria snorted and took it from him.

In three months the adobe walls were up; the vigas laid, hatched with aspen latillas and covered with earth; the dirt loor hardened with goat's blood. The new hut had one oom, one door and no windows, and faced the house.

"There. It is finished. I shall be married before the first rost. On the dia de San Francisco de Asis." It was the only ime that Teodosio had ever worked. He swelled with pride at his new house.

"It is not bad. It will do. But I expect the fireplace to smoke," said Maria quietly. "Now before you bring this gnorant rabbit of a wife home, where Niña can teach her properly how to live according to custom, you must move my things into this small humble hut. Thus you will enjoy happiness in privacy; while I, myself, will yet be close enough to keep an eye on all matters."

Teodosio, still sullen after two weeks sulking, brought his new wife home to live in the privacy of two rooms shared with Gertrudes, Niña and her child. The bride's name was Concha. She was small, big eyed and timid as a rabbit, café con leche in color, deeply pock marked, and with thick black hair drawn back over her small round head. She lived there two years. She was never much use in the fields: her back was too thin, and her feet never out of the squeaky, glass button shoes she had been married in—the symbol of village gentility. But she built fires and cooked, took care of Gertrudes and Niña's child, ran errands, fed Teodosio's team plastered the walls in summer and scraped the snow off in winter, cut wood and tanned hides. All very awkwardly, said Maria.

She died not from too much happiness, according to Teodosio; nor to escape work, according to Maria; but to flee the everpresent specter of Maria looming suddenly in the doorway.

"Concha! In God's name! Here in this doorway, behind you, I have stood for three minutes. You did not hear me on the path for I have no squeaky shoes, useless on such a warm day. But here I watched. I saw you put on the beans, the sopa. All without making the sign of the cross on top. How then do you expect success and flavor?

"Yesterday, unobserved, I saw you clumsily bruise your foot while cutting wood. I came over. I saw you washing it in warm water to take away the pain. Imagine! I did not see you lay that silver knife upon the bruise, which would have healed it according to custom. No! You do not know. You do not remember. You are a task."

So Concha mortally fled the omnipresent specter of Maria. It was omniscient as well.

She would appear suddenly at a remote mountainside hut, and stalk in without greeting.

"You are Crescenciana, wife of Filadelphio Aleman, whose newest child is backward in talking and walking as well," she would accuse the woman sternly. "What! have you no eyes to observe those natural facilities of bird and beast which can be transferred to ailing child with the proper remedies? Listen well. Rub the child's legs with rabbit grease daily; it will impart life to lazy limbs. To induce talking give him to drink

f the water left out overnight for the chickens. Take
eed.... Now when the crops are gathered, and this
ackwardness has been overcome by following my advice, I
vould have for a present a fanega of that barley your man
as planted. To Maria at the bottom of the cliffs in the valley
ou will send Filadelphio with it. Without fail. Understand?"

"Sí, Sí, Doña Maria. Gracias. Mil gracias, Señora." And the
voman would watch her climb into the buggy beside
Teodosio, and vanish down the cañon.

To other huts Maria went. To advise that the fingernails of
tiny babe should be torn off, not cut, lest the child be
ongue-tied. If it were ill with the mollera—if the soft spot on
he head was sunken in and the beat of the heart could be
elt by a hand upon it, she directed that it be cured by
ubbing with breast milk mixed with a pinch of salt. Mal de
:uerpo she cured, and recommended morubio for poultices
on yagas, the sores of the flesh.

From spring till fall she traveled, from Monte Aplanado to
La Jara, up La Cañada and across the Cebollitas. She
nspected the crops and herds, gossiped with the Indian
vomen as they all lay in the hot mud baths at El Alto de los
Herreras, exchanged wit and wisdom for seeds and herbs
hroughout the valley and even behind its walls.

Teodosio continued to drive her in the buggy, grumbling.

"From dawn till dusk we travel. Our road has no end. My
ife is jolting away over these cursed roads. My kidneys are
hattered. Now I must get out again."

"You are a sick pig without insides. Besides, now that you
do not have the responsibility of caring for a wife, it is well
hat you be occupied in greater matters lest your grief
overcome you."

Teodosio grunted assent to this mocking suspicion of grief.
It was the only way he could force himself to believe he had
had a wife.

In the winter Maria kept to her hut. She scraped and read
her goat skulls, prepared herbs and seeds, concocted

remedies, and kept her own strange calendar.

Three days after Christmas she went around to h
neighbors, borrowing their most prized possessions. Whe
they were not returned, two of the women trudged tl
snowy path to her hut and cautiously knocked.

"Señora, pardon the intrusion, but you will remember th
shiny brass kettle you borrowed. It distresses my heart 1
remind you of this shiny brass kettle, Doña Maria, but m
kitchen wails its absence."

" And that horsehair rope, Doña Maria. The one you g
from my man who bids me return with it. Three days aft
Christmas it was. You remember?"

Doña Maria lighted a cigarette from the fire with
sunflower stalk. "I remember. See, there is the pot, there th
rope. It was the Dia de los Inocentes. But you have forgotte
So now to get them back you must pay well."

"But we do not understand, Doña Maria. You will forgiv
our ignorance, but that is my pot which my kitchen wails.
have not forgotten."

"On the Dia de los Inocentes," answered Maria imperturl
ably, "one is permitted to borrow from his neighbors. Whe
they say, 'pero no por inocente,' then it is a loan. But whe
they forget, proving themselves innocent of the custom, the
they must pay to get these things back. It is the custom. No
that is not a bad pot. A little battered perhaps, but sti
useful. For it I must have a good price. And one also for th
rope. Thus you will remember the old ways which are bes
despite these changing times."

Even so, occasional valley folk traveled to her door.

"It is the first day of the new year, Doña Maria. As yo
know, we are poor, our crops have been poor. But even so w
have brought this little present of turnips. Perhaps it 1
possible that you can tell us what the new year holds
whether our oats will spring forth sparsely or in abundance.

Maria nodded. "Leave the turnips and return befor
midnight with a handful of the oats you will plant in you

eld. In this little pot, at midnight, I will plant them. It will
t in the window, a forecast of your crop. Thus you may
de by, day by day, and read your future for yourselves."

So her name grew, and her power. She was tolerated with
istian phrases, hated in whispers, and respected silently. Of
l the valley she was the most surprised to receive a
edaration of love.

Fulgencio Garcia y Valdes brought it himself. He drove the
uarter-mile from his own fine place in his best buggy. The
iorning sunlight made golden statues of his matched
iestnuts. His polished boots seemed copper pillars marching
own the path through the apple trees to Maria's hut. When
e took off his big sombrero, his thin hair gleamed silver.

"Todos Santos!" whispered Niña to Gertrudes and
eodosio peeking through the window of their house. "The
ian is made of money. What can Don Fulgencio wish of
oña Maria—this time of day?"

He stayed two minutes. When he drove away, they rushed
ut to Maria. She was still shoeless, on her knees and
plastering the fireplace.

"What?" she asked, smacking a handful of wet adobe into
hole. "Señor Garcia has requested me to become his
ife. . . . What!" she shouted, after a look at their faces. "Do
ou find it so strange as that? Get out! Can you not see I am
lastering before the spring rains?"

Women have as many ages as moods. When it comes to
iarriage they have only one. Its costume is procrastination,
id its masks are coyness, shyness, modesty, fear and pride.

"The Devil!" men echoed in stores, saloons, in town and
iroughout the valley. "I cannot understand why Maria does
ot make up her mind. She is wise and powerful, it is true.
ut neither young nor virginal. And Don Fulgencio as you
now is the best catch in the valley."

"Verdad. Verdad," whispered the women. "But there may
e many things to consider. She is shrewd. She will consider

them all.''

So they waited the union of the wise and powerful Mar
and the rich and powerful Garcia. Meanwhile he came twi
weekly to sit under the apple trees and press his suit.

Fulgencio Garcia y Valdes was a fine name and a po
figure. He was small, withered and brittle as a dead twig. I
face was sharp and sallow, his voice either curt or oily. I
was a politician and seventy years old; he called himself six
and ''an agent of the Government.'' His virtues were a sou
seat on a good horse, and the best piece of land in the valle

It happened to be the largest, and it lay adjacent to Mari
at the mouth of the cañon. There were rich flat varas f
planting, lush meadows, an orchard. But the landmark of t
valley was his great stone and adobe water mill located at t
turn of the river. Its huge burrs had been brought fro
France when the mill, under his father, had been built
grind on contract most of the grain for the fort. The run-c
was used as an acequia madre, and by an ingenious irrigati
system which engineers from Europe had come to stud
watered his rich fields.

But now the elder Garcia was dead, the fort gone with
fat contracts. The mill still ground grain for the people of t
beautiful blue valley, but only sporadically. There was
smaller, cheaper one north; and besides, something h
happened to the water. It only flowed half the time. So D
Fulgencio was content to work his fields, to strut throu
public opinion and local politics, and boast of his chestn
horses and horse chestnuts—he owned the only tree of
kind in the valley.

For all his wealth and importance, he lived like a peo
with an old blind crone, his sister, and in the back of the mi

''Don Fulgencio is a gentlemen of the old days,'' peop
would say proudly. ''A true caballero. He keeps his horses
his house and lives elsewhere.''

It was quite true. The long, beautiful adobe hous
crumbling through the years, he used as his stable. Where

s money came from no one wondered. The Garcias had
ways had money. This is the advantage of a reputation, that
persists in giving one what one has not.

All this Maria pondered. To others she seemed shrewd and
liberate. She herself was simply perplexed.

"Why is it you would marry me, Don Fulgencio?" she
ked him one afternoon.

Señor Garcia rose and bowed, hat in hand. "Doña Maria,
om the fullness of my heart. From the respect I bear you."

"Sit down, sit down," Maria demanded. Then chewing on
blade of grass, she said simply, "Now, Señor, to me this is a
range thing. Me you have known for many years and never
oke. Me you knew when the spring of life rose in our veins.
ow is it that the fullness of your heart did not overflow to
e then? Is it that the passion of your body now calls for
is old wrinkled flesh which has received many men and
ven many children? That I cannot believe. Nor can I believe
ou would be much of a man yourself in bed nowadays,
ulgencio. Our blood is no longer hot, mi amigo."

Garcia slapped his thigh. "Madre! My manhood has never
en questioned. But I grant what you say, Señora. The vile
sts of the flesh no longer possess me. The union of our
odies I do not desire. It is simply as I say: that I ask out of
e great esteem and treasured respect that such a woman
serves."

Now this was a strange thing, almost unbelievable, and
hen next he came Maria asked him, "This marriage, Don
ulgencio. I cannot see what good it would do you. I have
ood land, it is true. But you have better and more. Besides a
ill. I have influence perhaps, with certain herbs and
isdom. But you have the power of an agent of the
overnment. The new gringo government. There are many
en who mark crosses on their votes as you direct."

"You observe clearly," he answered. "It is one of your
ncounted virtues. A woman who observes clearly. Pues,
ou are a miracle! But see yet further. I have power from the

Government over men. You have power over the simple. Is
not fitting that we two unite and so give to all the unit€
leadership they deserve? How proud they shall be—and I, m
dearly esteemed Doña Maria! That I, Fulgencio Garcia
Valdes, have been given to wife that gracious and wise Doi
Maria whom all know and love. I dream of it nightly. Wh
do you say, Señora? What answer may I hasten away with?

And still another week she questioned him.

"I have not forgotten to think about this matter whi€
concerns us, my friend. I have remembered many things.
was a young ignorant girl of the hills. I wandered with m
goats. It was your father's men, and you with great cru
stones, who chased us from grass during drought. I rememb
when my man Onesimo died. I had the Niña and Teodos
when they were small. We were poor, we were hungry. W
had nothing at all. To you I went for permission to glea
your fields. You gave me scarce enough, where only th
reapers could not swing their blades. The years have con
and the years have gone, and we have always been the sam
You have been rich and I have been poor. You are of th
Garcias, and I am of the people. Your power is of th
Government, of politics, of important things understood on
by the intelligent. And they are good, doubtless. But m
power is that of the wisdom of the people who do not thin
but feel. And that is good too.

"Now it seems to me," she went on slowly, "that the
two powers are yet far apart, even in these changing time
The power of gringo ways and politics, of steel plows ar
papers to land and houses, that rests in you. And the pow
of the simple, of the old customs, of the earth and its herb
of the stars and the seasons, the power of the blood that res
in me. Perhaps it is not possible for these two powers t
unite. Perhaps it is not fitting that we try to unite ther
Señor Garcia, I am a simple, old and nameless woman. I hav
never learned to write my name. Why is it that you wou
wish to marry me?"

Fulgencio Garcia y Valdes still insisted. His honor was at
ake. Imagine! The honor of a Garcia with the only chestnut
orses and horse chestnuts in the valley at the feet of a
mple goat woman. People discussed it fully. Their sentiment
vung to Garcia.

"True, she has a nice bit of land," they said, "but what can
on Fulgencio get from this marriage, with more? She is old,
ean and shapeless. Perhaps he wants her to read goat skulls
 him, and the future. . . . Not that he has much of it left,"
ney added maliciously.

Garcia cast now his pride at Maria's feet.

"Questions, questions, questions! I can stand no more.
oña Maria, you look at an old lonely man. Without child,
rithout friends, with no one but a shriveled blind magpie to
eep him company. What is this talk of lust of the flesh, of
ower, of name and custom and wealth? We are no longer
oung. Let us grow together in our gentle age, and so be wise
t last."

Maria sighed. She felt her heart at last understood him.
Come to me yet once more. In three days. I shall have your
nswer."

Yet when he returned, her tongue was still sharp. "Señor
arcia, you desire marriage with me without the passion of
ne flesh?"

"Pues. I would not have it known, but my passion has
bbed. You may sleep where you will, as though a virginal
laid."

"You have your work, your mill and land, your power
rith the políticos. You understand that I too have my life,
hough a woman?"

"Goat skulls and herbs! I have never seen such a woman!
ut I shall be busy. I shall not interfere with your days.
hough I shall be censored for it, no doubt," he added
mely.

"Well!" Maria frowned. "This is stranger than ever. I can
nink of no reason for your marriage but the question of

land. But wait! I do not know what the new law says about woman's land. I do not want yours, nor shall you have mine. Tell me. Should we be married, on paper, would you first write a paper, a Government paper, that to me my land remains?"

Señor Garcia blinked. "The strip of your land from the cliff tops across the valley to the mountains. The land of your Antonio and Niña, your worthless Teodosio's. All your land in this valley. And you shall have your paper, besides."

Maria took a deep breath. "Then, Señor Garcia, I can think of no reason why you should marry me. . . . Nor can I think of any why you should not. It must be as you say, that you are an old and lonely man, though rich, who needs a heart with tenderness and pity. Perhaps I can give it to you, Don Fulgencio. . . . You may set the day for Santána."

She rose. Suddenly, with a strange gesture of compassion she drew his head upon her breast. "Imagine, Don Fulgencio, I have never been married!"

It was high noon. It was mid-summer. A long line of wagons, buggies, horsemen and pedestrians crawled down the wide road. The blinding sun muted the shriek of colored paper and ribbons. Thick swirls of dust tarnished the laughs and jokes. The procession smelled of perspiration and whisky. It was el Día de Santa Ana. It was Maria's wedding day.

She sat in the most dilapidated buggy of all, beside Teodosio in a new suit with the fly sprung open. Her short lumpy body bulged out a cream satin wedding gown for which Don Fulgencio had himself paid two hundred dollars. A high, jewelled, Spanish comb wobbled in her black coarse hair. Her cramped feet sweated in brown shoes with glass buttons. To her swart, indomitable face she held in stubby calloused fingers a tortoise shell fan to keep off the sun. She was staring down the road toward the crowded village plaza.

Herself at midnight she saw mounted on a plodding burro

nd carrying a small child. In back, on the rump, another sat
wathed against the cold. Leading them in front walked a tall
ean man, one hand thrust inside his leather coat. His face
vas raised to the gritty December stars.

"Mother of God!" ejaculated Teodosio. "Has there ever
een such a day and a wedding? Look at the plaza. Listen to
he bells. They sound as beautiful as the pesos Don Fulgencio
ingled to have them ring.

"'Roll me a cigarette," demanded Maria sharply. "It is not
itting that I do so. Besides, I forgot my tobacco."

For the third and last time in her life, she entered the
hurch. Nothing was as it should have been. She was no
onger poor, sinful and humble. The church no longer
emembered the tall lean man on his shaggy burro, or Him he
ad looked like, the gentle Jesus. Like her it gleamed with
he glory of Don Fulgencio's gold.

"Santána!" whispered Teodosio as they walked down the
isle. "What a wedding! It is better than a fiesta mass. The
ells, that was ten pesos. Don Fulgencio told me himself. The
rgan, that is fifteen more. Look at the candlesticks and the
andles—at a peso for each. Madre! Listen now at the voices
f los cantores. Six pesos more. To say nothing of those for
he priest and the holy water, the use of the church, the
lowers, the Holy Book, and God knows what else. You are a
ucky woman!"

At the altar waited Don Fulgencio. He looked as though he
ad been dragged out of his great carved chest at home, black
elvet embroidered with coroded silver, a little wrinkled,
crawny and juiceless, but satisfied and smiling.

When the priest came out, the music stopped. They knelt
nd rose. The priest spoke and prayed. They were married.
And now as they passed out, the bells began to ring again.

"Bravo! Bravo Don Fulgencio! Brava, Doña Maria! . . .
alud, Señor y Señora!"

Don Fulgencio took out his buckskin bag at the doorway
nd threw money to the people outside. He strutted into the

bars to leave more money for drinks. Then he escorted Doña Maria to his buggy and whipped up his chestnuts.

All afternoon they sat at home in the dreary back room of the huge mill. Don Fulgencio's old blind sister sat with them entertaining guests. The room was large, gloomy and stuffed with furniture from the abandoned house. It smelled of dust and flour.

"What a fine old chest!" a guest would say, thumping the stiff leather. "And that comoda. I have never seen such carving. From the old days it came. Up the Chihuahua trail. Pues, but times are changing. Still, Doña Maria, you are now a Garcia. It is a long way from selling goat cheese. No? I congratulate you."

The old blind sister sat pouring wine unerringly from a dusty decanter. Don Fulgencio talked horses and politics, water and crops.

"Doña Maria," another would point out, "your new husband has shown you the pride of his life? The great horse chestnut just outside? Such a tree! The only one in the valley!"

By dark they had drifted away, whispering. "Mother of God! Did you ever see such a bride? In that dress! That old herb woman, that peddler of goat cheese. And now the Señora Garcia. Who would have imagined our Don Fulgencio would come to such a thing? But it is said among the simple that she has a power. No doubt she cast a spell upon him. Well, we shall see what he gets out of it."

Inside, bride and groom and chaperon sat quietly in candlelight. It was nearly eight o'clock. Don Fulgencio began to figure the costs of the wedding. "Two hundred dollars for that fine dress. Then the shoes. . . . I gave the priest too much, but he wanted more. . . . There was the dobles—rung before and after, el organo and singers as well, la agua bendita and all the candles—did you notice how quickly they were snuffed? To say nothing of money thrown to the poor, and left at the cantinas. . . . Well, I shall get many votes for all is, mark my words! But an excellent wedding, eh Doña Maria? You will remember I spared nothing. . . . And you have your paper?" It was clearly a tone of dismissal.

The old blind woman sat staring, stonily, from her filmed-over eyes. "Come. It is time for bed. The Señor retires at such an hour." She got up, opened the chest, and began to spread the couch with blankets.

"And where do you sleep, sister?" inquired Maria gently.

The woman nodded her head toward the cramped kitchen where she slept on the floor.

"Go then and sleep, sister!" demanded Maria sharply. "Who else shall prepare a man's bed but his wife?"

When the woman had gone, Maria smoothed down the couch. Don Fulgencio sulked. He looked a little frightened, like one who is likely to choke from too big a bite.

Maria knelt silently and took off his shoes. Then she grasped him by the shoulders, gently, as one holds a child.

"Don Fulgencio. You have forgotten, but I remember the words between us. You are a powerful man, but you have been womanless too long to know that a woman has a power too. My friend, in me is that power and more. There is in me gentleness and pity for you, for never till tonight have I been wife properly, on paper. So to you I give it.

"Now I go home to sleep, as is proper between us. Adiós, my friend. We shall talk tomorrow."

Through the willows along the stream, around the cliffs she crept home. Carefully in the darkness lest she be seen and so disgrace Don Fulgencio.

In her hut she took off her cream satin wedding gown and glass button shoes, laid away her comb and fan. Shoeless, in her worn black cotton rebozo, whe crouched before a tiny fire built to keep away mosquitos. Between her knees she held a goat skull.

"What a strange marriage," she thought. "Who knows what it means? But there is something wrong in it that defies all my wisdom. What is it that Don Fulgencio would have had of me?"

Ay de mi! What an illusion that time is a moving flood. I changes the world and the hearts of men. But the beautifu blue valley and Maria do not change. They are like time itsel the one impregnable constant.

"And no wonder," people said of her. "She is not only to old to learn, but too simple to forget."

"She stayed long enough to put her spell upon him," sai others. "What more do you ask?"

Thus they explained Maria's return to her hut. Thei explanations condemned her. But her obduracy whicl prompted them aroused their secret respect. It is the respec with which one beats a stubborn burro.

Maria did not heed their talk. She was still perplexed as to what Don Fulgencio had wanted from their strange marriage

A railroad had come through the plains below the beautiful blue valley. Crews were cutting timber for ties in the mountains above. The great logs were freighted througl Santa Gertrudes. The valley supplied men, and the men witl supplies.

"I have been thinking," Maria had said to her husband "Business is good. Water is plentiful. You could run the mil every day. And that, it seems to me, is a very good thing That you should run the mill and so supply with profit to yourself the flour for all these men."

Instead, Don Fulgencio dismissed the man he had and closed the mill entirely.

Yet another year and Maria suggested, "Don Fulgencio, the water has been scarce this year. Now when you wanted to marry me I suspected this, that the time of drought would come when your land, being below, would want for water; and that mine, lying at the mouth of the cañon, would yet receive the stream's flow. Wherefore I suspected reasonably that you wanted my land to protect the water for your mill and also your land. Now it is no more fitting that a man's land go dry while his wife's prospers, than that hers be despoiled for his. But still you do not ask. Is it because of pride, because of the paper I requested from you? Shall I not instruct the Master of the Ditch to share equally between us the water in the cequia according to custom?"

But Don Fulgencio would not clean out his ditches for water, not that year nor thereafter, and let his crops prosper or wither as they would.

Thus no money came from his mill, no money came from his crops. But still, from somewhere, money came to him for everything, for buying votes and buying whisky for more, for shiny store clothes and riding to the city on the train which passed far below the beautiful blue valley. No one thought anything of it. Pues! The Garcias had always had money. Besides, was he not a político and an agent of the Government? But money he began to have for loans on land, and for buying land to sell again. This disturbed Maria.

"Of what use is land if it be not worked?" she asked him. "For land is land. Like women, it exists only to bear. It is a law above any on paper."

"Madre!" he answered irritably. "What does a woman know of business? To me my business as a man. To you your herbs and goat skulls. Let us not interfere."

But soon he ceased going to the city. He gave up his politics. He grew older, scrawnier, more brittle. His chestnut horses faded to buckskin shadows turned loose to pasture. But he still carried horse chestnuts in his pockets, and took immeasurable pride in the great tree outside, near the bend in the river. It became an obsession. Not a hand would he allow to touch it, not a foot to approach it. Under it for hours he sat nursing a secret fear and smug satisfaction that gradually distorted his thin sharp face. It was the look of a miser sitting on his chest of gold. He became feeble and crusty. He became unbearable.

"Don Fulgencio," said Maria. "Ours has been a strange marriage. You did not desire to possess my body, being too

old and manless, and myself without desire, so I have slept a
home unknown to the neighbors. You did not desire m
land, neither water for your own. I offered advice o
business, consulted the stars, read herbs and skulls that yo
might act with success when the time was ripe. You refused
all.

" 'Surely then, Don Fulgencio spoke truth,' I said t
myself. 'He is an old lonely man. Out of the fullness of h
heart and the respect he bears me, he desires for his last yea
on this earth the help, gentleness and pity of a wife.'

"This have I given you. Each day I have come. I worke
talked, prepared food, besides. For what? To be ignored, t
be treated like a blight? I, Maria of the Valley? No, Do
Fulgencio. So I go to return no more, not knowing what yo
wanted in marriage with me. Adiós, Señor Garcia."

The old white-headed man looked up with a scowl. He sa
vanish the last personal care and pity that anyone was to ca
from Maria. Like the land, she had been fruitful an
enduring, ever waiting for a master. But can it plow itself, ca
it bear without care? Thenceforth, crusted over, she kni
back together into an earth inimical and unbroken.

So she returned to her hut, resuming uninterrupted he
long rides with Teodosio throughout the valley and into th
enclosing mountains.

But once she stopped at Don Fulgencio's. The fields wer
full of weeds, the unpruned orchard sprouting suckers. Th
fences were falling. Crows were picking the eyes out of tw
buckskin covered skeletons in the broken corral. Under th
great horse chesnut a little wizened man with white hair sa
muttering to himself. He kept plucking handfuls of earth
letting the clods trickle from hand to hand like hoarded gold

"Doña Maria! Keep away from this tree!" he screamed
leaping to his feet upon seeing her. "Away! Accursed woman
wife who is not a wife. You have laid a spell upon me!"

She walked into the mill. The machinery had rusted. Th
great wheel was broken. Green slime filled the sluices. Rat

ill scampered through the empty bins. Cobwebs laced the
rafters. In the back room, in dust and silence, huddled the
old blind crone with her rebozo drawn up over her head.

"Maria? It is the steps of my brother's wife? You got my
message?"

"It is not your brother's wife. It is not her who got your
message and whose steps you hear. It is Maria. Maria of the
valley who comes here as she would to any other place."

"Ay de mi, Doña Maria. You have lived to see fall the
house of Garcia. But to you in your simple wisdom, being
less talkative than others, there is something I would say
before I die. Go quietly and unseen into the back garden . At
the foot of the grandfather apple tree, the gnarled old one
with the low crotch seven paces from the crumbled wall, dig
and bring me the small box you find among its roots."

Maria obeyed.

"You found them? Here, let me feel. Yes, they are the
heavy gold pieces. The same. The old ones. Do you find them
tarnished, Doña Maria?"

"Not tarnished, but dull. Neither are they round, but
square," answered Maria.

"But still gold which remains constant in all it forms, and
thus invaluable to the greed of men," observed Maria.

"Pues. Take them. Bury them again where you will against
the hour of need—the hour of my death. For all their corners,
being gold as you say, the priest will not refuse them for
nobles, for holy water and el sepulchro. It is not fitting that a
Garcia, even a blind childless woman, be buried without the
sound of the bells, and a proper entierro. If there be enough
for a candle or two, so much the better. I have been in dark
long enough. You will do this? I can ask no one else."

"I will not refuse," agreed Maria. "Console yourself against
the hour."

"Well then!" spoke up the blind woman. "Listen now to
what I would say. It is your proper payment."

"You observe him sitting forever under his tree—he, my

brother, your husband in name? You heard him shout at yc in madness when you approached. You hear me now rela how he beat me with a stick the day I went there to gath dry twigs. Look at the bruises on my flesh, feel the welts c my poor head, which still remain!

"Doña Maria, there are things to be said which one cann say. But you are a wise woman who can hold her tongue ar be patient. Do you not wonder how a man can be so rich ar yet so poor, and why he sits forever under a worthless tre Go then, and remember this box of gold pieces, myself ar him who guards an old tree not worth guarding of itself. I these words and your remembrance of them lies you reward. . . . Do not forget the candles! Being faithless yc can talk sharp business with the priest. One at the foot an one at the head, if possible, Doña Maria. Do not forget."

For months a somber gray had overhung the valle blotting the beauty and obscuring the blue. Fall it was an still raining—an incessantly dripping mist, a sparse quic splatter or the lash of a heavy storm.

The earth was soggy. Adobe walls kept crumbling. Anemi water-logged corn straddled puddles. Beasts and birds of th field dragged hoof and claw as if too discouraged to shake o the clinging mud. When the sky appeared to be clearing, th river bloated with more debris; there had been another heav rain up one of the tributary cañons.

"Mother of God!" a man would exclaim, tramping in fror the fields. "I have not seen it so wet in thirty years. For all feel it might be that long since I have seen the peaks agains the sky, the clouds lie so low and heavy."

Weeks ago when the crops were given up, Maria had pu away her goat skulls and marked willow twigs, had discor tinued watching for dry stars. She was a woman vigilant o the future, not unaware of the past, but wise enough to giv herself to the present.

So she sat quietly in her hut, head down and listening t

e orchestration of the day's storm. She was cooking beans.
he fire rubbed long red hairs against the pot. Its reflection
y like thin straw on the floor. Outside, the apple trees
ivered; fruit thudded on the ground like lazy thumps of a
rum. The rain on the roof was a pizzicato, the rumble of the
eek a sustained adagio.

At mid-afternoon came a violent crescendo. A bit of roof
irt trickled down between the rafters, followed by a steady
rip of water. Maria set a pot under it. Soon there were seven
ots filling on the floor. "Diablo! A seven pot rain! One more
an the worst!"

When the hard mud floor became sticky, Maria grew
neasy. She opened the door. It was scarce five o'clock but
ark. The creek roared beyond the little orchard. A sour
nell tainted the air. The rain was coming down, as it is said,
buckets. In the corral Maria saw lanterns.

"Teodosio!" she called. "What is the matter with you? It is
seven pot rain, and more, for I have none left. Come! Move
y things into the house."

"What is the matter with you?" he shouted back. "We are
arrying chickens into the house. We have lost two already.
re you blind? The corral is ankle-deep in water from the
eek."

Maria grabbed up her rebozo, and went out. The little
ream coming down the cañon was a torrent. At its junction
ith the creek, the water had banked up against the cliffs and
as creeping through the orchard. Above, the wall of stones
hich protected the corral from the creek was hidden by
ater.

Hurriedly she lugged out armfuls of things from her hut.
he house was already full of chickens, goats and a calf, Niña
nd her daughter, Gertrudes and Teodosio. The chickens
icked at her seed corn, the calf nibbled at her precious
erbs. The goats stared disconsolately at the heaped skulls of
heir predecessors. Gertrudes and Niña's girl examined her
ld clothes. Teodosio grumbled at the half-cooked pot of

beans, and Niña at the weather. The rain clawed at the wall
trying to get at them all.

"These beans!" muttered Teodosio. "Not only are the
half-cooked but full of water. Now I would not say yo
failed to put the lid on as you carried them through the rain
Carajo! You could make me believe it rained through the po
itself, so strongly it drives!"

Maria sat still, head cocked; there had sounded outside
queer splintering. "The hut," she said, rising, "it—" Even a
she spoke came the crash.

They ran outside; the path was shin deep under water
Maria's hut had fallen down. Water had dissolved the lowe
bricks.

"Well!" shouted Teodosio. "Now you will be glad to go
back to your beans, in warmth and comfort, be the
half-cooked and cold! Our Lady! You moved out but in
time!"

They trudged back. But not before Maria had looked long
and anxiously up the cañon. It was raining harder than ever

The roof of the house was the usual: large hand-hewn viga
laid across the tops of the walls, a cross-hatching of smal
aspens, on these a few planks, and covering all, two feet o
dirt. By eight o'clock water had soaked through. Everyone
and everything was wet.

"We are on a rise. The walls rest on stones. We are safe bu
miserable," observed Teodosio, with water running down hi
back. "But Madre mia! It is like trying to escape fate to
dodge these trickles. Even my cigarette papers are wet. I do
not have a dry pocket."

"Let us go down the road toward the village," pleaded
Niña. "We shall come to a dry house. The beasts here will be
safe. But I can stand no more."

Teodosio opened the door and stuck down a foot. He drew
back a leg, wet to the knee. "Mother of God! Go? How? We
should need a boat! But not this one. Why should he go
outside to get wet? There is plenty of water in here."

Maria stood beside him, holding up the lantern. She was smelling the air.

"Come! I have a certain foreboding. But leave the doors open for the beasts." With this she plunged out into the night.

The others waded after her flickering lantern. Near the road they heard the splash of horses, saw the light of a torch. It shone on a bedraggled family down from the opposite side of the valley.

"Teodosio! And Doña Maria!" exclaimed the man when they met. "Thank God for such good neighbors. You look upon ruined friends. Our house has fallen in. And here you stand in water to meet us, and lead us to spend the night in your own warm house. In this storm we might never have found the way."

"Jesú Cristo" answered Teodosio. "You mean to tell us that water floods the north as it does the south? Us, who are washed out like rats, even as yourselves? Cristo, Cristo!"

All straggled on in wet and darkness. "Maldito!" cursed Teodosio. "Is this road or river? I can tell only what it once was by the fence posts."

They came to the house of Santiago Jacquez; it was dark and crumbling. They came to the house of Mechor Sandoval; it was deserted, the chairs were floating out. They reached the house where Quiteria Pacheco lived with her three sons, the ranchito of Fidencio Romaldo y Trujillo, the long adobe wherein lived the three poor families of Santistevan, Espinoza and Donaciano Romero. They were all abandoned and besieged by water. It was midnight and still raining when they saw a light.

"Ójala! I know it now!" exclaimed Teodosio. "It is that old stable of gray stone near the bridge. Across from the mill of Don Fulgencio. We have come not more than a kilómetro! Imagine! Pues. Are we ducks, are we fish? Come! I smell coffee and tortillas, a warm fire."

But inside were only Santiago, Mechor and Quiteria with

their wives and sons, Don Fidencio and the families of Santisteven, Espinoza and Romeros. There was no coffee, no tortillas. There was not even a fire; there was no dry wood. There was hardly room to squat down. "So this is what a man gets, swimming like a fish a kilómetro that seems ten leagues!" grumbled Teodosio. "Not even a dry cigarette."

One by one more groups splashed in to stand dripping in the light of torches. From Tramperos, Cañoncito, La Corriera.

"What! Is it raining there too? You brought no dry cigarettes? No?" Teodosio asked each.

No one answered. They were a people elaborately dumb under misery and misfortune. All watched Maria who kept opening the door to sniff the air. The light from her lantern flickered out to the watery fields. All the stock had been let loose. Horses, cows, burros, goats, pigs and sheep splashed round the building, whimpering.

An hour after daybreak Maria turned back from the door. "It is coming. What I feared and suspected. A new smell and fresh mud. The creek brings down not only wreckage and willows, but fresh pine tips. Come! We must go! To the village."

They straggled out again. The pallor of dawn was reflected in their muddy faces. Their features were set like cement against sleep and hunger, fear and misfortune. A child whimpered with cold, their only voice. Behind them splashed twenty head of loose stock. No one seemed to notice that the rain had ceased. For at the bridge the creek was still swelling.

They looked back. The valley was no longer beautiful and blue. It was gray and slimy. It smelled sour. They looked ahead, and it was the same, soggy fields crossed by rivers that had been roads, and sodden adobes from which no smoke rose. But there stood the church tower of Santa Gertrudes. Down to it from the southern slope of El Alto del Talco, from the northern slope of El Alto de los Herreras, plodded more people across the fields. And down the little mountain pass from La Cuesta, Ledoux and El Oro, from the Cebollita valley, trudged a steady line of people and stock.

But Maria was staring back up the crescent valley, at the tall cliffs near the curve and the shrouded mountains toward the north. A man had stuck a stick down in the creek bank. He came running back with it.

"Mira! Doña Maria, look! The water was here when I placed it. Now it is here. A good two inches. The rain has ceased, but the creek yet swells. And swiftly. Look!"

Maria did not answer. Neither did she turn around. She stood staring at the swirling water. Fence posts came down, broken planks, dead chickens, willow branches and brush-pine tips. Then a drowned goat which lodged against the bridge piling. Maria waded down to it, and remained.

"Señora! What do you see? . . . Doña Maria! It is dead!"

"Of course, fool!" she replied, coming back, wet to the waist. "But I saw on it the burnt three bars of Filadelfio Eluria. He lives up the steep cañon beyond Los Alamitos. . . . Burro! Are you yet blind to its meaning? How do you suppose this goat came here? There has been a cloudburst on the pine ridge between the high cañons of Luna and Lujan. The first rise of the river is coming. Get the people to the village. Sound the church bells. God knows what to expect."

The people fled on—save Maria, Teodosio and two other men. "For why?" chattered Teodosio. "Why do we remain? Look! Mother of God! What fury! In ten minutes the water will be over the bridge."

"It will be enough!" answered Maria curtly. "I have business across the bridge. Are you unaware that that is Don Fulgencio's old mill?"

One of the men stepped up. "Doña Maria. A thousand pardons. I am not unaware that he is your husband in name, and that you feel a certain anxiety about him now that the old blind crone, his sister, is dead. But look. The flood will sweep round the cliffs directly upon the mill. Not only that but the bridge will go out. Besides, he is probably not there."

"He is a fool, and you. Look!" She pointed across the river. Below the mill and under a great chestnut tree stood a tiny old man waving a stick. "Will one fool listen to another? I must talk to him myself." Maria shook off his arm and hurried across the bridge.

Above the roar of the water, as she approached, she could hear Fulgencio's screams. His sombrero had fallen off. His thin white hair stuck to his bony head like wet silk. He was soaking. "Away, cursed woman, who has laid a spell upon me!" he screamed, dancing about with his uplifted stick. "I saw you. I saw all the people you brought to gaze at me. You sent them away to hide behind the bushes. You come alone. But I see you and them. Away!"

The great chestnut stood on a small rise. The acequia had burst, the empty sluices were filling; from the mill above, water was streaming down upon the tree. But around it Fulgencio had been heaping up a tiny barricade of mud.

Maria rushed upon him. "Fool! Will you be drowned with your gold? Here, give me that shovel! We shall carry it into the mill where the walls are strong."

The old man let out a shriek of rage. "She told you! That magpie with no eyes and a loose tongue. She guessed and told you!" With a stick he beat down her upraised arms. They fought, sliding in the mud. But it was the old man's insane strength which secured the shovel. With a mighty swipe meant to take off her head, he leapt forward. Maria slipped; her feet went forward, her head back. The blade of the shovel caught her a glancing blow on the jaw. Teeth flew out, blood spurted. Her cleft chin opened like another but vertical mouth. Maria dropped like a log.

But now the men came running across the bridge. The old man leapt for the lower branches of the tree, and scrambled up to perch shrieking above them.

"Blessed Mother!" shouted one of the men. "He would have killed her who would have saved him. But there is no time to lose. The water washes over the bridge. Come. Let us get her between us. She awakes. Jesus, the blood! It is a miracle that we waited not too long to save her."

Halfway to the village, Maria came to her senses. She was being pulled along between two men, her chin held together by a strip of torn rebozo. Teodosio, in front, kept turning around to throw handfuls of muddy water in her face. 'Blood and mud! You look like a slaughtered pig. And yet you keep mumbling of the gold necessary to rebuild our house. Mother of God! That day will never come. The valley is ruined forever. It is the day of judgment."

They reached Santa Gertrudes. The stub streets were filling with refugees from all directions, even from the pine slopes above. Among them milled horses, burros, cows, pigs and goats. The plaza in front of the church was packed solid with people. From the tower above, the bells were ringing. On the steps stood a priest, praying. Inside, a hasty mass was being said.

Suddenly the priest stopped his prayer. The bells stopped. In the tower a man had begun to shout. The first rise was coming down.

A cloudburst had broken in the high mountains to the north. Down the V-shaped cañons of Luna and Lujan the water rushed to an apex, grew into a flood, and swept down the one narrow steep-walled cañon into the upper end of the valley.

Here, from the high Sangre de Cristo on the west, it was joined by the swollen Rio de la Casa. A mile farther, the flood separated to follow down the river to the east and the creek to the west, and thus spread into the already soaked valley from both sides.

As the water crept up to the village streets, Maria roused from her lethargy. She plucked Teodosio's sleeve, spit blood and another tooth. "These bells! This praying!" she said faintly. "I myself would trust high land to religion. Hoist me upon a loose burro. Let us go."

Again they plodded on. Up the steep little pass between

the valley and Ledoux. Others followed. A long bedraggled line returning to the highlands whence they had come, if only to prove that while misfortune seeks company, danger calls them back to solitude. Here on the pine slope they looked down to see the second rise sweep down the valley.

Two hours later a strange thing happened on the opposite side. Just beyond the high cliffs at the curve of the crescent valley a white snake leaped forth. It was transparent. In it straws twisted and jammed and poked through the skin. The snake roared and flashed. It tore loose great boulders as it unrolled down the mountainside. Maria's apple trees lay down before it. Swiftly it uncoiled, stretched and dived into the creek. But still, unending, its body kept unrolling from behind the cliffs.

Maria discovered her voice. "It is as I feared! As I said, yet not as I said! It is worse! The flood comes down La Cañada also!"

The cloudburst had broken in the high mountains to the north drained by the Luna and Lujan which in turn empty into the valley from the northwest. But between these cañon and that of Guadalupita there is only a ridge of pines. The clouds had but shifted slightly. And now the water coming down La Cañada del Carro was sweeping into the valley from the northeast. Into mid-valley, at the center of its crescent beyond the jutting cliffs.

Maria saw her apple orchard sink, her barn float off in pieces, her house become an island. And now, six feet high, the snake rushed at Don Fulgencio's mill. The hewn stone held—a small gray pillar in a surging flood. Surprisingly, the old chestnut on its rise still stood, but half submerged in water. And now through the afternoon the clumps of people watched the water creep up into the village, a foot deep.

At dusk Teodosio found something to say. "They are having a wet mass down there in the church. . . . But Jesus! I cannot be so cold. . . . I shall try to light a fire. Did you bring matches? I have none. Not in that pocket, nor in this. . . . "

At dawn they crept down the mountainside, halfstarved
nd stiff with cold. The water was receding, the sun coming
ut. It was unbelievable. It was ugly. It was revealing only an
arth that was for them stricken and homeless, an earth that
tank.

Bodies were being brought in, and reports of others.
Emeliano saw something sticking in the willows. . . . Myself
nd Abrán buried him, Señora. The head, you will realize
. . . It is best to be truthful in misfortune, Señora. . . . He
 will not return. My sympathy, Señora. . . . There where the
rows and buzzards are already gathering. But yet the water
s too high. Patience! And prayer!"

Maria listened. That night she heard of Don Fulgencio. His
ody had been found nearly a kilómetro downstream. He
vidently had been swept from or fallen from the tree. "But
he chestnut?" she asked. It still stood, but weakly, gouged
ut to its roots.

Maria sighed. Her sigh included, perhaps primarily, the lost
ox of gold pieces he had buried at the foot of the tree. Now
here would be no money to rebuild and plant again.

In the morning she gathered together Niña and her
aughter, Gertrudes and Teodosio. "Let us go back," she said
tiffly, toothlessly.

"To what?" grumbled Teodosio. "Out of this you have a
car. A fine scar; nobody will recognize you. But nothing
lse. Mother of God! Not even a tooth! To say nothing of a
lace to sleep, a scrap of tortilla, a sip of water. Jesus! And I!
do not even have a cigarette. Not even a wet one. I tell you
his has been a flood. Without doubt, a flood. Why. . . . "

7

At the age of seventy Maria was living alone in a small mountainside hut. It was the old one that lay in the little clearing just below the tall weathered cliffs which jut out to separate the crescent halves of the beautiful blue valley, and just above a steep corn milpa sloping up from the rutty cañon road. Thus unseeing eyes placed it. Maria, whose eyes saw it in time as well as in space, saw it as the point of a completed circle.

But Maria was a character. Such is regarded one who has outlived virtue and vice, having proved invulnerable to both and more powerful than either.

"She is strange and wise," people said of her.

The strangeness implied her uniqueness among their orthodoxy. The wisdom reflected her ability to see through their opinions.

"But I do not trust her fully," added some in a whisper.

Such a secret lack of faith do people below have in the truth that awaits above them.

Maria was content to wait. Seldom she allowed Teodosio

o drive her down into the valley in his rattletrap buggy. She only saw to it that he came up often enough to weed the corn and to bring her salt, sugar and tobacco. What more was necessary? She milked her goats, split her own wood; was too toothless to eat meat, too contented to require conversation, too busy to relish interruptions. "Besides," she said, "I can watch from here the empty doings of you all."

So she thrived on loneliness, and proved that energy creates inert mass. This energy, this understood vitality in one so old and wrinkled, she had sucked from her loves and labors, anxieties and follies, the illusions of her life. Its inert mass sat hour after hour, day by day, on top of the cliffs.

Below her the valley grew, new houses rose from the earth. New roads crawled up the cañons where only foot trails had come down. Burros diminished, rattling tin automobiles appeared—to be pulled out of chuck holes by teams and wagons, the mean that held between these extremes of travel. She saw the valley green, yellow and whiten, the mountain peaks step forth and back again into mists, scant harvests and days of plenty. Gringo voices came back, greaseless wagon hubs squeaked on frosty mornings, the church bells tolled births and deaths.

It all went on outside her as it went on in memory inside, changing but changeless, and thus an illusion. What remained was their common core. It was the reality she pondered.

Wind and rain matted her straggly hair. Sun and frost made leather of her swart cheeks and cleft chin. Her black, bright little eyes took on a queer remoteness. At times her steady gaze seemed turned inward—as if it had rounded the earth only to return to the duplicate within her.

But occasionally her meditations were interrupted. She had gone long to the people of the valley; now they came to her.

"Doña Maria," a man would say, respectfully standing before her, hat in hand, "you will forgive this interruption, but something is wrong with my house. It is a new house. It

is a well built house. I built it with these hands. Ye
something is wrong. In it I have always a cold, my wif
sniffles, the noses of my children drip. It was not like this i
our old house, which is now a stable—where no doubt ou
beasts are better off than we with colds."

"This new house of yours. It has windows?"

"Of glass, Señora! And two doors."

"It breathes through the eaves?"

"An air space, as they say. It is the new way."

"Pues!" grunted Maria. "These new ways! These nev
windows of glass by which one would be outside and in, a
once! That is your trouble. Hereafter take care to stuff th
eaves and doors. Remember this:

> *"When a draft gets at you through a hole,*
> *Go make your will, and pray for your soul."*

Advice on all matters she gave, and new remedies for ol
ills. Especially she recommended for headaches pieces of blu
paper or the blue government tax stamps taken off tobacc
cans and pasted on the forehead and around the eyes.

So her power still grew, and her name. She was not only ;
character but an institution. The trail up through the steep
corn and pines to it wore deeper.

The fat, red-cheeked priest from the village church took i
yearly. He came up hopefully, went down discouraged
"Father in Heaven! Give me strength! This miserable an
faithless old woman is more powerful than a priest! Her fee
are surely fatter!" Once he nearly swore.

It had happened on his autumnal visit to convert her to th
faith, and so draw her power over the simple into the church
that he encountered her below the cliffs. She had driver
down to her old home and orchard where Niña's family lived
Teodosio having moved with Gertrudes up the cañon. It ha
been a good apple year; there was a huge stack against th
barn; Maria was in a tender humor.

"Let us have no empty words, Padre," she said kindly.
For twenty and more years I have heard your pleas, threats
nd arguments. They are all the same. I will listen no more.
ut of this heap of apples take plenty. Verdad! Fill your
uggy. Take them to your church—wherever you will."

Niña's eyes popped. Teodosio's jaw dropped. But over the
riest's red face crept a look of beatific triumph shadowed by
tiny irreconcilable doubt. Hastily, still smiling, he dropped
o his knees, clasped his hands.

"God, O Father and His Blessed Son!" he prayed rapidly,
efore Maria could change her mind. "You have rewarded
our servant's toil of twenty years and more. To me it is to
e given the baptising of this woman so long without faith
nd divine aid. Nor in my ecclesiastical joy am I unaware of
hose in this same church who preceded me in prayer for this
dmirable soul who gives this day in the name of the Father,
he Son and Holy Ghost . . . ."

"Momentito, Padre!" interrupted Maria harshly. "What is
ll this about? I said merely to take apples to your church.
The pigs will eat no more."

The story spread. Men in the cantinas roared, women
ittered in the stores; the whole valley shook with laughter.
The remark became a saying. "Take it! The pigs will eat no
nore!" Thus they joked when giving the unneeded to one
nother.

The priest's visit was followed by Pierre Fortier's. He was
o longer merely a shopkeeper who sold clothes and canned
oods, fresh meat, harness and tiny sewing machines; who
ought wool, hides and grain by the car load. He was
omething of an art dealer. Agents from the cities came to
im for arrowheads, for old tinwork, leather trunks and great
arved chests, for precious old blankets and lacework, and for
Santos of all kinds—the carved bultos and the retablos or
ablas painted on wood or tin.

Old Pierre had a nose for all these things. He had lived in
he valley a lifetime. Every hut in all its cañons he knew, and

if it contained an unknown treasure: an old carven chest
from Mexico half sunk in the damp earth floor, a browned
old Santo hanging above the rickety bed. Moreover he knew
the idiosyncrasies of their owners.

"This dirty old chest!" he would say, giving it a kick. "The
wood is rotting away! Bring it in some day when I am in
good humor. Perhaps I can find use for it as a wood box, and
give your wife a new dress on credit. In such a tidy house it is
a disgrace. But not today, compadre!"

Those places where the Santos were stubbornly clung to
by the old, he merely noted. This old woman would die soon;
her son liked whiskey.

What he had long wanted from Maria was an old
burnt-orange Chimayó blanket. One edge was tattered, it had
holes. It was dirty, it was thin. But whenever Pierre saw it
glowing in the sunlight, felt its weave and wonderful softness,
his mouth watered. "Mon Dieu! It is a blanket too good for
the top of a piano in a home of the rich. It is fit for a
museum. An old woman who yet knows the old way, to
patch the holes. Another to wash it in amole. Yes. Then for
this blanket I could begin to ask seven hundred dollars!"

But also every time he saw it he groaned. Maria used it in
Teodosio's buggy. When the blanket was thrown over the seat
the protruding springs poked through the weave. When it lay
over her lap she trod most of it underfoot. Always it was
assaulted by the sun and dust, by rain and hail and snow.
And Teodosio used it to cover his horses.

Where this old blanket came from Maria did not remember. She had never been without it, even as a child. So she
ignored first the gruff and then the polite preludes of Pierre
to buy it.

On the day he came up to Maria's hut, Teodosio's old
buggy was waiting at the foot of the trail. In its seat lay the
blanket. Pierre's eyes gleamed. He rubbed his long black
whiskers, and on his wooden leg stamped wheezing up the
slope. Maria he hugged and kissed on both cheeks.

"By Jesus, old friend! I tramp up this cursed steep trail to commiserate with another old and poor, broken in health and miserable. To find you sound as mountain beef, glowing with health and bubbling joy through bright eyes! Are you in love, have you found the fountain of youth? For shame, having not told me, your oldest friend. Why do you never come down to see me?"

To Teodosio he even gave a cigarette.

His visit was brief; he was buying cattle, he said. And when Teodosio left, Pierre accompanied him down the trail. At their adjacent buggies he stopped. As if on a sudden impulse, he jerked out of his own a new, bright-colored Navajo blanket, and spread it carefully over Teodosio's seat.

"We have been compadres for uncounted years," he said, slapping Teodosio on the back. "As a present I give you this fine new blanket. May comfort and protection, pleasure and joy, it give you both. . . . But I shall just take away this forlorn old rag that you have been forced to use all these years. . . . Adiós, compadre!"

When a few days later Maria asked for her old blanket, she was presented with the new one. She inspected it silently, its color, its weave and design. She drove down to Pierre's store with Teodosio.

Pierre was out in the mountains. She sat down on a sack of pintos. She waited all morning. She waited half the afternoon.

"What is it, Señora? Is it important, as surely it must be, that which keeps you waiting?"

"Well, it is about that faded old red blanket that Señor Fortier took of me. . . . I forgot to tell him that it was full of bugs. Bugs of sickness." Maria fixed the clerk with a shrewd look. I can trust you? Maria can trust a boy who seems so bright and helpful, who will keep his counsel? . . . Well then, listen. Those bugs of sickness were none other than the plague itself! Now! Do you see my anxiety, its importance? I shudder to think of the hands—whose hands, amiguito, have touched it?"

"But three, Doña Maria.—Thank God, not mine!—Those o Señor Fortier himself. Those of the old woman whom he gave it to mend, those of her who washes it now."

"Excellent! To them I shall go at once with herbs to relieve them of possible danger. Their names quickly! And to Señor Fortier when he returns, my thanks for his gift."

Maria obtained her blanket from her who had washed it "Pierre Fortier will pay as agreed. Give him my thanks for washing it, amiga. It has never been so clean and soft."

To the woman who had mended it she went with a message. "Pierre Fortier will pay. But give him my thanks for mending it, amiga. It is as good as new."

Maria rode home content. It was an old blanket, though mended and washed; it was true it had once covered a child with the plague. Yet she liked it, and thenceforth slept under it.

Behind her she left Pierre Fortier cursing in French and stamping his wooden leg. Throughout the village and echoed up the cañons shouted the gossip. "My thanks, compadre. But Pierre Fortier will pay."

"Mother of God!" people laughed. "What a strange and wise old woman! She fears neither God nor man. She has a mind of her own, has Doña Maria. It knows everything."

It is true that those who laughed the loudest feared worst the priest and owed Pierre Fortier the most. It is the tribute of slaves to bondage, that they never learn to use their strength in freeing themselves, but only to applaud others.

Maria sitting in silence on her crags neither heard nor needed their approbation. It was sunset. The valley before her deepened in color from plum to blue; it was no less beautiful when blue-black. Behind her in the little clearing among the pines waited her little hut—no larger, no more changed than it had been, off and on when patched, for seventy years. It was the point of her completed circle. She too had endured unchanged.

She had withstood the ebb and flow of the seasons; the sullen hostility of commerce and misfortune; the anaesthesia of religion, wealth and acclaim—all the passions that warp the mind, flesh and spirit of man.

She was immune from all but the ultimate destruction of her inessential outer shell.

At eighty, she heard of the dam.

It is late afternoon. The whole day in the valley has churned like a fiesta. Wagons loaded with people rumble down the cañons. Double-mounted horses too have passed: the front rider with left foot in the stirrup and leaning sideways, the rider behind him with right foot in the stirrup and leaning to the opposite side,—the old way, when mounts are scarce and must carry double over the rocky trails. Men have left their fields, women their houses and wood piles. The roads are full. Santa Gertrudes and San Antonio both swarm. From each, continually, a battered tin automobile chugs up one cañon after another and returns with a load of people.

It is not a Día de Fiesta. It is not a Saint's Day to be celebrated. It is Election Day in the beautiful blue valley.

Across from the courthouse in Santa Gertrudes stands a gaunt adobe. It is unfurnished save for a wooden platform at one end. Here each Saturday night, and all day during fiesta, sit the guitar players who pluck out music for dances. Today the floor is even more crowded. The walls are lined with tables partially screened by mosquito netting. Near the door sits a man at a table with two huge boxes. It is the place of voting.

The road in front is crowded. The sheriff and two deputies wear their guns outside their coats. The deputies are too drunk to use them. The sheriff cannot read the sign which says in English that no electioneering is permitted here.

When the crowded Ford sputters up and unloads, he makes way for driver and passengers and a político who meets them. The político smokes a cigar and wears a cloth vest.

"Ah, you brought them," he says to the driver. "Our goo friends from up the cañon! Welcome. Welcome, amigos."

The passengers have no shoes. They are rudely dressed i dirty gingham and black rebozos, in denims and leather vest: Their eyes shine like polished obsidian.

"To you our devout thanks. We have never ridden in máquina before. Our wits are turned by its swiftness. W were there and then here. A day's hard journey transforme into the flight of an hour. It is a miracle!" she stoops an kisses the político's hand.

"Por nada, por nada!" he answers gruffly. "Here are you papers."

They look at the sample ballots wonderingly. None ca read.

"What is the name of him for whom we mark the cross thi time, Señor? Is it a new Gobierno? Perhaps a new Presidente himself? Strange. We have had no pictures of him for ou windows. We have heard no talk."

"Bastante, compadre! It is not a great man you vote fo this day, but a great thing. Your hand is put to the paper s< that there will be no more floods to sweep cañon and valle with death and destruction, that there will be water for all i time of drought, that it will be measured, to each his prope share. The Government can do all this. But it wishes the sig of your will. . . . Here now! Each! See, I have marked o your paper the tiny crosses. Inside, Fidencio will give yo others like this, but empty. Fill them with crosses as these without mistake. Thus you will do your duty!"

Slowly the people file inside. Carefully, tenderly, the spread out the clean sheets on the little tables, lest they b soiled. Pencil stubs they lick with nervous lips, and hol< awkwardly in calloused brown hands. They talk through th mosquito netting. "See? I have made the crosses as in structed. Do they look right to you, primo? I would not hav the Government consider me too ignorant though I canno read."

At the center table they give their ballots to Fidencio. He
·oks them over casually, and stuffs them in a box.

Outside, the político gives each man a sack of tobacco and
ιch woman a stick of candy. They are hurriedly stuffed
ιck into the car.

"Have you got them all?" the político asks the driver in
nglish. "Know anybody else? Anybody, anywhere! If they
on't come get their names. Get the names of their horses,
ιeir cows and pigs and dogs. Where is that list of names you
rought from the graveyard? We might need that too. . . .
Jow get on! For God's sake! Give her another twist."

And til dark the battered tin máquina chugs back and
rth from the dark cañons.

Maria has watched it steadily, all day, from the top of her
iffs. She rises stiffly and walks down to her hut. In the
ιsky clearing she chops a few sticks. She boils tea, spoons
)me beans with pieces of a torn tortilla, puts up the tea
aves to use again with fresh.

It is eight thousand feet high, and already cold. Her mind
cold with foreboding, too. She huddles before the blaze
ithout moving. An hour. Two. Her thoughts begin to boil.
er old, dark and impassive face thaws into wrinkles. Her
·ose lips draw back from her one tooth. Suddenly, savagely,
ιe spits into the coals.

"Los Mofres! Those cursed Mofres!"

Many, many years ago when Maria was a goat girl, a
ranger had wandered into the beautiful blue valley. He had
lue eyes, fair skin and a sharp tongue which lurked behind a
erpetual smile. On his broad back he wore a pack. His hands
ere clever at mending broken pots, and dexterous at
arding off occasional knife thrusts with the staff he carried.
e was an itinerant peddler, an Irishman from County
onegal, and his name was Thomas Murphy.

Respect gathered round him with the walls of the beautiful
ιlley. Perhaps its own blue seemed green. He remained.
oon his brother came, bringing a wife for each. Shortly they

had land at the mouth of one of the little cañons. And befo
long, Tomás had a house and a store, and Roberto a hou
and a tiny mill for grinding the grain both raised and whi
Tomás sold.

It was amazing how they prospered. Their land grew a
was fruitful. The store enlarged, rivaled Pierre Fortier's. T
little water mill duly supplanted the big one of the Garci
Sons and daughters came in abundance, grandchildre
Finally, with all of these, came power.

The source of this power really lay in a hairline differen
between them and the people of the valley. Outwardly the
lived as all. Their Spanish was even better. The women cou
dish up costillas adobadas flavored to the exact heat wi
chile carribe and dance a varsoviana as gracefully as a
neighbor. The men could rope and tie a wild steer as quic
and hold as much liquor. To their own innumerable Celt
superstitions they added those of the valley. Their first bo
sons they sent to the priest as altar boys for training. And l
most they were accepted not as the only gringos to remain
the valley, but as proper vecinos. Their name was chang
from "Murphy" to the more easily pronounced "Mofre," ar
the little cañon they controlled became known as "El Cañ
de Mofre."

But inwardly they remained gringos and Irish. As gring
they held to a certain cold objectivity which enabled them
see themselves apart from the land and the people. /
Irishmen they felt it incumbent to always get a shade t
better of both. In trade, land and argument, they were st
sharp peddlers.

The one trait they inherently possessed in common wi
their neighbors was a natural gravitation toward politic
Drunken rows, cold scheming and hot arguments ov
candidates for a school teacher, a county clerk, a ne
sheriff—these offered a pleasure surpassing that in a go
trade. They became políticos.

Los Mofres then, through land, business and politic

ecame a power in the beautiful blue valley.

Maria did not trust them. year by year she watched them ence in a piece of land, a field here, a few varas there, and till another pasture. Year by year she heard of another aisano falling into debt to store or mill. She began to smell a at.

There is the power of the mind. It says, "There are no ribes, no races, no peoples separated by the color of their yes, their hair and skin. There is only mankind. All men are rothers. Each has the same passions, thirsts and hungers. he greed for gold and the greed for land is common to all. he Murphys of the world have it, as do I. I will not unjustly ondemn my brother."

But there is also the power of the blood which keeps eating, "There are many earths, and each has its own rreconcilable spirit of place. Now what is a man but his arth? It rises in walls to shelter him in life. It sinks to receive im at death. By eating its corn he builds his flesh into walls f this selfsame earth. He has its granitic hardness or is soft esiliency. He is different as each field even is different. Thus lo I know my own earth; I can know no other. I am greedy or my land, and that is right. Does not a child cry for its nother's breasts? But when the Murphys desire my land, it is alse. For they would not belong to it; they would only that t belonged to them. By this they refute their own mother, nd would enslave another's for a ransom of gold. So I uspect them."

Maria listened, and remained silent. But watchful.

Into the valley came talk of a dam. There came strange gringos who answered to no names as men standing on their wn feet, but whose mother was the same, "La Compañia de Agua y Tierra de Demora." With the Mofres they talked. Always.

A little longer, and the Mofres supplied beef and mutton or a fiesta down in the campo below the village. Many mportant men, they said, would be there to tell the good

people of the valley, our neighbors, about the dam. The dar
of which you have heard, no doubt. Has there not been talk

So all the good people of the valley assembled on th
campo. Maria went herself. And there were the importan
men who talked about the dam to all, men of th
Government, of the State, the nameless men of the Compa
ny, officials, politicos. And beside them, looking mor
important than all, the Mofres.

Instantly, intuitively, Maria distrusted the dam. She rod
home perplexed. She withheld judgment. But all the tim
she pondered the question up and down, back and forth.

The dam had its virtues, no doubt. There had always bee
floods, down one cañon, then another, and once fror
two—Madre mia! There had always been droughts which wer
equally bad. Now with a dam, as it was said, there would b
no floods and no droughts bearing death and destruction i
each. There would be water at all times, measured to eac
man his proper share.

But this dam is to be built only for the benefit of the goo
people of the valley, and the Mofres' eagerness for it, did nc
quite coincide in Maria's mind.

The Mofres loved the good people of the valley, thei
neighbors. They loved them, besought them with great cred
in store and mill. "Just sign this paper, compadre, to sho
that it is not your will to forget." And then, very quickl
they took away their land for payment.

Mother of God! Can one believe a man who says he love
his family, when he allows one member to starve? Can a ma
love his country, and yet neglect his own field?

There is no patriotism beyond the few leagues we woul
really die for. There is no love of abstract humanity. There i
only the love we show each man as an individual.

So Maria questioned the Mofres' intent to benefit th
people by the dam while they robbed them individually. Sh
wondered what they would derive from a dam that woul
control the cañon water for their mill instead of themselve

she wondered how they would exact payment for the beef and mutton eaten at the fiesta.

The election came. People waited to hear Maria's opinion. Some went to her. She was silent. So they listened to the busy Mofres and to the políticos who sputtered up the cañons, they accepted rides in the máquina to mark their crosses as instructed, candy and tobacco. The políticos came up for Maria.

"Just what is this election?" she asked quietly.

"Well," answered one man, with the ready formula. "It is for the people to express their will for a dam. That there may be no more floods, no more droughts, but water always, as needed. Is it not a wonderful thing?"

Said another who knew Maria's shrewdness, "Madre, it is the water district election, granted by our county commisioners whom we elected ourselves."

Maria rolled a cigarette. "Water District?" she asked slowly. "Is there not water in all districts?"

"It is like this, Madre. Allow me to explain fully. This valley is one water district of many in these parts. It is a judicial district. It is a County. Do you see? When one regards water, it is as a water district. When one regards justice and law, it is as a judicial district. When one regards government, it is as a County. And none of these districts, of which there are many of each, may be different and thus interfere with the others. Thus we are the United States! Now do you understand? We are no longer merely the valley."

"No, amigo," said Maria puffing deliberately. "It is you who are dumfounded with words. We are still the valley. Water is our problem; our fights over a stream's flow have always been the fiercest; too much of it has killed us also. We have out Masters of the Ditch. Hence also our need for justice, for government. But with all of these, and more, Señor, we are still the valley. The mountains enclose us, the earth feeds us. It is a thing of itself. Do not talk of a district on paper!

"But how—granting what you say—will this dam be built if it is the will of the people? Who will pay? We ourselves are too poor."

The político alternated between impatience to be off and the desire to show his great knowledge of these matters.

"Señora," he stated tersely. "You will not understand, nor is there reason to. The election for the dam will win. Its results will be an issue of papers worth money—bonds, the great men call them. These will be sold in the city by the officiales. This money will pay for half the dam. It will be given to the Government which will then supply the other half, and build the dam. The Government, Señora. For the people. For water conservation and safety."

"And what will the people in the city do with the paper they have bought? I cannot imagine . . . . "

"It is clear, Doña Maria, that you have no mind for such matters, despite being the widow of Señor Garcia whose knowledge of these things—and money—was profound. He himself was of this Demora Water and Land Company, as are the Mofres—two of them. Besides being, one of them, a Water Commissioner. . . . I may add, however, that this illustrious Company will no doubt buy much of that paper. They will then collect money from the people they save from death and destruction. In taxes. So much for the water they use. No more than reasonable, of a certainty. Are they not our neighbors? . . . Bastante! We must be off. No one else has asked so many questions. . . . Come now, Doña Maria. We will help you mark your paper with a cross for this great thing."

"I shall not vote," replied Maria wearily. "As you see, I am old and weak. That swift máquina would break all my brittle bones. . . . Go with God, Señores—you do not have far to go."

For two days she sat alone, studying this new problem. She had the miraculous memory of those who do not read and write. Moreover her years with Don Fulgencio had already opened to her the new world of worldly matters. She

as more shrewd than anyone—even Don Fulgencio—had
spected.

On the third day she had Teodosio drive her down to the
llage. The overwhelming results of the election had just
en announced. She also nursed the new fact that Don
ılgencio had been a member of this water and land
•mpany. She went to the courthouse, puffed up the warped
ne steps to the office of the recorder. He was an old man,
is Sanchez, with puffed cheeks and small eyes. He had been
friend of Don Fulgencio.

For twenty minutes they battled with elaborate politeness.
"To the point!" directed Maria sharply. "I come in haste
ıd in distress. I am old. I shall soon be dead. How much
nd do I own? Get out the papers. . . . We are going to have a
ım. Advise me, as a trusted friend of your friend, my
ısband, about this dam and my land."

Sanchez tottered over his maps as if he did not know that
e knew every tree, rock and ravine that marked the limits
' her land.

"Your strip of land here, from the tall cliffs across the
lley to the opposite mountains. . . . This piece, your share
om one Onesimo. . . . These pieces of your children,
efugio Montes, Gertrudes Paiz and Antonio de la Vega, yet
your name, as that of Teodosio and Niña. All in the valley,
:ñora. That without, you have already sold."

Maria brushed back her thin gray hair. "Sold? Yes, of
urse. But my memory fails. What land did you say,
nigo?"

Sanchez blinked his small eyes suspiciously. Maria drew
ıt from her tattered rebozo a heavy, yellow coin. It was
uare in shape, and gold. Her old wrinkled hands turned it
ly as she watched the greedy glitter come into his eyes.
ıen she slid the gold piece across the table. He clutched it;
was gone.

"Come, Sanchez!" Her voice was hard, metallic. "All what
nd? My memory weakens. Refresh it, Sanchez."

"Why surely you remember! All that land up in th
mountains. Beyond the valley. The share which was you
equally with that in the valley, according to the old Grant,
he went on complacently. "The original Spanish land grant t
the first seventy-six settlers in the valley. It gave them nc
only the land within the valley which they developed and wa
all they could use or want. It gave them all the land outside
nearly the whole Condado, which they forgot.

"Now the time came when this grant was confirmed by th
new gringo government. And the time came, as you remem
ber, when all the descendants of these seventy-six were give
titles to their land, and the Presidente caused these titles to b
made Patent. Now a title to every piece of land within th
valley was also a title to a share without—ten times the size
But who remembered? Nobody. Save Don Fulgencio, Señora

"Cómo no? He was simply shrewd and careful. It wa
business. Like this. A poor farmer comes to him for a loan o
his land, with land to sell. My wise friend takes title to all hi
land—the piece within the valley the man knows he owns
and the larger piece outside that he knows nothing about
Pretty soon the man raises a little money, he wants his lan
back—it is the Devil the way they hang on to their land! S
my friend simply transfers back to him his valley land, an
retains title to the rest. No one is the wiser."

"Ah!" sighed Maria.

"Ah, indeed! What a head he had on those narro
shoulders of his, Don Fulgencio, my friend, your husband
Most of this land was mountainous, fit only for grazing. Bu
he smelled the new railroad approaching, which neede
timber for ties. . . . But more important! This land was on th
watershed. With it water rights could be controlled whe
eventually a dam was needed. There was even a Compañí
forming. And Don Fulgencio had the land. So he became on
with the Compañía. Only one piece more was needed. You re
member? Title to that long cañon draining into the valley pas
the tall cliffs. The perfect site for a dam that must be buil

"My memory returns, Sanchez," said Maria soberly.

"As I thought!" he replied shrewdly. "A great price Don Fulgencio must have got for it, too, from the Compañía. Why, for ten years I myself watched pass the timber they cut from it to sell the railroad. To say nothing of all the other and like it he got from these dull people, our neighbors. I myself arranged the papers of title for him—at very little profit to myself, for keeping a tongue in my cheek. Though he promised more. But died too soon." He was eyeing Maria steadily now. "Of course you are poor according to custom, Doña Maria. As was he, being wise. But a little of that gold now. . . ."

Maria stood up. "Enough! Well do I recognize my husband's shrewdness in being a politico to maintain you in office. You who are so cunning yourself. But I think not too poorly paid for what you have done. No doubt these new politicos, the Mofres, who have taken up the dead one's power, pay you less than he. Verdad?"

"A little but not enough. Cristo Rey! But when the dam is built, and they have the water to measure and sell, and theirs is the new electric plant, and taxes moreover—well, it is best to bet on the winning horse. . . . But now. About this land of yours. That in the valley. The piece by the tall cliffs. It is good with respect to the dam. Very good, I will say to you with the memory of Don Fulgencio between us. But, as you say, you are getting old. If you would sell, to the Mofres I myself . . . ."

"No, amigo. No, my cunning friend. I have decided not to sell my land. Not a vara. Now I must go. To you I leave the memory of Don Fulgencio and a piece of his gold. I would not know what to do with either."

Sanchez looked at her curiously as she went out.

Winter crept down the mountains. The valley paled from a lake of blue to a lake of white. Cold clutched and throttled it. And then its white turned blue again with the shadowy reflection of the peaks upon its icy crust.

So do men, their deeds blanketed, still reflect the natural color of their lives.

Maria from her cliffs watched the mutations. She knew at last why Don Fulgencio had desired her in marriage. But so long ago! It meant nothing to her now. He was but one of many, his shape a shadow mirrored for an instant upon the one enduring earth.

For days, a week, she was snowbound. It gave her time to properly consider the dam. There was this about it, it was more than a dam, it was a step in progress. And progress men define as that step toward giving the greatest good to the greatest number of people. Now Maria believed neither in the majority nor in the minority. She believed in all men. Good for the strong at the expense of the weak she saw as a natural inevitability. But also she saw that intentional wrong dealt the few can never be paid for by the right derived from it by the many. Maria believed in fulfillment instead of progress. Fulfillment is individual evolution. It requires time and patience. Progress, in haste to move mass, admits neither.

So she pondered, beating her way up the snowy trail to her seat on the crags, and wrapping herself in the soft burnt-orange blanket.

The suspicion never entered her head that she was philosophizing. She thought that she was making up her mind about the dam. It merely shows how abstract are all things in perspective when seen from a height. In dimensional time and space nothing is only what it seems.

Over the icy fields below her raced a spot of black. It had length and breadth, form and movement. Yet deep ravines did not halt it, nor rocky slopes, nor fences. It was the shadow of a crow in swift flight overhead.

The dam too would cast a shadow. The misfortune of men who would lose their land would not stop it. It would flit across their lives with fear and suffering, anger and evil. All shadows of the shadow of the dam itself. But can you tell a

an who starves that his hunger is unreal? Can you tell a man
at his own life is but a shadow when he has no eyes to see
e real?

Maria sighed. How long it had taken her to climb above it
l, this valley of illusion with its pain and incomprehension!
et to it she was still bound. There is no philosophy of value
hich would deny the earth below. For it is life with its
justice and cruelty, and its patience to suffer both, which
ves us even the philosophy to lift ourselves above it.

The wind had come up again. It curled round the crags
reamers of snow. It shrieked through the pines, whistled
ver the rocks. The leaden skies dropped and crushed its
ice and action. The pandemonium became a pause.

Maria trudged back to her hut. Another snow was coming.
he would need plenty of wood.

The snow came, a foot of it and more. Another came, and
et another. A day of sun welded the layers together. The
arth became solid as a frozen peach. And still the cold
ersisted. Twice a night she got up stiffly to replenish the
re. For water she had to chop up the stream. The pine
utside split open with cold. In the clearing, gaunt, heavy-
eaded deer stood up to their bellies in snow. With them
Maria shared her own corn.

Late in February winter broke. The earth began to soften
ke a spoiled peach. Its muddy juice ran down cañon and
ountainside. The roads began to open. Soon came
eodosio. She could hear the squeak of his greaseless hubs a
ilómetro away.

For an hour they sat talking in the hut. Then Maria got up
nd placed a bag of pesos in his hands.

"There are twenty pesos," she said sharply. "You will say
here are not enough. But with them I want that old buggy
xed. A new tongue. Rims for three wheels. A bit of leather.
Much grease. Perhaps a lantern to tie behind. No less! The
st time I rode, the wheel broke; I would not fall again."

"Mother of God! Such expense. To say nothing of the

work to me. Why, to fix it as you say would require a fortune. Do you think it has remained the same? Jesus Madre! Now the top is gone. The seat is hard with chicken droppings. Its. . . ."

"Enough! Let it be fixed with your work and my pesos."

"For why? By all the Saints. . . . "

"Because," answered Maria slowly, "because I have remained up here alone too long. Spring comes. We ride down through the valley as before. There are things that need my attention. Especially this new dam. I do not approve of it."

8

The first cocks were crowing into the darkness when a faint, low chanting murmured across the fields. Unhurried and throaty with sleep, it moved slowly up the valley growing in volume but not in tempo. Under this polyphony beat another rhythm, an undertone of shuffling feet and the muffled allegro of still more running from out of the scattered adobes on each side. It was a centipedal procession of voice and feet.

Near the bottom of the jutting cliffs the lifting darkness revealed its body—a long column of shivering legs, thinly wrapped thick torsos and bare bent heads. The procession turned right and straggled up the curving cañon. A kilómetro and more up, it turned left out of the pallid gray road. The narrow trail wound up through a steep corn milpa freshly plowed, into pines, past a little hut in a clearing.

Voice and foot became louder now. Dislodged stones rattled down the mountainside from the more steeply rising trail. Breaths came shorter, hoarser. But still all sang, raising their eyes to stare upward and forward toward the looming crags.

At their head climbed four old men alternately carrying o
two of their shoulders a statue of a fifth tottering on a litt
wooden platform. The latter was older than all four. H
wooden cheeks were cracked, his painted skin peeling. Onl
his eyes were bright and timeless, little marbles of shin
agate. In one hand, for a staff, he held a wooden spade. A
his feet stood a yoke of oxen no bigger than rabbits.

"Courage, San Ysidro!" panted one of the old mei
respectfully, stopping to steady the statue with a hand almo:
as brown and lifeless. "It has been a long climb. But we are i
time. Mira! The day is just breaking."

They reached the top of the tall cliffs. On the top-mo:
crag sat an old wrinkled woman wrapped in a fade
burnt-orange blanket. She did not turn around at sound c
their chanting, nor to watch them group around the rock
below her. She pushed back her thin, flying hair, an
continued staring fixedly down into the beautiful blue valley

The sun was rising. Little javelins of sunlight struck th
opposite wall of the mountains, were deflected back by clii
and rock, or fell split and broken down the water-gashe
hillsides. The air grew luminous with spears and arrows c
gold. Pine needles glistened metallically. Micaceous rock
glittered like cut diamonds. Streams flowed silver. Far off,
window glass gleamed crystal.

Then suddenly the mist lifted. Down below spread out th
squares and rectangles and strips of black, fresh plowe
earth—the fresh, deep, soft earth of spring.

"The Salida del Sol! Look, San Ysidro!" a deep voice criei
out in the pause. "It is your day, el Día de San Ysidr
Labrador, the blessed saint of farmers, the precious patron o
our fields and crops. It is your day, and sunrise of that day
Now we have brought you to these high cliffs so that yo
may overlook all our fields and see that our fields are ready
our crops in. Bless them therefore, San Ysidro, on account o
our devoutness, our readiness and labor, that they may thi
year bear fruitfully."

The deep, slow chant burst out afresh. The old men hoisted the little platform still higher, carried it to the edge of the cliffs, turned it slowly this way and that, all ways. And San Ysidro from his bright, shiny little eyes of agate stared down at Santa Gertrudes and San Antonio, at El Alto de Talco and El Alto de los Herreras, at all the little clumps of adobes in the long blue crescent, and saw that all the land between was black and fresh and ready.

"Lift him higher, Padre!" shouted a paisano pointing to a narrow cañon mouth. "My land is high. It is partly hidden by those pines. But I want him to see it is ready, for all those cursed stones that chipped my plow."

"Turn him this way! No, that!" demanded another crowding to the front of the crowd. "I would have him know that it is yet too early to plant my crop, being but the middle of May, yet see that my land is all prepared and ready for the seed. Gracias, Señores. Mil gracias."

Through all this singing, these exhortations, the old woman above did not stir. Nor did she turn around at silence when all knelt on the rocks in a prelude to prayer. She continued staring down into the sun-flooded valley.

The men rose from their knees. They flashed quick looks at her above them, and then plodded in noisy groups back down the trail. The Santo had done his duty as they. Now they were men hungry for porridge and tortillas, and he was a piece of wood. So they passed him cumbersomely from arm to arm, and unmindfully cracked the little wooden platform against protruding rocks. But the woman, having both the qualities of saint and man, they still respected. They did not speak until they had passed her hut.

Two old men remained on the cliffs. They approached the topmost crag.

"Well, Doña Maria," said one, respectfully enough. "It is the middle of May. It is el Día de San Ysidro Labrador. It is just past the rising of the sun. Now we have done as you suggested, according to the old custom. Did we not do it

right? Did we not do it well? What do you think of it, Doña
Maria?"

"And what do you think of the future of our crops?"
added the other shrewdly. "Will we have a heavy harvest?"

Maria screwed around in her seat on the rocks, and focused
on them her small bright eyes.

"Pues! How now do you feel about this thing, yourselves,
compadres? Have you no feelings in those brittle bones that
you must ask me for mine?"

The two old men stepped back. One of them began to
study his feet. Said the other, "Well, I, Señora. . . . Well now
I will say this. I feel very good about this thing. It is queer
but so. I feel like the young man I was when I first climbed
up here on San Ysidro's day. How many years has it made?
Quien sabe? I know only that it was my first piece of land,
the first wife I had to feed from it. Now the blessed Santo
did not fail me that first year. He has not failed me
since—only off and on, perhaps, for which any Santo can be
duly excused, this being earth and not heaven. So I say, and
truly it is my opinion, that it has not been a good thing to
forget this old custom of late, and that it is a good thing to
continue it again. . . . Madre! I had forgotten how beautiful
the fresh black earth looks from here on high, in spring, with
the crows busy already. . . . Not only I, Señora. I saw other
eyes and in them the wonder. Did you ever see so many as
came? At a suggestion. At a nod. So far too. So steep. . . . It
makes me hungry for hot coffee. For an egg, perhaps. . . ."

Maria spat. "There are no eggs! There is no coffee! Am I
rich that I can eat thus every morning? But in my house there
are no doubt tortillas. And tea. I have used it but once. With
a little fresh it will be black enough. And hot—if you cut a
little wood."

She began to unbend, very stiffly and slowly. Then
suddenly, one foot down, she spoke to the other old man.
"Señor! You ask of the future of your crops. Pues! Tell all
who so bade you ask, this: It will be a good year. The best in

ve. Is it enough? Now come. We shall have that tea. For two
nen who must depend on an old woman for their faith as
well as their breakfast, you have not done badly with this
rocession."

When they had gone, Maria lay down underneath a pine
or a morning nap. The stream beside her gushed full and
oisy with melting snow from the peaks still white above.
ven with little rain the acequias would be full all summer.
he belched, then sighed with wisdom.

It is impossible to fight the new with its own weapons. But
o go back, back to the dimly understood truths that lie
ormant in dead faiths and living bloodstreams—that is the
ecret of seers and dictators, of power and success. For
nechanical progress, being change, is evanescent. What
ndures is only the enduring.

So she began to fight the dam: not opposing it with any
eason, but calling forth the feeling for the land it would
upplant.

There was much time, for still the season paraded, and
here was no dam.

"What is this?" a villager would ask. "Where is that dam
or which we marked our crosses as directed so long ago? The
overnment has failed us."

And soon they almost forgot it.

But always, at dawn, noon or night, one might glimpse an
ld buggy stopped in the middle of a road. Over forty years
ld it was—that part of the original which still remained to
queak and groan and flap in the wind. Automobiles jolted
ast in whirls of dust which choked the old woman stiffly
pright in the tattered seat. Bands of horsemen, groups of
omen, plodded by. But oblivious of them all, an old
hite-headed scarecrow of a man in a rusty suit stood at the
de letting water.

"Sacred Heart of Jesus!" she would exclaim when he
ambered up again. "Have you no control over your water?

It makes three times already that you have been out. An
those pantalones! Have they no buttons?"

"Of course, of course," grumbled the old man. "But it
cold. How can I wait? Besides, my kidneys are shattered wit
all this traveling from dawn to dusk. Cristo!" He slapped th
skeleton horses into a walk again. "Andelante! Nosotros n
somos congrejos! We are not crabs!"

It was a specter, this rattletrap buggy drawn by a skeleto
team, and containing an old white-headed man and a dar
wrinkled witch—the specter of Maria fighting the specter of
dam.

Suddenly both assumed more reality.

The rich people in the city had finally bought those paper
of the Compañía. The papers from which the dam would b
built. Much money it required. Not a thousand pesos, Seño
Ten thousand! And more, though I cannot imagine more.]
has all been given to the Government. Now the President wi
build the dam. He has not forgotten, after all. Imagine tha
compadres!

The Mofres and the Compañía gave another fiesta. The
shot off fireworks. These, beyond words, were beautifu
There were stars of hope, flowers of fire, flashing blades c
passion, bright streamers of desire arching the heavens. An
all in color. Such colors. Magnífico!

Old Tiburcio, he who was called "El Tigre," saw ther
from his hut in the mountains. He lashed his horse to town i
a lather, and flung off to grovel on the church steps. H
thought that the end of the world, by fire, had come.

"Courage, primo! Have no fear!" he was counseled, wit
many reassuring thumps on the back. "It is but these ne
fireworks you see for the first time. Hah! Great days a
coming. You will see greater things yet no doubt when th
Government comes to build this dam."

Maria continued to drive around in her buggy.

"A fine stand of oats you have," she would say to a ma
"A beautiful piece of land. There is none better. We

easure it and find comfort in it while you may. Soon it will
e nothing but a lake. You will have to make your living
shing, though in winter you will probably starve. You have
oted to give up your land to this new dam."

To another with skin trouble she would recommend this
remedy: tierra blanca and raw frijoles ground together.
Beans you may obtain from any man. But this tierra blanca
ound on your own ranchito is the best I know. As you
now, half the walls in the valley are washed with it. Such a
name that you would give it up for this dam."

As she rode away each stared after her with a look of dull
ewilderment.

But now the day was set; the day when all the people were
o come to town for a big talk. Little posters appeared in
ore windows, on fenceposts, adobe walls and tacked upon
eat pines. Officers of the water district had called a meeting
o ask landowners to agree upon a price for their land.

Maria set her jaw, ignored her rheumatism, and rode
oggedly from house to house. This time she talked plainly.
hen a man saw her coming, he hastily summoned his
eighbors. They gathered round her buggy with hats
removed.

"Doña Maria, I have called my primos to listen also. We
now you do not like this dam, but we have forgotten why.
ou will pardon our short memories, for you know that we
e simple. Now tell us again what we should think."

Maria spat over the dashboard. "Are you men or are you
uildren? Listen! You have heard that the dam is good. It is
ood because after it there will be no more floods, no more
roughts, but water always for each man according to his
eed. Is not that what the políticos told you, los Mofres, the
gents of the Compañía?"

"Verdad! Not a word has she left out. What a memory she
as. . . . Sí, Sí, Señora. It is as they said."

"All right, Señores," said Maria patiently. "Let us say that
is dam will do all these things. Now answer me this. Think

well, amigos." On each simple face in turn she fixed her gaze
"Guadalupe, would you have your land with floods an
droughts according to the will of God, or would you have n
land at all?"

"Why, Doña Maria—what is this you ask? Surely a ma
would have the poorest land to none at all. Why, withou
land a man would starve, be it overrun with grasshoppers an
full of stones to test his strength and patience."

Around him ran a murmur of approbation. "Verdad. H
speaks truly. He answers for us all."

"Good!" replied Maria, rolling a cigarette. "Now answe
me this: Of what good is this dam if you have no land t
benefit?"

The hopeless bewilderment settled on their stolid, unline
faces. "But Señora!" spoke one solemnly. "We do no
understand. We wish our land, of course. But why will no
the dam be good for it?

"Fools! Burros!" spat out Maria. "Because if there is
dam you won't have any land! Will the dam be built in th
empty air? No! It will be built on land. The water it will hol
back will cover more land. The roads to it will require sti
more land. A lot of land, Señores. Whose land? Antonio
land; Guadalupe, your land; Trinidad's, Casimiro's, Be
abe's—the land of you all. Now without land what will yo
care if there are no more floods and droughts? What will yo
do with the water? You will have no crops."

There was a moment of silence. "But Doña Maria!" It wa
a sharper-faced man who spoke. "Much land the dam wi
require. But not all the land in the valley. Is there not roo
for all, even with a dam?"

"True, Trinidad," she answered. "You think well but no
far enough. Now think this far. You sell your land, you
house, your barn. You and your wife, your children, a
homeless, without land. But you have a bag of silver peso
You walk down the road. You come to Policarpio's house.

" 'Policarpio,' you say, 'I have sold my land. Here is m

oney. Let me buy a piece of your land to live on.'

"But Policarpio says, 'No, Trinidad. I have but enough for yself. Look, here are my six sons. When I die they must ave land, too. I am sorry, amigo, but you see how it is.'

"So you walk down the road to the ranchito of ncarnacion, here. You would buy a piece of his land. Now ncarnacion is a wise man. He says, 'Trinidad, I cannot sell y land. This land is my mother, as it was my father's and y father's father's. What would I do without land in these anging times? I would be homeless, like you.'

"So you go to another house, to yet another. You go roughout the valley, and you can buy no land. Your oman has no place to make tortillas. Every mouthful of od you must buy. Your pesos dwindle. Will you leave this eautiful blue valley, your tierra, to return no more? Will you ork on the railroad like a common labrador? You will be omeless as birds. You and your wife and children can roost the pines. You can live on piñones, perhaps?"

In silence Trinidad stepped forth and faced the crowd. His ace was red with anger. He beat a fist into his palm.

"Mother of God! So this is what you would do to me? ou, Policarpio! You, Encarnacion! You pigs who would ake a man homeless! Step forth if you dare and test the eight of this fist. See if I have forgotten the feel of the knife my belt!"

"Gently, amigo!" purred Maria leaning out from the buggy pluck his sleeve. "This is what would happen to each of ou who would sell his land."

"Who says that I would sell my land? He lies!" shouted ne from the back. "I will not sell my land. Not for silver. ot for gold. Not to any man here!"

"Not to any man here?" repeated Maria softly. "But there no man here who wishes to buy it. Each has his own land ke you. . . . Those who would buy it are not here. They are town waiting for you to come to the meeting. On Sabado is. To them give your answers, compadres. . . . Now adiós.

My own land waits. I must return to see that all is well."

It was not. Antonio de la Vega had not paid his taxes. S
Maria called on her son, his wife, his son and his wife, the
children. In the small dark room they crowded about h
with coffee and homage. Maria sat back stiffly, keeping the
at bay with thrusts of an angry gaze.

"Antonio, it makes three years you have not paid tho
taxes on your land. Do not lie. Now it is not a matter
eighteen pesos which I have ascertained. It is a graver matte
It is a matter of principle. You do not care for your lan
Therefore I have come to tell you the land is no longer you
Be off of it by the next sinking of the sun."

Indignation and protestation, pleas, tears—nothing avail
against her. She drove them out with a set, stern face, a li
of kinsfolk filing across the fields with blankets and pots
beg refuge of a neighbor.

To be sure, the next day they all drove contritely up to h
hut, Antonio with eighteen borrowed dollars. Maria allowe
him to pay his taxes and move back as before. But the less
remained.

"See?" observed the neighbors. "Doña Maria keeps h
own house in order. You should have seen how Antonio an
his kinsfolk came to us. They were weeping and homeles
They had not a roof over their heads. Just as the wise Seño
said. To any of us it might happen. Husband, are we owi
any of this tax money on our land? Now you wi
understand, it is little but important. Muy important
Verdad?"

To three races and four generations, through all its man
names, it has been known simply as the beautiful blue valle
But to some men, one day each month, it is something mor
It is a judicial district and a county seat.

At sunup the plaza begins to fill. By eight o'clock th
hitching racks seem solid leather; the single dusty street
choked with wagons and horses; the exasperated honk of a
automobile is less heeded than the honk of a stray goos

edaling through a forest of legs. Men crowd the cantinas and
ie sunny side of adobe walls. Squatting women cover the
ourthouse lawn. At ten the bells begin to ring.

It is true, there are three courthouses in Santa Gertrudes.
ine faces the inn, at the turn of the Guadalupita road. It is
ld as the memory of man. The floors sag, its huge vigas are
ropping with the roof, the thick adobe walls are crumbling.
xcept, of course, the little patch of gray stone built into one
de. "That," one hears, "was the wall of the calabozo. A
ood stone wall it took to hold El Tigre in his prime! His
nife could cut through adobe as if it were cheese!"

Of the new one the people will be very proud when it is
nished. It will resemble no building ever seen in the valley.
: is cold and tidy as an algebraic equation, inelastic in line as
w, modern as a stiff collar. It is a temple of that progress
·hich recognizes no inherent qualities in different earths and
ices.

The second courthouse, chronologically, reflects a bit of
oth the others. It too was standard in its time, when a
rown stone front portrayed the dull respectability of the
ringo eighties. But life and time have mellowed its gaunt,
tern body. Its hollowed stone steps hold rainwater. The dry
ir has cracked its woodwork. Cottonwood limbs hide its tin
oof. Its brass spittoons spout stubs of hand-rolled cigarettes.
. rag stuffs a crack in the front window. It, like the first,
rouses the suspicion that even the Gilbraltar of law and
rder is not impregnable to the assault of justice.

To this one the people turn, lazily mount the steps to the
ourtroom. The cracking of piñones and the sucking of stick
andy is in order. It is a show room big enough for all,
hough some must squat in the aisles. Cómo no? These are
ut more for the local políticos to impress.

But court raps its little hammer.

Jesús Alarcón is in the clutches of law. He was drunk that
ther Saturday night. He kept riding his horse up and down
he flagstone portal of the old inn, and beating in the wooden

shutters with his whip. Jesús Alarcón is fined five dolla⌐
Señora Alarcón sobs buckets. She is going to get a beati⌐
tonight, because it is she who brings out from her rebozo t⌐
five dollars in a glass jar. God knows where she got them, b⌐
Jesús will want to know.

Jacinto Mondragon! You stole that white heifer from yo⌐
neighbor Ismael Trujillo. You admit it. To Ismael Trujil⌐
you will return that white heifer and give also that litt⌐
Jersey calf of yours.

Ceferino Valdes! The case of El Estado y El Condado ⌐
Demora against Ceferino Valdes for stabbing with a knife t⌐
person of Mechor Santistevan. Mechor Santistevan may di⌐
he may recover. The case is carried forward till God decide⌐

Maria del Valle. . . !

What! Mother of God! Can it be so? Our Maria? Do⌐
Maria in the clutches of the law? In God's name, for what?

Feet shuffle. Heads crane forward. Consternation rippl⌐
through the room. Also eddies of satisfaction, people bei⌐
what they are. Why, it was supposed that Doña Maria w⌐
greater than the law. And now. Look! She is no greater th⌐
the least.

Yes. Maria is sitting down in front like a captive haw⌐
Without doubt a hawk in its cage resembles little the one th⌐
flew so regally in freedom. Maria looks ragged, cramped an⌐
ugly. But still she is wild, wary and imperturbable. Her o⌐
tooth is clamped down indomitably on a cold cigarette. Sh⌐
might be sitting on her crag.

Don Teodosio sits besides her. It is he who feels the bar⌐
He scrooges. His trembling hands pick at his sombrero.

"Maria del Valle! Remove that cigarette from your mout⌐
It is unseemly in a court of law."

Maria removes it to hide in her rebozo for later lightin⌐
She does not look at the judge, but watches the político wh⌐
shouts his charges at her.

"Yes! This witch of an old woman we have caused to b⌐
arrested. This very morning. In the very street outside. In h⌐

uggy she sat gathering men about her. Like flies about a
oney jar. For what? To deceive, to ensnare with lies. Against
ne dam she talked. The good dam which is the will of all the
ood people of the valley. The very dam of which we will
lk tonight in meeting. . . .Is it not so, old witch, traitress?
ow you will pay!"

"Caramba! Burro! Fool!" answers Maria. "What man here
as heard me say a word against the dam? I say build this
am. Build it I say! But find your own land to build it upon.
ot ours. Build it in the air where all the promises of
olíticos are built! Is this not what I said? What man denies
?"

Bravo, Señora! Bravo, Doña Maria! Look! This captive
awk has ruffled her feathers. Watch out there, compadre,
or that beak, those quick talons.

A small pandemonium breaks loose.

The judge raps for order with his wooden hammer. The
om stills. Maria watches him now, respectfully.

He is tall and stooped, but he is younger than Teodosio.
e is a good judge. Maria knows it. She had switched his little
ehind with a willow twig for stealing apples in the days
efore he went away to return a rich and learned abogado.

"What have you to say to this, Doña Maria? Rise, as is
tting, to address the court."

Time it takes Maria to unbend, straighten and try her stiff,
neumatic legs. And more to lasso the crowd with a look of
old contempt.

"The accusations are false, Don Eliseo . . . . "

" 'Your Honor,' please," interrupts the judge. "You
ddress not me, but the robes of authority which cover me in
nis court."

"Your Honor," begins Maria again. "No man denies what I
ave said. You heard me ask. You heard silence answer."

"It is true, Señora, that you caused a great crowd to
ollect about you in the street this morning?"

"Your Honor Don Eliseo," says Maria slowly. "You

remember this old courthouse of ours. How its floors sag, i
vigas drop with the roof, the walls crumble to rise no more
You observe this courthouse in which we stand. It is almo
worn out. It can scarcely hang together. Now out th
window you see the new courthouse soon to be ready. Th
third courthouse in this one valley. Pues. It too will wear ou
and crumble to dust. No doubt there will be more, and the:
too will sink back, outworn, to earth. It not that so?"

"The court questions Doña Maria, not Doña Maria th
court, Señora," replies the good judge dryly.

"Pues! This then is what I observe." Maria glares round th
room; she is not without a sense for the dramatic force (
pause. "The steps and cries of men for justice have worn ou
even the wood and stone of the first courthouse. They hav
worn out the wood and stone of the second as well. They wi
wear out the third and all those to follow. The need of me
for justice, Señor Judge, endures forever. Wood and stor
cannot stand against it. Neither men, nor words, nor law
Thus I say."

The good judge wipes his mouth. His hand hides a smile
but not his twinkling eyes. His raised hammer silences th
angry políticos. He appears to consider both the wisdom (
Doña Maria and the political expediency of the situation.

"Doña Maria. The court fines you two dollars for ob
structing traffic on the main highway through town."

Doña Maria turns and stalks out of her cage without
word. Teodosio digs a dollar out of his pockets, borrov
another, pays and hurries after her. They get into the buggy
Teodosio whips up the bony team.

"Mother of God! What a scene! We have defied not onl
the officials of the Compañía and the políticos, but the lav
itself. Before the learned Judge himself. And on the very da
of the meeting, when all were there to see how resolutely w
faced disgrace, destruction, a day in the calabozo or even
great fine. Santána, how they will talk about it! Our courage
our strength of will. Wait until the meeting tonight. Word

ill be hotter than chile seeds. . . . Ándale! . . . I must
urry back.

"Ah. . . . That Señor Judge, Don Eliseo," murmurs Doña
aria. "He whom I have switched for stealing apples not
nce but often. It shows what success and fame do to a man.
'ith less fear of others' opinions he might have fined us only
ne peso or even none at all."

Usually by dusk the roads from Santa Gertrudes were
·owded with people returning home from court.. That
aturday they were empty: all had stayed to attend the
teeting. Maria, facing from her crag the sun sinking behind
ne Sangre de Cristo, saw it all below her as she had
ways—as the beautiful blue valley.

But this was only its stark reality. All day it had been a
tdicial district. Tonight it was something else, a water
istrict.

This latter premise the políticos duly expounded to the
cople in meeting. Behind the speakers sat two of the Mofres,
me officials of the Compañía and several engineers all
odding agreement. Behind them on the wall hung great
taps of the valley to further attest it.

The room was packed; townspeople had brought chairs
ad benches from home to fill the aisles. Bewilderment and
sentment struggled with comprehension and acceptance on
teir dark simple faces.

The necessity of the dam and the benefits to be derived
·ere being explained. Its location was pointed out to them
n the large colored maps: there at the mouth of that cañon,
ere where the cliffs would provide anchorage. Up this way
 it a new road, and through the valley still another. And
chind it, a beautiful blue lake.

This lake people could understand. It sounded almost
tiraculous. There were claps and yells. Imagine, a lake where
tere had never been one before! As if God Himself would
t it down. As easy as that!

During the applause Teodosio appeared. His battered

sombrero was askew, the fly of his rusty suit gaped open, h wrinkled cheeks were flushed pink as a babe's. "Ah, Do Teodosio! Doña Maria's Teodosio!" People respectful huddled against the wall to let him pass. He staggered dow the aisle and collapsed on the floor.

He was late, but not too late. Just as he had driven up his buggy, he had met the good judge. His Honor had bee much impressed with the wisdom of Doña Maria th: morning. It had deeply pained him to fine his old friend. B alas! He spread his hands in mute eloquence. One of the came to rest on Teodosio's arm. It contained two silve dollars. Teodosio, himself an understanding man of year pocketed them without a word.

"Law is law, and I uphold it," said the Judge. "Bu friendship is friendship, and I do not forget it. So to the wi Doña Maria, my good friend of years, deliver my profoun respect and great esteem. Now come. I shall buy a drink. N for myself who drinks no more and who must drive h máquina away this very night. For you. In memory of tho days when we chased cows together through the thickets."

So Don Teodosio had sat with Don Eliseo and drunk h drink. It warmed his blood, stirred his tongue. He recalle those days—that day—"But I must go now, amigo," said th Judge rising. "Remember my message to Doña Maria. Als those two pesos. Forgive my mentioning them, but we are a forgetful."

"Of course, of course. I shall just remain here a moment i respectful silence while a great man leaves." And Teodosi had sat there in the dim and empty little cantina. Yet in th: moment a friend had come and the two pesos had gone. The were not in this pocket nor in that. Nor would the bartend serve him another drink on credit. Teodosio unraveled h thoughts as he rose. He must go to the meeting. Wit something to tell Maria, and the Judge's message of esteen perhaps he need not mention those two pesos.

So Teodosio sat on the floor listening. There were speake

nd interpreters, oratory and bombast, facts and figures.
esús! A man could not remember one. He squirmed about.

In the middle of a speech something happened to
ʼeodosio, it happens to the best of men at the worst of
ʼimes. He got up and struggled out through the packed mass
ʼo the shadow of his buggy. The speaker glared at the
ʼommotion, then resumed. In a moment Teodosio returned
ʼo make another fuss. The people let him through respect-
ʼully as before, whispering to each other. "It is all right. It is
Don Teodosio. Without doubt Doña Maria waits outside in
ʼer buggy. He has been out to tell her what is being said."

It had all been explained, the necessity of the dam and the
ʼenefits the people will receive, where the dam will be and
ʼhe new roads, the amount of land it will all require. Now a
ʼew speaker rose before them. "Such is the will of the good
ʼeople of the valley. You remember how you marked the
ʼrosses on your votes? Well, the Government observes your
ʼwishes, and is ready to build the dam. Now we are here in
ʼhis great meeting called by these your officials of this
ʼllustrious water district. All the landowners of the valley. To
ʼgree on a price for our land. For the dam must have land,
ʼhe roads, the lake. Some will need to sell. But at a fair price.
ʼs it not reasonable that we agree on one fair price for each?
ʼVhat do you say, compadres? Shall we say four dollars an
ʼcre for grazing land, the rocky mountain hillsides? And
ʼhirty-five dollars an acre for the vegas, the fields in the
ʼalley—the upper end where the dam will be, where the land
ʼs not so rich?"

A thick silence eddied in the wake of his words. It was
ʼtirred by the clatter of a chair, a noisy stumbling, the groan
ʼf one with a foot trodden on. Teodosio was hurrying
ʼutside again.

"He is hurrying out to tell Doña Maria!" the whisper
ʼirculated. And when Teodosio came back in the people took
ʼeart. "He says nothing. He sits with a bowed head. But look.
ʼHis face is grave. Doña Maria doesn't like it."

The men on the platform were having trouble. It was as they were shouting down the throat of an empty cave, n one answered. "Come, come! You must agree on a prope price for your land. It is why you are here. Have you n speakers? Have you no opinions? Don Policarpio! Do Encarnacion. . . .Trinidad. . . .Casimiro. . . .Berabe! As lanc owners, speak. You are among friends."

Feet shuffled. Eyes looked furtively at others. At last man rose. "Four pesos is very little," he said. And the apologetically, "But I don't know how much is this a-cre Still, perhaps I would not sell my best varas for four pesos Where would I get more?" Thus he remembered Maria' words.

The ice was broken. More shouts, more men rising to thei feet. Curiously, as if for confirmation, they all looked towar Don Teodosio who had risen and was holding to the back o a chair. His face was gray and sweaty; he was eyeing the bac doors again like a man suddenly ill and contemplating a quic exit for relief.

It was the pose proper for the gravity of the situation. Hi refusal to answer shifted the responsibility to their ow courage. His pale cheeks betokened fear that they had none His posture of ready flight indicated his readiness to fle outside with news of their capitulation.

For behind him, presumably outside in her buggy, sa Maria—their common conscience, the invisible and invincibl backbone of their solidarity.

It was a profound and significant moment: the momen that in all battles determines the tide of victory.

Teodosio turned, choked, excused himself.

At his first step, a man in the audience watching hin shouted out in a great hoarse voice. "Policarpio! Encar nacion! Casimiro! Berabe! Do I speak for you? Do I speak fo all of you, compadres?" He had jumped on his chair. Hi heavy muscular body seemed to rise out of his denin trousers, above his wide, brass-studded belt. He flung up a rm, pointed to Teodosio. "Don Teodosio! Do I speak for ou?"

Teodosio's thin stumbling body stopped halfway up the isle as if blown against a chair. He turned around, jerked up is head.

"Then!" shouted Trinidad at the speakers' stage. "Then, eñores! Listen well. We will not sell our land for four pesos or for thirty-five. We will not sell our land for silver or for old. We will not sell our land for any price!"

With an appealing look of bulging pride and indomitable tubbornness, he swung around to make sure that Teodosio ad heard and would so inform Doña Maria.

Teodosio did hear a roar behind him, waved his scrawny rm, and weakly, hurriedly stumbled out to the nearest ottonwood. In a few moments he emerged from its shadow. Iis fly was still open, possibly wider. The lapels of his rusty oat he wiped off carelessly. Then, staggering a little, he nade for his empty buggy and crawled into the seat.

A half hour later he was awakened. The pandemonium nside had burst into a bedlam. There were not only a undred men shouting, but women screaming. There came he crash of a chair. Teodosio sat up and rubbed his eyes. The loors flew open. Out of the opening poured interlocked hadows cursing and yelling. They parted to let one stagger oward him. This shadow became a man with a shadow taining his shirt. Past Teodosio he staggered toward the antina. Teodosio smelled blood and violence.

Hastily he laid a whip to his sleepy team, backed into the oad, and turned for home.

Mother of God! What a meeting! There would be plenty of news for Doña Maria without mentioning those two pesos.

9

Maria tottered toward ninety.

She resembled an ancient Santo on one of Pierre Fortier's shelves except that her robes were threadbare and tattered black cotton instead of dusty motheaten silk. Under them her body had shrunk like seasoned wood. It was knotted and cramped from rheumatism. Her flesh was a dark, lifeless brown that had long lost its gelatinous sizing of boiled cow's horns and gypsum yeso, its paint of oxide and ochre mixed with egg yolk, its sheen of polished mutton tallow. Her white hair was thin and brittle as straw. Bent over, when erect, she posed a question mark supported by a cedar stick.

The fingers which clutched it were the prehensile talons of a hawk. But in her face still lived all the sorrow and fecundity, the passion and wild violence of the span of life measured by that human receptacle recognized by men as Doña Maria of the Valley. Its powerful and primitive feature faceted them all. Her promontory beak of nose, high cheekbones and solid, cleft jaw jutted out from her dark wormwood face a savage, sad visage battered by time but still inviolable, a look that only an old Indian can encompass.

Her eyes refuted it all. They had gone dead. Their bright blackness was dulling to a smoky gray which only a brief flicker of the spirit behind could light up like milky opals. Perhaps they had been in-turned too long and deeply to focus readily on the surface life outside.

So when walking she began to poke ahead with her stick. It was a habit few observed. She received vistors while seated in front of her fire.

Maria, then, gave to all simply the aspect of a citadel beleaguered but still impregnable. She so regarded herself.

Yet, because the families of Gertrudes, Niña and Antonio anticipated her weakening blows with an axe, she was persuaded to accept the companionship of a grand-daughter.

"This Piedad of ours and yours," they lied, "is a good girl but a little wild through ignorance. She needs counseling. We wish you to take her, Doña Maria."

"I will accept her for the winter. To instruct her," Maria lied in turn.

Piedad's exercise book was a jag of frosty piñon and a rusty axe, her schoolmates a few shivering goat-ewes whose teats were torn by briars, her reward a bowl of porridge and a few leathery tortillas. She was small, sixteen, quick as a squirrel and more inquisitive. She was simpática. Maria liked her.

At night they crouched together before the fire. A white-bearded storm shook the hut and blew his frosty breath down the chimney. Piedad shivered, drew closer to Maria.

"Mi abuela, my grandmother Doña Maria," she asked, "why is it that children call that frightening boogie man whom none have ever seen 'El Abuelo'—a grandfather? Surely you frighten me not at all."

"My child," replied Maria. "To youth, age is incomprehensible. To ignorance, wisdom is frightening. So that El Abuelo having age represents the learning which the ignorant child fears. Now this is wrong. But even grownups have it. They possess learning and knowledge, and still fear the wisdom which they have not attained. We must all learn to be unafraid of the dark, the child of learning, the man of wisdom. Hence we shall all reach the true maturity which is eternal youth."

The fire writhed into a heap. Piedad threw on another stick. The flames uncoiled, rose up and shook like snakes. The resin rattled. The glare outlined pinkly the rows of goat and ram skulls on the rafters.

"Doña Maria," spoke the girl again, "it is said by all that by skulls and herbs you could read stars and weather, foretell good crops and misfortune, the future of man. Why is it you use them no more?"

Maria sighed. "Ay de mi, child! For many years I have ceased to read them. They were helpful in those days of my youth when like you I mistrusted the unseen trail ahead. It is true I had a knowledge of the signs and the events they portend. But not wisdom—the wisdom to perceive the future in each moment, in each stone and blade of grass. The past also.

"It is like this. A child looks at life as a wolf at the trail of his quarry. He has no sense of the past, only a hunger to devour the future. Thus, to pursue it with success, he soon stops and raises his head. He sniffs the wind. He observes the signs—even those on goat skulls. He listens to all the world around him.

"Now, you understand, he is at middle age. Having memory, he can see part of the trail behind him as well as the present he treads. But still the future winds unseen before him, up toward the cliff top shrouded in mist. He reaches it. Pues! That dreaded and hungered for future is no more than the present which resembles the past. They are all one. His fears were nought, his predictions useless.

"Entiende, muchacha? I will say it again for your simple ears.

"Life is a great white stone. You, a child, stare at it and see only one side. You walk slowly around it. You see other sides, each different in shape and pattern, rough or smooth. You are confused; you forget that it is the same great white stone. But finally you have walked around it, stare at all of it at once from the hillside above. Verdad! Then you see it: how it has many different sides and shapes and patterns, some smooth, some rough, but still the one great white stone: how all these sides merge into one another, indistinguishable: the past into the present, the present into the future, the future again into the past.

"Hola! They are all the same. With wisdom who knows one from the other? There is no time, which is but an illusion for imperfect eyes. There is only the complete, rounded moment, which contains all."

And Maria, with gray filmed eyes which saw more, clouded, than when they had been bright, reached blindly for her little sack of tobacco. "Ay de mi! Often I hear steps outside. I look up to see a man in the doorway. It might be Onesimo as he was called, a certain gringo soldado, Don Fulgencio himself, dead these many years. No! It would not surprise me if he were any of these. There are shapes of men less alive than shadows of men. So do even I confuse what has been and will be again with what is."

Thus in her wisdom she taught that winter the lessons which must be learned by each alone, and did not see the incomprehension in the girl's sleepy eyes.

But everyone else throughtout the valley paid her homage with extravagant praise as they plowed and sowed their fields again.

"Well, well, primo. We will have our land, thanks to Doña Maria. In our ignorance we voted for a dam. Then, with the Señora's wise advice, we refused land for it. Now there will be no dam. Ah, how black this loam is. How it smells!"

Maria had reached the peak of their regard, they almost called her Santa Maria. Yet she had no ears for their praise.

She heard only the gaping silence behind it—the lull before a storm. And far off, the faint rustle of that paper which was to build the dam.

To the families of Gertrudes, Niña and Antonio she said, "This Piedad of ours. She has learned the old ways. Let her leave me now. To go down into the valley and observe the new ways. Thus will her faith be strengthened."

To Piedad, alone, she said, "You have helped me well here, child. You can help me more, away. So leave this hut. Go down to the village. It is said that a criada is needed in the old inn. I would that you do the work."

Piedad was shocked. "A servant in a public inn? To strangers and gringos? It is not our way. We have always remained on our land, for better or worse, having no other master. What will happen to my modesty, my dignity, my pride?"

"As you know," went on Maria quietly, "that old inn has been empty for years, save on court days. Now it is full of gringos who are no doubt talking about this dam. Make their beds, serve their food and wash their dishes as instructed. But keep your ears open; you understand their tongue. Here!" She passed the girl an old square gold piece. "Buy yourself a horse. An old one but well breathed. From one of Antonio's neighbors. Ride up here to me weekly with news of what you hear. Teodosio is sick again. Besides, it will save his old buggy from falling apart and breaking your neck. Sabe? Listen to all, tell only me."

And Maria again drew back into the loneliness of her mountainside. She never left it.

The beautiful blue valley was changing swiftly. A new road had been built to one end from the city below. Another leading from the upper end over the high pass had been straightened and graded. The link between, through the valley, was filled in and tamped down so that the increasing automobiles would no longer stick in chuck holes and slide off slippery adobe into fences, cows. The new courthouse was finished and admired. Young people no longer danced gracefully to a few guitars the varsoviana, the vacquero and buckaroo. They hugged, squirmed and distorted their bodies to the blare of brass in dances enumerated to the old as "The Step of One" and "The Trot of the Fox"—though, to be sure, they still carried knives in their belts and razors in their coat pockets for ready use. Most of these dances took place a half mile up the road in a large new adobe intended for a later school gymnasium. It was called "La Casa de Gym."

"Who is this Señor Gym?" they asked.

Soon great saws, like steel beavers, leveled the row of old cottonwoods flanking the road past it. Only a few were left to stand back of a narrow cement walk built into town— drooping forlornly as if with immeasurable regret, not for their vanished companions which with them had shadowed the parade of hot, dusty, barefoot travelers with their bundles and children, the quarrels, seductions and rapes of a half-century, but for their own fate. They were the real tragedies; they had outlived their usefulness.

Still a red rooster, a line of geese, stray stock ambled down the village street deaf to honking cars. But the town had changed. Its pulse beat faster.

People generally were satisfied. Women learned to wear hats and squeaky shoes. A man had money to pay for them by working between seasons on a road gang. Children were taught English, though still the only school was not a State public school but one conducted behind the church by the Sisters of Loretto.

So they forgot the dam. They almost forgot Maria. Like all Saints she was left in her niche to be recalled in times of stress.

The long flagstone portal of the old inn faced Pierre Fortier's store across the road. Beside his front door he sat on his loading platform awaiting customers, jumping up to swat a fly and tally it, with a pencil stub on the wall. This appeared to be the gringo guests' only amusement as they waited for supper. Soon they drifted inside the inn.

It too was changing. The long bar now served as a hotel desk. Above it hung Kit Carson's brass kettle, a sword once worn by an officer at Fort Union, Jicarillo Indian baskets and Picuris pottery, old horse-hair lariats, faded French prints. The gambling room was a dining room, the green felt of tabletops replaced with checkered oilcloth. The dreary parlor still boasted the James Holstrom grand piano brought by the Colonel across the plains in an ox cart, with its fly-spotted scores of "After the Ball" and "Over the Garden Wall." An old tabouret was covered with a faded, velvet-lined Paisley shawl. On it stood a conch shell and a brass bound Bible. Over it, from the ceiling, hung an old round porcelain lamp painted with red flowers.

The men went out to their rooms, through a little square placita paved as the portál, its flagstones thrusting up from the roots of a giant locust, through a narrow zaguán into the large back garden flanked with a wing of the rambling building, sheds, and a crumbling adobe wall. Here, somewhere, were buried two men with their mules and a chest of gold, no longer dug for but remaining as ghosts to haunt the greed of credulous strangers.

In their dark narrow rooms the men washed in porcelain basins, combed their hair before crystallized glass framed in old tin. In all were large spool beds with feather mattresses, a great comoda for hanging clothes, a battered chest full of firewood for stove or fireplace. In one was an old rosewood cabinet covered with a doily and used as a dresser. No one lifted the lid to see the broken, rusty machinery inside, the bent crank and perforated music rolls of polkas, valses and French quadrilles.

But now through placita, zaguán and garden walked a young Mexican girl ringing a bell. The men came out, strolled lazily through the great greasy kitchen with its battered beams and roaring wood stove, and sat down in the dining room The girl lit lamps, served food.

The men were surveyors, engineers, laborers, clerks. They talked, an unceasing and vehement assault against the dusty silence and strange remoteness of their surroundings. The young criada was a part of both—a lithe, slim shadow in soft huaraches moving in and out among them without a word.

But once a week Piedad rode up to talk to Doña Maria.

"These gringos!" she said with a shrug. "They betray their ignorance daily. 'Hand me that gringo,' the woman will say in the kitchen when she wants the rolling pin. 'Señor Bolio', that is what we call a gringo to his very face. And he, being ignorant of the idioma as of everything else, only laughs at the insult as if at a joke."

"These Anglo-Americans," corrected Maria, staring stonily across the clearing. "Yes, they are ignorant of some things as we Spanish-Americans are ignorant of others. So do not condemn them unjustly. When we both see all, then there will be no difference between us. There is little now. The good judge, was he not a ragged little chamaco? Is he not respected now by the Anglos perhaps more than by us? Simply because his eyes, through learning, have seen both ways."

This tolerance seemed unwarranted; she was getting old.

"But come, Piedad. What is it you hear?"

Week by week she heard, and so did everyone else. The Government was making a survey of the valley; old titles, queer old measurements were being investigated. Since the people could not agree on a price, the District Court had obtained appraisers to value their land. Finally there was a Court condemnation suit.

"What is this?" grumbled the people. "We have refused to sell our land, yet these strangers walk over our fields, they look at our papers. They say our land is worth this, now that. But that we will have to sell. No. We do not understand."

The day came when each received a little printed slip of paper advising him that his land had been appraised, condemned, and that he must move off.

Lines of men knotted in fields, in streets, before the bars. "Sacred Heart of Jesus! Get off your land, compadre. This is what it says to me, this paper. The impertinence! Do these gringos have a wish to test my strength and courage, the steel in my blade?"

"The same, compadre! It is exactly what my paper says according to Filadelphio Baca who can read. Come. Let us get another to read both papers at once."

They remembered Maria now. Daily they rode up the trail. "What does this mean, old mother? That I must get off my land! Carramba! Did we not follow your instructions? Come, Señora. We will not be betrayed."

"Señora! Good Doña Maria! To you we turn again in fear and ignorance. We do not wish to leave our land. Advise us again, Madre. For the love of God, Señora."

Maria sat bent over the fire, her warped bony hands clutching her stick, her filmy gray eyes unblinking as the papers were thrust under her nose. To threats and pleas alike she was obdurate. To all she made but one answer.

"Señor. . . . Señora. . . . Amigos. . . . Listen: I shall never see this new dam."

To her one day came the good judge, Don Eliseo. They met alone in her tiny hut, Maria crooked and bent, the Judge straight and brittle as an old pine, both wise, both wary.

"I am the Court and still your friend, Doña Maria. In me you see a personal man robed with the impersonal authority which he would not betray. So give me your hand and speak frankly. The truth is good for all, though for the weak it is often too strong to bear."

"You are always welcome, Don Eliseo," replied Maria sadly, "though it is you, cloaked with the robes of justice, who deals injustice to many."

"The dam cannot be stopped," went on the judge. "It is not a dam alone. It is new roads, new food and clothing, new customs to add to the old, education for all; it is the progress of the world which sweeps all nations, all valleys of men. No man can stop it, for it is of man himself.

"I tell you this, mi madre, for you are wise and understand. I tell you that you may tell the people, you who have a certain power over them beyond all others. Thus we may prevent fear and trouble, perhaps even bloodshed. Our people are quick to strike at what they do not understand."

"Speak on," assented Maria. "Say fully what you have come to say."

"The talk spreads," continued the Judge, carefully brushing specks of ash off his sleeve. "The talk of certain injustices. Now the Mofres, it is true, will be great gainers from the dam. They own the best land in the valley. They are members of the Compañía. Being rich they have bought much paper in the dam, and will thus derive a certain profit. Now this is not injustice. As you know, gold breeds gold. In every litter there is the stongest. And they have been sharper than most. That, Doña Maria, is inevitable.

"But this is untrue, that while the people will be paid thirty-five dollars an acre for their land, the Mofres will receive a hundred. True, they ask two hundred and yet pay taxes on fifty. But that is the custom, even with Pierre Fortier. I speak this truly: all people will receive equally what their land is worth. It is the Court, above all men, which has decided.

"Now all this is what I have come to say. And to ask you to say to our people to prevent fear and trouble, perhaps even bloodshed."

Maria laid down her stick, rolled and lighted a cigarette with a straw of popotito. She smoked it through deliberately, then again took up her stick.

"Don Eliseo. Two days ago the Mofres came to me—their enemy. They spoke like friends. They offered me gold for my land. Twice what the Court has said it is worth on paper. It was bribery; they knew my power. So I dismissed it as I dismissed them. I also dismiss and will not repeat what you have said about this talk of injustices and the Mofres. Those things, if they be true—and surely they must be, for I have heard them from you, my friend—must be corrected in talk by the Court itself. That is business. And I have nothing to do with business.

"Pues. Let us come to the truth that lies behind all this. What you say is no doubt so; it is not a dam. It is new roads, new customs, the progress of the world which sweeps all valleys of men in turn. You say I cannot stop it, that no man can stop it. I fear, Don Eliseo, that is true also. And yet I cannot bring myself to aid it."

Maria stopped, and rubbed her eyes before continuing.

"Let us consider my refusal to countenance my reason. I have opposed the dam, this progress. Now suppose I aid it. Pues! The people who trust me will jump the fence blindly as sheep to follow me. Or else they will turn upon me crying, 'Doña Maria! You have betrayed us,' and thus I will lose my dignity, their respect.

"That, good judge, is a selfish reason. I am above it. I am too old to crave men's acclaim and to fear their judgment.

"Let us consider it more fully.

"I do not oppose the dam, new customs, a new vision of life; I oppose nothing. But I uphold the old ways for they are good too. I awaken in men their love for their land for they are a people of the land. It is their faith. And so I place that faith above all the lesser benefits they might derive from that which would oppose it. Do you not see? I mistrust these benefits, they may prove temporal. But faith endures. It makes no promises, offers no rewards. It is whole and contains all.

"My friend, good judge, Don Eliseo. We move through time. But the moment comes when each must stop and assert that truth of which he is a part. It is not the whole truth, for man himself is yet incomplete. But it is the only truth he has. It is his integrity.

"For me, compadre, that moment has come. I see the good

in the future. I see the good in the past. But I am of my time, and must assert that which I am, and the faith behind it.

"So we must part. It is for you, being younger, to move on. I, being old, will stand for what I am.

"No. It will do you no good to talk further, Don Eliseo. Besides, I am tired and desire sleep. So go. But remember this, one can not do evil to save the good. So I will help you counsel peace if necessary. No more. Adiós, amigo."

Troubled with forebodings, Maria watched him cross the clearing. But where there had once been great pines and spruces there was now only a milky blur. She could only hear his receding footsteps.

At noon a big truck covered with a tarpaulin rumbled up into the valley from the railroad town on the plains below. It stopped in Santa Gertrudes before a tall adobe house with a peaked tin roof. A long wooden sign hung across the gable. On the porch pillars stuck paper posters: they were noticias containing the date when the people must be off their land.

A crowd of loiterers on foot and horse watched the driver unfasten and throw back the dusty covering, heave three large canvas sacks on the ground, then drag them inside the house. They followed to stand in a long line before a window in the tiny front office.

As the mail was distributed they came back out into the sunshine. Their hands held long envelopes which they slit open with calloused thumbs to reveal printed slips and long important-looking pieces of paper. Frowns beclouded their somber brown faces. They muttered to each other, stared angrily or dully at the papers in their hands. Then they began to crowd into stores and cantinas.

Next day Teodosio, Niña and Antonio with their families drove up to show Maria their own letters.

"Look! Here is one for you also, Madre. Open it. See if it is not from the Government like ours and all men's."

"Open it and speak!" Maria directed her granddaughter

testily. "You know I cannot read!"

Piedad obeyed. "It is as the others, Doña Maria. It is from the Government. It is to pay you for your land."

"I see no gold, nor silver either," grumbled Maria. "Am I a burro to be fooled with a piece of paper?"

"Los cheques. That is what they are," stated Teodosio oracularly as a mummy come to life. "It is what the gringos use for money nowadays. Now here is what is best to do; I have listened to the talk in town.

"We take these checks to a político who writes our names on them, we mark our crosses on them also. Then they are ours. Mother of God! A thousand pesos! We are rich! We can buy fat cows, new clothes, we can buy a new buggy, perhaps a little bottle to celebrate and to warm our old cold bones."

"Enough! Burro. Fool. Pig—and the sick one of a litter at that!" cried Maria. "What will you do with fat cows if you have no land? What will you do with a buggy, having no shed? Will new clothes be a roof over your head? And a bottle! Cristo Rey! If you had sucked more milk from a goat's teat when young, you would have no need for the strength of whisky to make you imagine you are alive.

"But tell me this wisdom of the street and cantina. Who would give you all these things for a piece of paper?"

"I see you do not understand," said Toedosio blandly. "We can take these checks to Los Mofres or Pierre Fortier. They will mark down the amount in their big books. Now when we need anything we go to the store and it is ours. Without money. With just a wish. Pues, as they say, this credit will last for years. Perhaps forever. I tell you we are rich!"

Maria nodded. "Yes. You are rich and homeless. So go wander into the setting sun until you die. . . . But as you go say this to all those who have also received these papers of money for their land. Listen well, Piedad, for you will go also to explain.

"Say this, 'Do not take your papers of money neither to

Los Mofres, to Pierre Fortier, nor to any store. For then these stores will have all your money; they will cheat you out of half and give you poor goods for the remainder.'

"Say also this, 'Do not sign your names or mark your crosses on these papers. Thus you will have to give up your land. By refusing, it may still be possible to keep your land.' Do you understand? Now go."

There were many who did not heed Maria's counsel. For there had come a bank to the valley. True, it was the same old, sound and unused adobe granary they had seen for years. But it had a new roof and iron bars for the windows. It looked strong and important. Two of the Mofres and Pierre Fortier were directors, and thus able to explain its new use and importance.

"You see, compadres, it is a big strong box like that in my oficina—strong against night and thieves. But big as a house and open for all of you. It is the kind they use in the city below. In it the Government and the Compañía will keep money to pay the men who build the dam. In it you may keep your own money, with proper instruction. Now to be true, it takes a man with knowledge to use it. But if it is your will to give me these checks of yours, I will get the money from the Government and put it in this bank for you. When you need anything—good shoes with glass buttons, fat meat, nails . . . for you know my tienda contains all of the best—then I will give it to you, and obtain the money for it from the bank at no trouble to yourselves. Sabe? Thus I assure you of safety against thieves."

Yet there were those who neither gave their money to the stores nor to the bank to keep. They hid their checks in an old boot, in a box upon the rafters, in a buried glass jar. It was these to whom two Government men came with the sheriff and an interpreter.

"Look here!" they said sternly. "It is a month since you received your checks for your land, and yet you have not got your money from the Government. The Government knows this; it has its eye upon you. Now soon you will have to move off your land as directed long ago. Do you think to keep both money and land? So get your money quickly. You will need it to find new land, another house to live in."

To Maria they said this; and Teodosio, the families of Gertrudes, Niña and Antonio were there to listen also.

"Señores," answered Maria resolutely. "Here is my piece of paper. I will not accept it. The Government, the Presidente himself, knows better than to treat me thus. If you would take away my land, then give me silver, gold, money that I can see, feel the weight of in my hand, bite between my teeth. Here!" She tottered to a dark corner of her hut and brought back an old, warped, wooden box which she dropped on the floor at their feet.

"I must have this almur filled with silver pesos. Full and level with the top, Señores. It has always been the custom when selling and buying land. An almur—sometimes less, sometimes more—of silver for good land."

Vainly they threatened; Maria was obdurate.

They drew off together, outside the hut, to talk the gringo "This old witch, this old fool!" explained the sheriff. "An almur is about a peck. I doubt if it would hold fifteen hundred silver dollars. And look. Her check is for twenty-two hundred dollars."

Vainly now they returned to plead; Maria was still obdurate.

"An almur of silver. Full and level with the top, Señores. It has always been the measure when selling and buying land. I will accept nothing else."

"Mother of God!" mumbled Teodosio when the men left "It is you who are a fool. Money that you can see, feel the weight of in your hand, bite between your teeth! Our Guadalupana! You are getting too blind to see it. You have no teeth to bite it with. Besides that, where in this world nowadays can even the Government get a thousand silver pesos? To say nothing of those for us, for others also. We shall ll lose our land, our money and credit too."

Yet within a week the Government gringos returned. This ime in a shiny new carro containing not only an interpreter nd the Sheriff but a strange man from the city who held a hotgun across his lap. For Maria they filled the almur with ilver; she herself blindly passed her wrinkled hand over the op to see that it was full according to custom. To Niña, Gertrudes and Teodosio they gave also little bags of silver for heir share of land at the bottom of the cliffs and the astures above, and to Antonio for his fields and vegas.

In the dim light of a candle in Maria's hut all sat in silence taring at the silver; Antonio dully; Niña and Gertrudes vonderingly; the primos and the children open-mouthed; and Teodosio, bent over, letting the coins trickle through his ingers to fall back with a gentle, metallic tinkle. "Madre de Dios!" he whispered. "I have lived to see it. Silver that flows hrough my fingers like water, like moonlight, without end. Ve are rich at last."

Maria stood up, crouching over her stick.

"It is nothing!" she said wearily. "So take it all. It is yours. Divide it equally among yourselves, and bury it against the our of need. When the time comes that I leave you say imply, 'She had no land to bequeath to us. Only this silver vhich is meaningless without land.' Mark my words. In them ies your future and my directions to it."

Now to all the others the Government carro went in turn, o those who had heard of and followed Doña Maria's xample, to Berabe and Trinidad, Policarpio, Encarnacion, Donaciano Romero, Quiteria Pacheco and the rest.

"Give us the check the Government sent you," they lemanded of each. "Now make your mark upon this paper. There! Here is your bag of silver pesos. Now, Señor, the land s no longer yours. Be off it with all you own by the day set y those who come to build the dam."

This was the way it was. They hid their silver untouched or pent it according to their natures. Yet none of them could

believe they would lose their land until the new road curve
up into the valley.

A cluster of six dark red huts at Cañoncito stood before i
Two days later the fences were down; cows, horses, goa
were loose in neighboring fields and lost in the hills; free
chickens and geese ran squawking to be flattened on th
roadway; the houses and barns were heaps of smokin
timbers and shattered adobe bricks. With all this disappeare
Jesús Alarcón who had suffered a cracked skull under th
weight of argument; he had been carted down to a hospit
by a company truck.

The families fled shrieking to near vecinos, awaiting new

It came straggling up the road; four barefoot childr
Filadelphio and Señora Baca loaded down with pots an
blankets, who had walked forty miles back to the valley afte
an absence of six weeks. Filadelphio was no longer the cock
rooster who had taken his family to the city to spend th
money from his land. His new feathers were bedraggled. H
was surly, and sat outside muttering to the men. Inside th
house Señora Baca talked and shrieked between tears.

"God forgive us our sins, our pride and arrogance!" sh
wailed, not unconscious of the new power she had derive
from them. "To the city we went, as you know, to live th
life of the rich gringos; Filadelphio to work on the railroa
and thus add more money to our riches. You see us no
humbled to dust, groveling at your kind feet. Returned to th
valley, our tierra, penniless and shamed, without friends. A
de mi! You will be wise to turn us from your doors, we wh
have not had a tortilla since dawn. To refuse us your roof fo
this night. . . . What! An egg you are preparing? Cheese an
tortillas, even coffee. . . ."

Soothed, she held up to all ears their six weeks in the city
A little house they had lived in. Near the railroad tracks
Where they could watch by day the wonderful trains, an
hear the whistles and bells at night. Such a ferrocarril! I
shook the house. Of wood it was. Pues. That was the trouble

Of course, Filadelphio worked on the tracks. Very hard. A laborer. But money he got to buy canned peaches, canned tomatoes. You have tasted them? Seen those shiny cans with the beautiful pictures on them which can be pasted on the windows? Too, they walked the streets and saw the lights. All colors, burning at night as bright as day. They looked in the windows. Everything was in those windows. Mother of God! They went to the moving pictures. Not once. Many times. You have never seen a cinematografia? Well, that was the trouble.

It was true Filadelphio did not like his work. There was nothing of the good rich earth about it. It was true the señora did not like her neighbors; they were very common. It was true the children were sick from eating too many peaches and tomatoes out of the shiny cans. Sí, that was the trouble.

"What was the trouble, amiga?"

"What trouble? Verdad! Are we not penniless, homeless, starved and shamed? Listen, as I have said, all this was the cause.

"Filadelphio did not like his work, so when he came home he was tired and cross. I did not like my neighbors, they were too busy to talk. The house was wood, not thick walls of adobe; it was always cold and required great fires. So we hid our bag of silver, and went to the cine. That's how it was.

"You see the night came when we returned to find our wooden house burned down. There was no bag of silver to be found in the ashes. Our riches, our future, were gone in the flutter of an eyelid, as quickly as the cine. so we have come here. We do not like the city. But where is there land for us now? What shall become of us?"

So the people began to mutter. Should they lose their money in the city like Filadelphio? Or remain in the valley to be cheated out of it by the Mofres, and have their heads cracked by the bolios like Jesús Alarcón? Meanwhile they retreated before the advancing road.

Unlike the old one which crawled along the side, following

the contour of the mountain wall, the new one cut straig
up the valley. Nothing stood before it, neither fences, adobe
log corrals, nor fresh plowed fields, a hogback of slate, a dee
arroyo. It was a furrow which split men's families, fields ar
hearts. Its geometrical precision taught the unteachable, th
the shortest distance between two points is a straight lin
this struck terror into their souls. And in its wake lumbere
huge trucks and scrapers, winch-driven buckets and concre
mixers.

The French had come to the beautiful blue valley wi
steel traps; the Spaniards with their dead god nailed to
cross; the gringos with long emphatic rifles to punctuate the
taciturnity. But now something greater than all gods, a
persuaders of peoples, had entered the valley to entrap ther
It was the Máquina of progress.

They began to turn against Maria. When they came
taunt her with failure she still answered with her curt phras
"Courage, amigos. Meet fate with faith. I shall never see th
dam!"

"No! You will not see it!" they shouted with derisio
watching her wrinkled hand groping for a little tobacco sac
"You are going blind. Blind as well as toothless. Mother
God! So this is how you would betray us with your cunnir
words!"

Maria faced them like a rock. "Burros!" She spit at the
feet. "You yourselves will never see this dam built."

Wonderingly they retreated down the trail.

"She has said it! Doña Maria has prophesied. We sha
never see this dam built. Even now she says it," the
muttered in confusion. To be answered by braver voices
"We did as she told us, and yet we are losing our land. Ca
you doubt it? Look at Jesús! Listen to Filadelphio! No! Wi
all her wisdom and foreknowledge, she cannot stop this dar
She is a witch who has lost her power. She is nothing but a
old woman!"

Their mutters against her were waves that left her spewe

ɔ on her cliffs in silence. Their cunning against the Máquina
ɔbbed it nightly of shovels, monkey wrenches, air in tires;
ɹnctured gasoline tins, cut ropes; spit after receding
ɔotsteps. Their rage at the Mofres flamed up redly against
ɹe dark mountains and the skies of night.

Maria from her cliffs watched the roof of the store blaze
ɔ, the shed in back and two trees in front burn down before
ɹey could stop it. She heard shouts, a shot in the dark, a
ɾream, and the clatter of a horse's hoofs splitting the night.

At morning she was still there. She was unable to see
ɕearly the ashes below, but she could taste them on her
ɔngue. They had the same taste as defeat.

Dawn-dusk lifted slowly as a curtain from the valley.
ɑalfway up the mountainside the pulleys stuck. Darkness still
ɹrouded the tips of tall pines and spruces. Below them, on
ɹe edge of a little clearing, stood a man with his head
ɔraised above the noise of a waterfall; he thought he heard a
ɔund. He was an engineer surveying the stream, up early for
 trout for breakfast. Unwinding his line, he stared through
ɹe brush.

A small hut loomed clearer in the glade. From it as he
ɑaited an old crone hobbled out. She was naked and carried
 long stick. Her flabby breasts hung dry and wrinkled, her
ɔbs stuck out from skin brown and brittle as leather. In the
ɾeeze her long gray hair rippled. She shook all over.

Down to the stream she poked her way in the graying
ʒht. Her stick rapped on the stones like an early wood-
ɔcker overhead. The current in a pool she tested, then
ɕepped bravely in. On her thin flanks she crouched in the icy
ɑater, then ducked deeper to full immersion. Great gasps
ɹook here as she rose, groped for her stick, and slowly
ɔbbled back across the clearing to her hut.

The watcher in the bushes shivered in his high boots and
ɑather jacket. Then catching up his line, he stumbled
ɹrriedly downstream out of sight.

Maria in her hut dressed shaking before a fire. For a long

time she sat huddled in a faded, burnt-orange blanket. The
sun was high when she prepared tea and porridge. It was
warm and bright when she sat down in the doorway to feed
her birds. They chirped and squawked, ran, flew and pecked
at her feet. A cottontail came up, ears erect, to sniffle the
grain and hop lazily away.

It was the first day after the summer solstice. It was June
and morning. Maria felt warm and well. She slipped readily
into her morning nap.

Shortly after noon she called on her stick and strength to
carry her up the trail to the cliff top. In an hour she was
settled in her seat on the crag.

Vaguely she could distinguish the outlines of the valley
below. She could smell the rich plowed fields, hear the chir
of a thousand blackbirds and the caw of crows. But when she
stared above the mountain walls, at the sky above, she could
see nothing but a milky gray mist. This was good; there were
really a few tumultuous clouds rolling across the blue sky.

Near four o'clock rain fell, a short quick splatter on her
head and blanket. Maria raised her face, let the drops run
down her wrinkled cheeks. This was very good; it was what
she had waited for. She felt baptized and refreshed.

By sunset she had poked her way back down the trail. By
dusk she had eaten a bowl of posole, and drunk weak tea
from the morning's leaves. Now, content, she rolled a
cigarette and sat smoking before her fire.

It was el Día de San Juan de Bautista, and she had kept the
faith.

On this day all the waters of the earth are blessed, the seas
the rivers and the ritos, the clear forest streams and all the
muddy acequias meandering through the fields. So at break
of day you must go down to the stream and bathe. Thus you
will be immersed in the one living mystery, the waters of life
blessed by St. John the Baptist, he who baptized the Cristo
Himself.

For this day all week you have hoed your weeds, prepared

our fields that San Juan, the patron of waters, may favor our crops. Now this is the sign of his blessing to them and to ou, who need equally the waters of life to grow and prosper, at at four o'clock, according to custom, it rains.

Water is like life. It is life. It permeates everything. The and of God drops it at birth. It trickles down the snowy eaks, the little streams feed rito and acequia, the great rivers sh down to the sea. And the deep sea too feeds with mist d vapor that great blue lake of life unseen by us all, to be newed again and ever.

What is life without water? What is life without faith? So l the waters of the earth are blessed, and all the flesh of the arth is permeated by its flow, and all the earth of the flesh is nctified by faith.

For faith is not a concept. It is not a form. It is a baptism the one living mystery of ever-flowing life, and it must be newed as life itself is ever renewed.

This is the meaning of any dam, that it would obstruct the ee flow of faith which renews and refreshes life and gives it s only meaning. It is self-enclosing. It means stagnation. It eans death.

Faith is not to be dammed. It is not to be measured and eted out when timely. It must be free to penetrate every ll and germ of the whole. For it is the obstructed whole at finally bursts the dam, brings destruction and misery, vamps the temporal benefits of the past.

There are dams. There will be more. But all are temporal d unwhole. For they, like us, are spattered, swept and ndercut by an unseen flow—a flow that is stronger than sual benefits, that never ceases to permeate and undermine ur lesser faiths, and which can never be truly dammed.

10

There was no procession carrying San Ysidro to the cliff top
that May. Should he look down upon unplowed fields, a
earth bare and bitter with change?

The people did not invoke the blessing of San Juan tha
June, nor congregate on the hillsides to watch it rain on h
day according to custom. Of what use water when there wer
no weeded crops awaiting it?

Even the Corpus Cristi procession through the villag
stopping at shrines of pine and spruce branches, was broke
into segments and disrupted. Can people march four abrea
chanting, kneel and pray in the road when huge trucks hon
imperiously for passage and clog nose, throat and eyes wit
dust?

The earth was bare, water was disregarded, men's faith wa
broken. The Máquina of progress overrode them all.

From strange cities it came. Up from the plains of tall gra
and short grass where the buffalo had rolled, and the lon
horns had tossed their square bows. Over arroyos and mesa
into scrub oak and piñon, into pine and spruce. Through th

orest it cut a swath; through the little mountain meadows
vhere the deer had come down at night from the picachos to
·ound lazily over log fences and stand, ears up and unafraid,
stening to the sound of squeaking wagon hubs. With iron
irders it straddled the lower river. On white concrete and
·lack asphalt it lumbered through the blood-red adobe of
·uena Vista, the yellow clay of El Questo, the chocolate
·rown hillsides of La Cueva and the whitish talc near
·omeros Corner. Into the beautiful blue valley it came.

These mountains would never echo the sound of a train,
·ut the Máqūina assaulted them with more than a far-off,
·hin and muted shriek. It clanged and jangled, bumped,
·attled and banged. Past El Alto de Talco and El Alto de los
·lerreras, through Santa Gertrudes, Cañoncito, over La
·orriera and Tramperas. To the tall jutting cliffs it rumbled
·onderously, stopped and spread from wall to mountain wall.

Such a Máquina! It was iron and wood, steel and stone and
oncrete, bolts and long cables. It whistled, shrieked, snorted
·nd clamored with blow and shout; it smelled of gasoline and
·rude oil, whisky and good coffee. It was terrible with power.
·t was wonderful with the new and strange. It was unreal.

So down the cañon trails rode people to watch it. From
·una and Lujan, from Vallecito, from Guadalupita and
·urquillo and Lucero, from La Cañada del Carro. Men wary
·nd flint-eyed, in hand-dressed leather vests, sitting their
·estless mounts. Women staring wonderingly from out of
·heir cowls of black cotton. Children squatting transfixed in
·ld box wagons.

"Ah, the Máquina of the dam, no less. It is worth traveling
· day to see so strange a thing. Mira! I do not believe it!"

Of them all a bony little skeleton with white hair, and
·ressed in a greasy black suit with the fly sprung open, was
·he most bewildered and entranced. From morning till night
·e stalked the workings. His coat tail got caught in a winding
·able reel. A wheelbarrow bumped him to splatter his shoes
·vith concrete. A rising timber knocked off his little black

hat.

"Jesus Christ! Get off that gangway, you old fool!"

"Hey there! You Teodosio! Watch out for this load!"

"God Almighty! You here again? Over there. Out of th
way like I told you yesterday. I'll take you up in the ne
bucket but you gotta keep yer head down. Savvy?"

Don Teodosio smiled. He lifted his little hat politely. Ou
of his pocket he took a horse chestnut from the only tree i
the valley, and presented it to the gang foreman. "Sí, Seño
Mil gracias. I have never seen such a thing before. I a
overcome with awe."

There was this difference between them. Not that one wa
an ignorant, clumsy old man always in the way, and th
others careful, efficient workers. But that they were childis
slaves of the machine, their mother, while he was a
individual unbroken to its will.

So this Máquina, this monster, labored to give birth to
dam there at the bottom of the tall cliffs which jut out t
separate the crescent halves of the one long valley s
beautiful and blue.

Steam shovels squatted in the fields, careful attendants t
feed it. Great trucks rolled down and up the long macada
furrow bringing more supplies. The Mofres' little powerhous
was being built to warm and light it. Shops and a tool hous
became its nursery. A long mess hall and bunkhouse spewe
nurses in dirty denim. The old inn held its doctors, fillin
with engineers and construction bosses and vapid wives t
gawk at its souvenirs and bewail its lack of plumbing.

All waiting, like the people, to see born this child c
progress, this new dam of the Máquina.

Ay de mi! Nature travails alone in the thicket, being hard
and not to be denied. But the machinery of progress need
much attention; it has no faith; anything may break down.

And all—strangers and people—watched anxiously th
calendar and the posters which littered the valley walls. Th
people had been granted by court an extension of tim

efore they must move off their land, and it was ebbing
viftly. . . .

Maria could now hardly walk. Yet each morning her stick,
er grand-daughter and her own will carried her up the trail
) the cliff top. She stayed all day—lying on her blanket
nder a pine and rousing from time to time to sit looking
own into the valley. She was completely blind.

A dull rumble shook the hills, and then a clap of thunder.
"The great white-bellied clouds are gathering over the
erras?" she asked. "It will rain soon?"

"No, Abuela," replied Piedad. "The skies are stainless blue.
: is the thunder of gunpowder. The men are blasting away
1at big rock across the valley."

Maria nodded. A moment later she asked, "And what do
1ey today below us?"

"As yesterday and the day before that, Doña Maria. Those
ig máquinas are scooping up the fields. It is the sound of
1eir great iron mouths you hear. As much earth they hold at
nce as the size of a house. And that clatter, Señora,
ollowed by a whir. It is the carros swiftly hauling it away."

"I see, " said Maria soberly. "I see great iron gophers
igging. I see great iron squirrels with their pouches full of
irt scampering away to come again. . . . Now that far-off
vhine and the sudden crashes of trees. Help me to see
urther, child."

"They are great round saws. Also run by small máquinas.
'hey are clearing the hillside of trees."

"Like great shining gray beavers, no doubt."

"Sí, Señora," assented the girl listlessly. "Now come. It is
ime for your nap. I will rouse you when something strange
1appens. Then from the fire I shall make, you may have a
:up of tea. It will make you strong for the walk home again."

"You are my good eyes, child. I will do as you say." And
he lay down serenely in her faded, burnt-orange blanket.

Who knows she did not see aright this strange máquina?

We see in outer nature only that image which corresponds to our own inner nature.

But below her continued another unseen struggle. The people fighting time and gringos till the day when they must move off their land. Daily there were cracked heads and knife thrusts to be salved in court with patience and large fines, to be compensated for with days in the calabozo.

More and more men surlily rode up the trail to Doña Maria.

"Listen at that thunder of gunpowder; they are blowing up the hillside where I pastured my cows. Look at that patch of felled pines; I had been saving them for new vigas. Mother of God, Señora. Am I to stand by and see my land laid waste?"

"Peace," counseled Maria. "It is no longer yours. You have sold your land."

"Jesú Maria!" cried another. "That Campo Santo where our dead are buried. They are digging it up. They are carrying the old broken coffins, the gravestones, to unsanctified ground."

"Peace!" cautioned Maria. "The dead are dead. Remember your own living instead."

"This dam! You old witch! You said we would not see it built! Well what is going on? Are your ears deaf as your eyes are blind?"

"Enough! Fool! Has yet one stone been laid upon another? Has yet one timber been raised upon another? Remember what I say, you will not see this dam built."

And still the days thrust at them swiftly that day when they must move off their land. They became wild with fear and anger. They sharpened their knives. Their glances cut sharper.

"Look, old woman!" they shrieked. "Antonio's fields are a mess of machines; there is not space enough to harvest a turnip around his house. Niña and Teodosio's house is gone, their orchard cut down. They are living with neighbors. That is your land at the bottom of the cliffs, Señora. Where you

ived a lifetime. Mother of God! Are you too old to love your
land? Are you juiceless of feeling as a dried plum? Well let me
tell you this, old fool of a woman. You won't even have this
but when the day comes. Now what do you think of that?"

"Good!" she replied calmly. "I almost starved a lifetime
on that old piece of ground, to say nothing of Niña and
Gertrudes and Teodosio. It was too full of rocks to escape
with a plow. Now we have a good price for it. An almur of
silver unspent, like yourselves. Peace. I counsel peace. Bury
your knives with your silver. I will tell you when to use
both."

Thus she counseled peace, remembering her promise to the
good judge Don Eliseo.

The people went away angry. Their anger was fettered by
their incomprehension of Maria, their incomprehension made
fearful by her absolute disregard for her own fate. This was
the secret of Maria's hold upon them, for it is complete
freedom from self which alone makes possible complete
creative power.

Yes! It was ununderstandable. For years Maria had fought
this change and progress; she herself had aroused their love
for their land, their fight against the dam. And now—Mother
of God!

"It is as they say, Señora," confided Piedad alone with her
on the cliffs. "You are not alone my grandmother. You are
not only the oldest of the old among us. You are Doña Maria
of the Valley. Men speak the name proudly to strangers.
They speak of it as one speaks of the old ways, the wisdom
of the hills, the manner of beasts and plants, the movement
of stars and seasons, whom none know as you. Have you
forgotten all this—though I beg you to forgive me if I remind
you of those days when you were not quite so old? Have you
forgotten, that you turn upon us?"

Maria lay back against the rock; her weathered face, tragic
and timeless, seemed cut of a piece.

"No, child," she muttered softly through her gums. "I

have not forgotten. I have not turned upon you. I remember and thus give you the wisdom that rests in me.

"I see now that no man is greater than his time. I see now that nothing will stop this Máquina. So this I know, it is for each man and all peoples to become one with their defeat and so rise above it. This dam has defeated me. I give in to it wholly. Thus I am free of it; it cannot touch me."

"But Teodosio, so old and bewildered and feeble, Niña and Gertrudes and Antonio, our good neighbors, our primos and compadres, all the good people—what will become of us all?"

"Enough, enough! Do I forget my people? Listen. You are of one time, like myself. But you have not exhausted its meaning, and so must belong to it awhile yet.

"For there are to your eyes two times. The time of the land, and the time of the machine, this great Máquina which replaces it. Now the time of the land has its faith, and we belong to it; it has taken long to root in our hearts, our blood has watered it. But the time of the Máquina has yet no faith and so we must refute it.

"Do you see? No man can belong to a time until it has also a faith he can belong to. That is what our people do not like about this dam. It has no faith behind it to give it meaning. And so you must accept your own time which has a faith until the new time has also given rise to a faith, and you are ready for it.

"Pues. I myself am old. I have outgrown one time. I have superseded another. I shall soon die and be timeless. So it is only of you, of my people I think. Now plague me no more for I am tired. I have thinking to do while I sleep.

"But meanwhile send me Antonio and Gertrudes' youngest son. And then the good judge. In my hands, as tools of my foresight, they will mark your future."

Piedad shook her head. "Have you forgotten, abuela? It makes two days that they came at your bidding, in secret and with good horses. Now no one knows where they have gone or why."

"Pues," answered the old woman imperturbably. "When one sees into the future one may confuse the past and present. But send me the good judge, and tell him I would speak once more of a certain Don Fulgencio and the Sanchez you both know.

"Thus I shall insure my prophecy that you will never see his dam built. Now go."

So the days went. But Gertrudes' youngest son and Antonio did not return.

The day came; the day marked on the posters, in the hearts of all.

From the Court the carro came. To all the people in the valley who had been made to sell their land. In it were the sheriff with his gun worn outside his coat, a construction man in boots, a politician of the Compañía in patent leathers, and a stranger who carried a sawed-off shotgun.

The sheriff carried a paper of the Court. From it he read and spoke.

"Señora Quiteria Pacheco, the day has come. The day when you must be off your land. You have sold your land. You have received full payment for it. It makes a year and more that you have been living on land that is no longer yours. Now today you must be gone. With all your belongings. Before night."

Señora Quiteria Pacheco fell on her knees. She clasped her hands, the sheriff's knees. She wailed. "Madre mia! So it has come to this! That you would take away my land, my house! Where shall I go? To which of my three sons who have women of their own, with pots and kettles, blankets all needed to make a home? Who shall carry all my goods?"

The carro drove up the road to the ranchito of Fidencio Romaldo y Trujillo. The sheriff got out. A man walked out of the door to meet him, idly thumbing a long shining blade. At his heels stalked a shaggy mastiff. "Stop! Not one step more!" he cautioned lazily. "Or you come for trouble."

"I come with the paper of eviction, compadre," announced the sheriff kindly but firmly. "You have had a year or more to move out of your house by your own free will. Now, according to the law, we must help you."

The man spoke softly to his dog. It lunged forward growling—to be met by a blast of the shotgun and roll over torn and bloody and still.

"I am sorry, my friend," said the sheriff. "I know how you loved your beast. But you see what lies behind me. It is the power of a law stronger and quicker than any knife. By nightfall be gone from your house, lest your own blood be as needlessly shed."

Through the valley the carro drove. To the house of Donaciano Romero, to the families of Santistevan, Espinoza and Montoya, to Policarpio, to Berabe, to Trinidad, to all the people who had been made to sell their land.

At each they were met with tears or dry stolidity, with noisy pleas or silent stubborn faces. "Mother of God!" shouted the sheriff now. "What have you been doing all year when you should have been buying new land, moving your houses, your furniture, your animals? Today is the last day. By nightfall you must be gone from your houses and land, though you pile your things beside the road. You have heard me. It is the law."

Late that afternoon the car drove in turning off the road and stopped; the lane was blocked with driven stakes. The four men got out, clambered through the fence, and walked slowly across the field. It was their last visit. The long, low adobe beside the dry acequia was that of Antonio de la Vega. But outside stood a crowd of men, Trinidad, Berabe, Policarpio, the men of the families of Montoya, Espinoza, Santistevan, Donaciano Romero, Fidencio Romaldo Trujillo, the three sons of Quiteria Pacheco,—all the men who had been made to sell their land, all together, all at once. Behind them stood the women.

The four men stopped. One unslung his shotgun. Two

tepped behind him. One stepped forward and raised his
and.

"I would speak with Señor Antonio de la Vega."

"We have delivered your message," he was answered
uietly. "The same you have delivered to us all. Do you not
ecognize us?"

"Just the same, I would speak with Antonio. It is proper
ccording to law."

A woman pushed her way to the front of the crowd, spat.
'Well enough you know my Antonio has been gone these
wo weeks or more with Gertrudes' youngest son. Where?
Quien sabe? He is not here!"

"To you then, this same message. Be off your land by
nightfall. It is the law. It is the last day."

The woman's black glance contemptuously whipped him
where he stood. "It lacks no more than two hours before the
un sinks. Am I to move not only my own things, but those
f Niña and Teodosio, and also Gertrudes' who have moved
in with me? And to where?"

"To a kind neighbor's house—one whose land has not been
old," suggested the sheriff. "Surely friends will help. Perhaps
ne of them will sell you a piece of his land."

"There is no land to be bought in the valley. Would they
ose their land like us?"

The crowd of men washed forward, like a wave, to engulf
ier. A tall paisano spoke.

"Pues. You see how it is. There is no land to be bought.
We will not beg shelter like stray dogs. In one day we cannot
:hange our lives. So here, all of us together, we wait the
nightfall when you would drive us from our homes."

The sheriff rubbed his chin—a sign of weakness, no doubt.
_ike all men who shrink from might, he appealed to reason.

"I am distressed by your folly, friends. That you would
accept money for your land, and yet not give up that which
you have sold. That is not right, as well you know. But I am
only an officer of the law. I do my duty as bidden.

"Now what man here doubts my courage? You saw me
that day when alone I went after that old bear which had
come down into the Campo Santo. In the cantinas you have
seen me vanquish a borracho with drawn knives. Today also I
will do my duty.

"There are forty of you with sticks and knives. My short
gun will stop six of you. My compañero here will blow two
of you to heaven or hell, according to your conscience.
Which of you are these eight dead men? Suppose the rest of
you kill us this day. Tomorrow is another day. Soldiers will
come. They will destroy you all. Your children will not only
have no land, they will have no fathers. What do your hearts,
your minds, say to that?"

"We are waiting for the sun to set behind those peaks,
compadre sheriff," came the soft, wary answer.

They waited. It was not the red flare of the sinking sun
which came, but the thudding hoofs of a horse. Down the
cañon road, up the lane, across the fields. To the crowd itself.
A straggly-haired girl of seventeen on an old well-breathed
mare. Piedad. Doña Maria's Piedad.

She slid off the bare-backed mare, looked sharply at the
four and at the forty.

"It is exactly as the Señora foresaw!" she cried to all,
sounding a little excited from shortage of breath. "The
sheriff, the law, the Compañía and the gringo dam builders
have come to put you off the land. There is trouble brewing.
Is it not so?"

"What word does Doña Maria send?" gruffly enquired a
spokesman of the forty. "Or are you here as a mere child to
get in the way of serious business?"

"Let her speak," demanded the sheriff, as if she were the
only straw left to clutch at weakly.

The girl spewed at him a curt and contemptuous message.
"The Señora tells you to go away without trouble. To the
court and tell the good judge he will be obeyed.

"To you," facing the crowd, she cried, "Doña Maria says

to get off your land. You have been too long at it already."

A murmur rose like wind in the pines—and as swiftly gone. No man listens to another's words. He listens only to that unheard but revealing voice of doubt, indecision and emptiness, of courage and faith and command, which is the voice of the one of many gods dwelling within us each. The people, then, did not listen to a seventeen-year-old, stragglyhaired girl standing beside an unsaddled old mare. They listened helplessly to her who had been their master for a lifetime, to her faith and irreconcilable authority—to Doña Maria, whose voice was Piedad.

"She is blind but she saw you here," went on the girl, as if forgetting her commands but remembering clearly their contents. "She is weak but strong. So she commands you to peace. Move your things, this night, without fail, off your land. Anywhere! Into the vega, on the hillside, among the unfelled pines. Everything! Save all. You will need it for new homes. This she says. More too! Doña Maria will see to it that you have these new homes, new land. She is searching for them even now. Her own Antonio and Gertrudes' youngest son are her eyes, her hands, her feet. Now! Do you doubt?"

No. They did not doubt. Their credulity of the impossible sustained them. But they saw the shadows lengthen, felt the first faint stirring of the night breeze.

"My man is not here to help me. How can I move in an hour a life's home?" wailed Antonio's wife.

"How can I move this night? We have no wagon, no place to go?" grumbled another sullenly.

The man with a shotgun relaxed. The man of the Compañía talked swiftly to the sheriff who translated to all.

"The político of the Compañía says he will himself arrange with the law to give you not only this night, but another day. Is it not well?"

And now the construction chief murmured to the sheriff, who further translated.

"This ingeniero!" he shouted, slapping his companion on

the shoulder. "He is a friend also. He compliments you on your sagacity, and offers to help. Listen well!

"That vega there between the old road and the new one. There you can place your things. It is close to wood and water. More! To all those who have no wagons, no man, like the wife of Antonio here, he will send big bellied carros, his empty trucks and men to help them move. . . . But first to Donaciano Romeros', for that land he must use first and not delay his work."

More mumbling between the four; a faint flush had crept back into their cheeks. The tenseness drew out of the forty.

The sheriff raised his hand. He grinned happily. "Compadres! We are all friends. We will help one another. This very night let it begin! The ingeniero here, the big Jéfe, will send his men and trucks to help you move. Let the women build big fires and arrange their sleeping places. The político of the Compañía here, he will provide good coffee for all. It shall be a fiesta! We will all work and drink good coffee. Perhaps we can even find some fireworks to shoot off. Thus you shall move into the vega against the day when Doña Maria's Antonio and Gertrudes' youngest son return with news of your new land and new houses.

"Is it well? Are we all compadres? Shall we ourselves hasten away now to do all this? To tell the good judge, the law, as Doña Maria instructed?"

That night fires bloomed on the plain. Through the glow of leaping flames huge trucks rumbled like ghosts of buffalo, black shadows moved like ghosts of gone Comanches. Old comodas, great chests, heaped on the ground. Women spread feather beds and corn husk mattresses, cooked beans and slapped tortillas thin, sang children to sleep under the naked stars. Men cut wood, lugged water, unloaded and stacked furniture. The camp spread out. A great bivouac. At its edge nibbled tethered stock. A horse neighed to another; a cow bawled heavy with milk; a stray ewe blatted. From fire to fire crept mangy dogs to be beat away from cooking meat with stick and kick. The smell of coffee tinctured smoking cedar. There was whiskey too. So much the better: it made the fireworks seem more beautiful arching and breaking against the sky.

Maria up above saw and heard nothing of it all. She sat in her hut, ear cocked toward the cañon road down from the mountains.

Antonio and Gertrudes' youngest son had not yet returned.

The people waited homeless on the plain. Dust came in clouds, flies in swarms. Sand got in the sopa. Somebody fouled the sluggish stream. The sun beat down. The wind shook loose canvas roofs. It was no longer a fiesta. It was misery. The fourth day poured rain on stacked furniture, on sleeping mats, on food, on people. Then it was hell.

They did not grumble now. They sat with sullen lowered faces sharpening knives. When one did look up, it was toward the tall misted cliffs.

On the sixth day two horsemen sloshed down the cañon road to Maria's clearing. Their clothes were torn, their faces black with whiskers. Their eyes were bright.

"Doña Maria!" cried the younger, leaping from his mount. "We have found it! Our new valley. It is beautiful."

"It will do," supplemented the other. "I have looked at the land."

Maria roused from her blankets and rubbed her sightless eyes.

"To your people," she directed Piedad. "Antonio and Gertrudes' youngest son have returned. I would have them here to listen to what they have to say. . . . But first more wood on that fire. Put on coffee or tea, whatever there is. Your primos have wet clothes and dry tongues."

That evening they gathered in the clearing before Maria's hut. A single great fire had been lit to keep at bay the somber, pressing pines. As if oblivious of their presence,

Maria dozed in her doorway against Piedad's shoulder. She awoke with a start, groped for her stick and rapped loudly.

"For what do they wait? Let Gertrudes' youngest son talk first; he has spirit. Then Antonio. He can temper it with prudence."

The younger man had been talking already a half hour. To groups about him, his dark brown cheeks flushed rose; his eyes shone; his tongue, like a running stream, rolled obstacles out of their way. He gesticulated with enthusiasm.

"What a valley we have found!" he cried. "It is beautiful. It is untouched. It is ours."

A hidden little valley behind these mountains walls, up the Lucero. Rock walls enclosed it; it was dark and triste; it was high and cold. But a little stream ran through it. There was adobe for bricks, aspens for corrals and lattillas, pine and spruce for wood, for vigas, for lumber, for log corrals. A rutted road ran close; the one up the Lucero and the Coyote; six months of the year one could get down it by horse, perhaps with a wagon, for supplies.

This was what his hope painted to them all.

Antonio talked. He was old and cautious.

It was all true, what his compadre said, he acknowledged. But there was this to be said. To get into it with a wagon aspens must be cut down. For homes they must build their own, first of logs for this winter, till the adobes were made and hardened, the vigas cut and seasoned. There was no mill the women would have to grind their own corn the old way. There was no stone. There were no neighbors—only that old Indian woman and her son who used to live at El Alto.

"But that is how we found it; we saw the smoke of their chimney," he said. "They have a cow, they have goats. The woods are yet full of game. Now listen. They have a corn milpa. The ears are small but well formed. I saw the earth The leaf mold is a foot thick. It is rich. The land will do. Now compadres, consider all these things. It is a great step. Shall we make it?"

What was there to consider? When people are homeless they make homes of their desires. Hardships whet their appetite to enjoy frugality. So they began to build their dreams.

This land. It is untouched. It can be bought for four dollars an a-cre, according to the new measurement. The good judge will give us papers to it. Now we have unearthed our bags of silver pesos. They are yet unspent. It is not as if we are poor. We are rich. We can buy not only land; we can buy seed and nails, a new wagon, food to take with us. We shall have new homes and they shall be as before. No doubt when these neighbors of ours see our new valley they will also sell their land in this valley overrun with the Máquina, and come to join us. Verdad? What do you think of it, compadre? Does not your hand ache for the feel of a plow, an axe? And your old woman. Does she want a chimney and a place to hang her pots?

Maria began to mumble. She could not get up. The people crowded about her, squatted at her feet.

"What do you wait for?" she grumbled pettishly, punctuating her exasperation with the rap of her stick. "I have fought for life, and soon death conquers me. Do you doubt it? Pues! Am I fool to doubt it also? So I accept it calmly, and make ready to go to a better world.

"You have fought for your land, and now the dam has conquered you. Will you doubt it? Look at yourselves standing there homeless as stray dogs! So accept it calmly, like men, and make ready also to go to a better place.

"Where? Does an old blind woman have to show you? Mother of God! Your weakness overpowers my last strength! Antonio and Gerturdes' youngest son have told you; they will lead you. But I myself have seen it. As a young girl wandering with my goats long before you emerged from the womb. All they say is true. The land will do. Who confirms me? What man trailing a wounded deer has also seen this hidden little valley so close and yet so unknown? So go! You are a people of talk. Make action of your words, homes of your desires. It is I, Maria, who makes this her last wish for you all, her people."

They thronged down the hill leaving only Piedad with Maria's hand upon her arm.

'Momentito, child. To you only I have something to say. Let us go into the house. I grow cold quickly with dark."

When they were seated, the old woman stretched out on her blanket and smoking a cigarette, she said to the girl, "This Liandro who has been up here so often of late while you stayed with me. I have never seen him, but my ears know him well. While I slept you left me to hide in the bushes with him. Is it not so?

"No; do not catch your breath in shame, child. You will soon be a woman, as he a man. The spring of life rises in you both. It cannot be denied. It would be wrong of me to attempt to dam it. There is no dam but, in the end, is wrong, the dam of stone which would obstruct the flow of water, the dam of harsh morality which would retard too long the flow of life. But this flow must be sanctified by your faith in it or it is equally wrong. So dig in the earth below the bed—under that corner nearest this fire—and bring out the box you find."

In a moment the girl returned and placed the box in Maria's lap.

"No. Open it and receive in your lap the square pieces of gold it contains. They are few, all that I have left, but they are more precious than when I received them. Replace two only and bury the box as before. The rest are yours and this Liandro's. With them be man and woman together, buy a piece of land in this new valley, a wagon and the few things you will need. Thus your faith will be sanctified. If you would be husband and wife on paper first, so much the better. Though it will take a precious bit of your money for that lazy priest which might be better spent till you can afford it. For I would have you look at life more closely than at convention. For convention changes, but life endures. Your baptism in it, together, creates a faith that nothing alters. But you must accept that faith and never dam it.

"Now." She lay down weakly on the bed. "Leave me if you will. To ride down to this Liandro—if he does not wait already in the pines. Get ready to make your preparations. And be back again tomorrow: I need more wood as you know.....Now before you go, roll me some cigarettes. My hands shake. I waste half my good tobacco.

"Madre de Dios! I must be getting old!"

They were the defeated fleeing the advance of progress, their conqueror. Their failure brightened their eyes with longing, stiffened their backs to bear its burden. Long firm strides pushed regret behind them. Jokes leapt from their quivering lips. Hands strong to grapple the future waved tremblingly at the past. A cow tied to the back of a wagon set up an anguished bawling. They hooted it down with nervous laughter, and whipped their teams up the rutty cañon road. Their hearts clung to the poignant, their voices to the trivial.

"Mother of God! It makes three times that broken pot has fallen off, and yet she clambers down after it. . . . Hey there, Crescenciana! What will you carry in a cracked pot? It won't even hold your young one's water!"

"Mire! In the wagon ahead! Old Pedro still hangs on to his first wife's little sewing machine. Now he has no wife. Not even his third. Does he think to marry next the old Indian up here? Or will he sew curtains with it to hang between the pines?"

They plodded up the cañon. Old wagons squeaking under high loads, and drawn by straining horses. Horsemen riding ahead, and boys astride stray mules. Women walking to rest teams on the upgrade, and fading aside to squat in the brush like great hens under their black rebozos. And behind each group, a few head of stock: a lumbering cow with a calf trying to get at her swinging teats, a hobbled horse, some plodding sheep and blatting goats.

The steep cañon walls resounded more faintly their slow passage. The light, clean air, redolent with pine and spruce and rain-washed cedar, muffled their noisy cries. The swollen stream, pouring over the rocks at the rising trail, obliterated the shuffle of their anxious, plodding feet. Now only a magpie screamed from a branch that they were gone.

All morning they passed, a string of wagons, another.

"Adiós, our Señora! God go with you, Doña Maria!"

"It is as you said, wise old friend. We shall not see this dam built. But we will return when our houses are built. Sí, Señora! For you, wise old friend. It will not be long. . . ."

The old woman squatting against a rock on the hillside above them, stared blindly at the passing cavalcade. Her only answer to their last farewells was a sleepy nod and a thin, emaciated claw which lifted unsteadily and then fell back heavily into her lap. The sun poked through the fir above her and shone on hair gray and rumpled as the dead moss she leaned against. Her dirty black rebozo seemed streaked and rusty as the oxidized iron in the rock. She wiggled a bare toe in the green grass. A beetle crawled across her leg. A robin chirped.

It was these she really felt and answered. Men pass on, and their shadows follow. But the heaving earth and its blind vitality remains changeless and indestructible.

Near noon the last wagons stopped below her with their stock. People hastened up the trail.

"Doña Maria! Awake! It is us. La familia."

"Pues. I waited for your passing. You are late enough."

"Have you changed your mind, mi madre? Why do you not come? Now look. In the first wagon I myself drive my wife and children, Niña and hers, Gertrudes. In the second, Alfonso and Gertrudes' youngest son drive all our things. Never fear! We have lashed tight the good beds, the chairs, the cómodos, the stoves—all the big things are safely tied. The third is full of straw. It carries our pots and pans and

Santos, the breakables. In it sleeps Teodosio, and there is room for you. What do you say?"

"No, Antonio. Perhaps when you return in a week for another load I shall go. Perhaps not. I am not eager to travel. I like my own tierra."

Down in the third wagon a scarecrow sat up and rubbed his eyes. He shook off straw from his rusty black suit, put on his hat. Very stiffly he clambered out of the box. For some moments, back turned and legs spread, he stood contemplatively at the edge of the road. Then he squeaked slowly up the trail. His fly remained unbuttoned.

"Well, well, well," he chirped, blinking his rheumy eyes. "So Doña Maria still refuses to go. Sangre de Cristo! Look at me, Madre. I am old but courageous, weak but wise. They cannot get along without me. So I obey their will in this matter."

"Old?" rumbled Maria. "And courageous? Pues. You sick pig of a litter. You are too lazy to sit up. I have heard you need half the wagon to sleep in. And now you wish me beside you to listen to your snores!"

"Abuela, my grandmother, Doña Maria," begged Piedad. "With me you shall ride alone. In Don Teodosio's buggy which I drive. Will you believe it? It is able to travel again. Besides, Liandro drives our own wagon behind me. So we can see each other, not being together. I shall watch over you, and he over us both."

The old woman let her hand fall kindly and casually on the girl's head. Slyly she kicked the shin of Liandro beside her. But to the others she spoke harshly.

"Ándale! Get along with you! Has it ever been said that Maria did not know her own mind? Now go! You are long behind the others. But this I must say which comes to my mind, Antonio and Gertrudes' youngest son have staked their claims, there is not such need for hurry. So I would say let this Piedad and Liandro ahead of you in their wagon together lest all the good places be gone. Is there not an extra man

among you to drive Teodosio's old buggy? Caramba! It migh
break down. It might shatter his kidneys. But that is more
fitting than that a young bride be forced to ride alone in
back."

"It shall be as you say," answered Antonio. "Now we go
to return shortly. In your hut is wood and food. Is there
enough?"

"Too much! Too much!" Maria cried irritably, sinking
down on the grass. "Now go. My nap I shall take here now in
the sun. Adiós. My blessings. Go with God."

Adiós, adiós, adiós. . . . They were gone.

"She is a wise one, no doubt," grumbled Teodosio as he
was hoisted into his straw-filled wagon box. "We shall not see
this dam built! Hah! She was right at that. But how about
herself? True, she won't see it, but she can hear it, which is
the same thing. Mother of God! You can hear that blasting
from here. The trouble with her is that she has always known
her own mind. And no one else. How can they? With all
meanings in the same words. Pues. . . ."

The wagon rumbled up the hill, shaking. Don Teodosio
flat on his back, lay mumbling to himself under the clear blue
sky. Soon his mumbling changed to grumbling; he had been
refused a match.

"Let him smoke," whispered a wife to her husband on the
front seat. "He is old and sick and weak. He ate nothing this
morning. I fear his grave will be the first in our new valley.
Jesús! Forgive me for saying it."

"No," replied he softly but sternly. "A cigarette in all that
straw—God forbid! We would all be burned and buried before
we got there even. . . . But what I fear, wife, is that Doña
Maria herself—Did you observe how her knees shook, her
hand trembled, her voice failed? She—No, I will not say it!"

He crossed himself quickly before shaking the reins again.
So did the woman. They did not look back. Toward life the
wagon rolled on, squeaking.

The lofty little valley was her cradle. The mountains rimmed her life. Clairvoyantly she saw in them now both her birth and death.

The sun was sinking behind the Sangre de Cristo. The snow-capped picachos were red as blood. This blood was ebbing swiftly. The peaks grew anemic; a slow pallor beclouded their faces. Then suddenly a strange effulgence lighted up the dusk—a light that came from nowhere, but as if from within, like a brief resurgence of life flickering up in a dying candle.

Maria rose shakily from her bed. She had slept all morning, again that afternoon. She had slept away the two days previously. There was still wood and a stack of twigs, food and tea, even a little coffee. Yet she had not eaten, nor did she eat now. She wasn't hungry. But she felt in good health and spirit—more resolute and cheerful than at any time of her life.

Quietly she toddled out of the hut. Life moved in a sustained adagio. The night breeze awoke in the pines. The little stream played its arpeggio on the rocks. A deer bounded over a string of logs, its quick hoofs striking a pizzacato. A few pigeons murmured on the roof. Two old goat ewes stalked across the glade and entered their corral.

Maria paused, breathing heavily on her stick. Noisy footsteps came up the trail through the brush, across the clearing. She could feel the warmth of a lantern when the two men stopped before her—men from the dam.

"You have come again?" she asked in a low clear voice.

"And for the same reason," one answered in good Spanish. "To tell you for the last time that you had better be gone. The blasting begins on the cliff tomorrow. There will be many men here to camp till the work is finished; it is a likely spot. All this will distress you, old woman. It may be dangerous, seeing that you are blind. Besides, you will be in the way.

"Now will you send word to your friends below to come

after you? I would take the message myself this night; I am going to the village. I am sorry, good old woman. But that is how it is."

"Yes, that is how it is," Maria replied in her low calm voice, without anxiety or regret. "My thanks, friend. You are considerate. It is a long walk here, after you have worked all day. . . . But I shall not burden you with a message. It is not necessary. By tomorrow I shall be gone."

She stood listening to their receding footsteps.

Slowly now she tottered to the corral and fed the two old ewes double measure. She did not shut the gate as she left, throwing the peeling aspen bars to keep out a chance coyote. She propped it open with heavy stones so they could get out at morning. Thus she did at the hen house for the three chickens that remained.

At the door of her hut she stopped, emptying a can of corn meal on the ground for the birds at dawn. She shut the door behind her as she did each night to keep out the evil spirits which fill the night air. Also, but for the first time in her life, she latched it.

The old woman was breathing heavily now, but no more than usually; such exertion always taxed her strength. Quietly a while she sat on the bed till her legs and arms ceased to shake. Then she got up and lit a candle. The one that stood before an old Santo in his niche, the one that she had cracked and mended a half century or more ago.

The pale guttering light made travesty of her putterings. She dug up the little box with its two remaining pieces of square gold, patted flat again the earthen floor. she smoothed the bed after removing from it the faded, striped, burnt-orange blanket.

Now with a little brush of popotito she swept the floor in a dark corner. Over it she pulled an old petate of woven tules. On this she lay down, and covered herself with the faded, burnt-orange blanket.

The candle stub burned steadily now, without a flicker.

Maria breathed steadily, without a gasp. It was as though she controlled both with an inner tranquillity, and the whole room hushed with her resolute assurance.

After a time something stirred beneath the blanket. Her wrinkled, scrawny hand emerged with the two square gold pieces. One each she placed carefully on her gray filmed eyes. They lay heavily, quietly, in the deep sockets between her high cheekbones and bony Indian nose. They pressed the calm assurance that they would not fall off.

These only were left her from a lifetime. There is nothing ever lost but unreal, evanescent images; nothing ever gained but a perception of the enduring reality behind them. This is difficult to learn. We must first learn that there is only one time, and that it contains all, eternally. Maria, having learned it, was content. She lay quiety, without moving.

A faint candle-lit darkness, and on the floor the shrouded shape of an old woman with gleaming spectacles of square gold. Like eyes of gold whose value could never be diminished by change, which could never be blinded by age and evil, or corroded by weather and misfortune. Steadily gleaming eyes that burned through time with a faith which could not be dammed, and with a gaze which saw neither the darkness of the day nor the brightness of the morrow, but behind these illusions the enduring reality that makes of one sunset a prelude to a sunrise brighter still.